PRAISE FOR DELIA EPHRON

Big City Eyes

"[A] really funny novel . . . A screwball comical tale of adultery and murder."

—*Talk* magazine

"*Big City Eyes* is the witty, touching, sometimes zany story of a single New York City mom who moves to a sleepy Long Island town to help her teenage son, who's still reeling from his parents' divorce nine years earlier."

—*New York Daily News*

"Ephron supplies ample doses of inventive characters, winning prose and interesting morality issues to calm the nerves."

—*Newsday*

"A novel that sparkles with lively characters . . . [Ephron's] talent for witty dialogue flourishes."

—*Publishers Weekly*

Hanging Up

"Compassionate, funny, and tremendously satisfying. Among the many pleasures of *Hanging Up* is the way grave and ludicrous events ricochet off one another, scattering sentiment and anger and hilarity in all directions. . . . Ephron's comic timing is flawless. *Hanging Up* is full of life and ultimately . . . love."

—*The New York Times Book Review*

"Quietly comic . . . with gentle humor and deadpan observation . . . Ephron handles it with a deft, delicate touch, never allowing her characters to descend into caricatures."

—*The Boston Globe*

BIG
CITY
EYES

ALSO BY DELIA EPHRON

Fiction

Hanging Up

Nonfiction

How to Eat Like a Child

Teenage Romance or How to Die of Embarrassment

Funny Sauce

Do I Have to Say Hello?

For children

Santa and Alex

My Life (and Nobody Else's)

The Girl Who Changed the World

BIG CITY EYES

DELIA EPHRON

Ballantine Books • *New York*

A Ballantine Book
Published by The Ballantine Publishing Group

Copyright © 2000 by South of Pico Productions, Inc.

www.ballantinebooks.com

Library of Congress Cataloging-in-Publication: 2001117073

ISBN 0-345-44345-4

This edition published by arrangement with G.P. Putnam's Sons, a
member of Penguin Putnam Inc.

Manufactured in the United States of America

First Ballantine Books Edition: September 2001

10   9   8   7   6   5   4   3   2   1

FOR

JERRY,

WITH

LOVE

BIG CITY
EYES

I MOVED to Sakonnet Bay to save Sam. I woke up with the idea. It had been one of those problem-solving nights. Having fallen asleep in a state of intense distress, I awakened with the notion that if I uprooted my life for three years, I could avert disaster.

I'm a journalist, a small-time, freelance magazine writer, and there is no telephone number I can't wheedle out of someone, no tidbit I can't unearth. If the front door is locked, I know how to sneak in the back. Now I would simply apply my creative doggedness to the problem of keeping my teenage son safe.

Once I made this decision, I rented a car and drove out of Manhattan. I felt virtuous, even noble. I turned on the radio and was able to listen. For the first time in weeks my mind was at rest, which is to say lying in wait for the moment when it could become agitated once again. Agitation is normal for me, calm is unexpected. I veer toward agitation, list naturally in its direction. Taking action, almost any action, calms me, regardless of whether or not it is the correct action. I assume this is true for everyone, a small measure of peace secured when one goes from worrying a thing to death to doing something about it.

I felt noble and virtuous because I love Manhattan, and even before finding my new town, I had committed to giving up New York. To sacrifice. For a time. I had moved there originally from Los Angeles to attend Barnard College. I don't remember my first sighting of a New York City street, or my first glimpse of its magical skyline, but I fell deeply in love. Every single time I left my dorm, later my apartment, and walked outside, I felt a rush: I live *here*. I get to live in this amazing place. It's very strange when a city can do more for you than a husband or a lover, but for me, that was always the case.

I drove 495 east, then cut south and prowled the Long Island coast, trusting that someplace would strike me as the solution. On one of those roads that jumped to fifty mph between towns and then abruptly announced thirty mph as it became a main street, I found myself in Sakonnet Bay. It felt like Brigadoon, a village that came to life for only one day every hundred years, so perfectly was it a dream come true.

Sam needed order and this town was orderly. Main Street, which formed a T with the only other commercial stretch, Barton Road, was lined with charming nineteenth-century buildings of clapboard construction—a visually comforting style, each narrow strip of wood tucked obediently under another, everything painted in refined grays, whites, and blues. Awnings shaded display windows, giving shops a proper, well-mannered look. There were no chain stores, no outlets that felt transient or common.

In my present condition, I was willing to leap to many conclusions to believe this move was right. Still, Sakonnet Bay's harmonious façade appeared to be a statement not just about its architecture but about its inhabitants. I had read Sherwood Anderson, knew that odd behavior could fester beneath the surface of small-town life, but that did not seem relevant. "Pretty" was the word for this sweet place. It was immensely pleasing and at the same time innocuous. This town could not possibly attract or foster trouble.

I stopped at a real estate office and in one afternoon located a house to rent and a future best friend. In my mind, meeting Jane Atkins, my Realtor, elevated the discovery of Sakonnet Bay from luck to destiny. The first person I met was simpatica. A former New Yorker, sharp and witty. I would not be lonely.

Jane toured me through town to see the sights that would make a New Yorker happy: the perfect food—doughnuts (plain and powdered-sugar), deep-fried and flipped automatically for everyone to see on the old-fashioned doughnut machine in the window of LePater's Grocery; a produce stand featuring local goods, which reassured me that Sakonnet Bay was country, not suburbs; and the bookstore, selling new and used—this was no intellectual wasteland—owned by an ancient sparrow of a woman, as quaint as the doughnut machine, whose thinning white hair was twisted into a tiny knot.

White hair. In one day, I noticed more than I had seen in a year in Manhattan. And permanents. Curls all over heads, turning older women into lambs. Fashions dating back in time. No, that's not quite accurate. No sense of fashion. A sort of immutability in women's looks. But not Jane's. While her approaching middle age might be visible in a certain widening about the waist, her hair remained a flashy honey yellow, a color that could be created only artificially. Hair dye alone identified her as a transplant.

In Sakonnet Bay, people aged and looked it. I had auburn hair and there was no way I was going to let nature take its course. At this time of my life, age thirty-seven, the only thing I had to do about gray hair was extract one strand at a time, but I already had plans to eradicate one irritating vertical crease between my eyebrows. I'd read in *Elle* about this magical remedy, Botox. A little shot of botulism. No beau of mine would ever boast, Lily doesn't wear a lick of makeup.

But many women here didn't wear a lick, and I found it cozy. Sam and I were moving into a village of grandmas.

After we walked the business district, Jane took me on a ride through the pricey area. "The ocean-side of Maine," she called it. An elegant landscape of groomed gardens and sprawling houses, but deserted, lifeless. It was late April, a month before the weekenders and summer residents from Manhattan would begin their occupation. Then we went north into my future neighborhood.

Here locals lived on tree-lined streets in two-story shingled dwellings on identical quarter-acre lots. The houses appeared to have been built at the same time, because they resembled one another like members of a large extended family. Jane said they dated from between 1875 and 1920. Each had a bit of personality—a path bordered in whitewashed rocks, dormer windows edged with gingerbread—but only personality, not eccentricity, and that was further confirmation of solidity, of a world that fads passed by.

I wrote about our move for *Ladies' Home Journal,* in a cheerful upbeat piece, which was what the magazine always wanted. I described my going-away party at a SoHo bar, claiming that my friends had sworn to visit. They did promise—that was true—and we all kissed and cried; but they were like me, diehard Manhattanites. To leave the city, unless it was to go someplace thrilling like Paris, they would have to be towed. I said that the traffic, crowds, and noise were driving Sam and me away. In fact, I thrived on chaos. It was unlikely we'd be back, I insisted, neglecting to mention that we'd sublet our rent-stabilized apartment month to month, to a writer friend who needed an office. I also enthused about how glorious it would be to see stars at night, when actually a grand sparkling night sky would turn out to be intimidating. Fodder for my overactive fearful imagination. Until I moved to a quiet place, I didn't understand how fears and fantasies could expand to take up all available space. So in this article, I was as inaccurate in projecting my tranquil future as in describing my troubled present. I omitted that my fifteen-year-old son was sneaking out to Manhattan clubs. Several times I'd caught him returning at four in the morning. And I certainly didn't mention the incident that had triggered my panic and subsequent break with the city: I had found a knife in Sam's underwear drawer. A steak knife, imitation-wood handle and blade with serrated edge. I'd been hunting for drugs, been prepared to uncover a baggie full of grass, when I discovered the knife instead.

I removed it and mentioned it to neither Sam nor his father, whom Sam visited in Massachusetts every fourth weekend. I couldn't imagine waving and yelling, What was this doing there? Besides, I thought I knew. Its presence was consistent with a crayon drawing Sam had made as a six-year-old, after the divorce: a stick figure of a boy under a sky filled with long narrow triangles.

"What are these?" I had asked.

"Missiles," he told me.

I showed the picture to his pediatrician, who announced, "Sam doesn't feel safe."

Nine years later, he evidently still felt unsafe. Perhaps his club-hopping was a way of seeking danger. He was going after an experience that would confirm an existing feeling. Mulling the situation, that's what I concluded. The knife was not a weapon but protection. I didn't think that anyone else would necessarily accept this interpretation of the facts, but I didn't care. I knew Sam. What I couldn't determine was whether his late-night expeditions to clubs where alcohol and drugs were readily available marked the beginning of a downhill slide.

I continued to obsess until I made the decision to leave Manhattan. Until Sam was out of high school, when his fragile teen years were over, we would live in a missile-free town.

"We're moving to Sakonnet Bay because I think you'll be better off there," was all I told him. I came armed with a map so I could point out our coastal town.

He didn't bother to look.

I started to fill in the details, to describe a place he'd never been able to visualize in his childhood drawings, but I choked up. He hadn't stomped away in anger. There was no one he wanted to phone, no friend to bitch and moan to.

Four months and no questions later, that August, we moved. *Ladies' Home Journal* wanted to accompany my peppy article with a photo of Sam and me attempting to install a hammock in our first backyard. I remember this day fondly, my pounding a nail into a tree while Sam held the hammock aloft as if it were a giant fish he'd landed. Sam, my baby, was now six feet tall, his flesh as pale as mole rats I'd seen on the Discovery Channel, animals that never once encountered the sun. He wasn't fat, more soft and squishy from a disinclination to move except when absolutely necessary. Still he was sweet-looking. Impish blue eyes, and brows that curved comically over them like quarter-moons. Nose straight and fine, a strong chin with a dimple. As the photographer snapped, Sam squinted into the sun, his head cocked back as usual. He led with his chin, walked with it tilted up and out.

I had stuck a copy of the photo in a frame, a reminder of the last time I could look at my son without wincing. The morning after that lovely afternoon, when he had, incredibly, swung in the hammock, and Jane had arrived with housewarming presents—candles and a transistor radio for the inevitable power outages—Sam shaved the sides and back of his head and pulled his remaining dirty-blond hair into a rubber band so it looked as if he had a spout on top of his head.

In Manhattan, Sam had gone through a phase in which he wore a set of plastic werewolf fangs to school—they fit neatly over his upper teeth—and that was fine. That was, in my opinion, in the normal range of teenage behavior. But one evening he had confessed to forgetting his algebra homework. This was well into his freshman year, and when I suggested he call someone in class, he said, "I don't know their names."

"Any of them?"

"No."

Not in the normal range.

I tormented myself with this code of measurement. No friends. Not in the normal range. Hair spout: NNR. I longed for normal range, lusted after it. When I signed the lease for our new home, I envisioned Sam strolling down Main Street, laughing and talking to other kids, munching a doughnut, powdered sugar misting his neatly-tucked-in alligator shirt. Within months, he would be as pretty inside and out as Sakonnet Bay. I caught myself, wanted to bang my head against the real estate office wall, dislodge a few pictures of ocean-front houses to knock some sense in. I must keep my expectations reasonable. Still, in the recesses of my heart, where reason did not dwell, a boy was talking and laughing, walking with friends, munching doughnuts. Having a wonderful time.

Our transition was initially easy. I worried that Sakonnet High might reject Sam because of his hair spout, but the registrar handed over the forms and he enrolled. This surprised me so pleasantly that I stopped at a nursery and purchased tulip bulbs. That evening I planted, measuring an exact six inches from one bulb to the next. The following day I started work at the weekly paper, *The Sakonnet Times.* A piece of good fortune, landing this job—the editor, Art Lindsay, happened to be the uncle of one of my city friends. Each week I would write a column on a subject of my own choosing, as well as several articles on assignment. I was thrilled to give up freelancing. It's an outsider's existence. With this work, I could set an example for my son. I would join the community, be part of the life.

On October 4, the day events took an unexpected turn, Sam sat at the kitchen table ignoring his bowl of cereal, which he had saturated with so much milk that the Cheerios floated around like pool toys. NR—normal range. One leg was pulled against his chest, permitting a crusty size-twelve foot to rest on the chair seat. He picked at the cuticles on his toes. NR, but disgusting.

"Isn't it beautiful out today?" I was reduced to weather talk with

Sam. Weather talk had turned out to be a big activity here. Commenting on how crisp it was, or how great the air felt on one's cheeks. Sam didn't bother to reward me with his usual grunt. I tried a more provocative approach. "I saw a fox the other day, hanging out down the street, near the corner." Sam poked the Cheerios with a spoon, sinkiǹg them and then allowing them to bob up. "I think the fox had a baby in its mouth."

He made the strange noise that I heard from him a couple of times a day: he opened his mouth as if to yawn, but what issued forth was somewhere between a sigh and a wail. I hadn't yet settled on a rating for this behavior—NR or NNR.

I really had thought the fox had a baby clamped between its jaws. In a foggy twilight, I was driving home from the Italian deli when I spied the animal by some tall shrubs. First I noticed the flat bushy tail—unmistakable, definitely not dog—then how surprisingly lithe the fox was. Just as it vanished, I thought I saw . . .

As a part of my job on the paper, I was allowed to peruse the log, the town's official computer printout of reported crimes. I went to the police department dispatch office and looked:

Ellen Franklin, 245 Cummings Lane, complained that a sport utility vehicle pulled in and out of her driveway three times in approximately fifteen minutes.

Victor Marcum reported that he had received one hang-up call a day for the past three months.

An intruder entered Stanley Lamb Housewares, 106 Main Street, via an unused doggie door, rearranged some merchandise, but removed nothing.

I loved the log. I loved the innocence of the crimes and the idea that crimes could be innocent. In addition to mining the log for ideas for my column, I read selections from my notes to Sam at dinner. "Listen to this: A kitchen door was stolen. Someone's mailbox. Three Dr Peppers were lifted from the refrigerator at Oscar Limpoli's chicken ranch."

I laughed gaily, alone, about these incidents. But I have a theory that just because a child isn't reacting doesn't mean he isn't listening or appreciating. I was influenced in this belief by *Enchanted April*, the only movie I have seen that is about being in love as opposed to falling in love. It explores the power of relentless kindness. Even though Sam was not my husband or lover, I believed the film's message still applied. One day he would not be able to resist my stories, my enthusiasm, my jollity, and would end up, against all inclination, having fun.

"I checked that log," I continued, despite Sam's manifest lack of interest. "I scoured it from top to bottom. No missing baby. I must have imagined the whole business."

Without any assistance from his hands, Sam worked his feet into laceless sneakers. He got up from the table.

"May I please have your bowl?"

He passed it over, and milk slurped over the side onto his hand, which he licked. I put the bowl in the dishwasher, opened the cabinet under the sink to get some Cascade and discovered a dead mouse.

I slammed the door closed. "There's a dead mouse under the sink."

"This place sucks," said Sam. He disappeared into the hall, his jeans drooping off his hips, the bottoms drooling around his toes.

After pacing, trying not to wish there was a man around the house, I opened the cabinet again, this time squinting so that whatever was in front of my face would have a vague shape. The gray blob, undoubtedly the mouse, was between a blurry green—the Cascade—and a yellow blotch, probably sponges. With a wad of paper towels, I reached in and seized the soft gray item, which stiffened and squirmed. I screamed, throwing the wad into the air. The mouse landed on the floor, ran across my feet and under the stove.

"What was that?" Sam called, his voice remarkably flat given my shriek.

"Nothing, nothing, forget it, nothing." I didn't know that mice slept. I had never heard of a sleeping mouse, except perhaps in a children's book where mice wore aprons.

The front door rattled as Sam left. My son never did anything gently. In our New York apartment, drawer pulls were falling off his bureau, his window no longer shut properly, the bathroom doorknob no longer worked. Out the window, I saw him kick up some dirt for no apparent reason as he passed several deer chomping bushes in the front yard. Did deer ever charge, did they bite, did they carry rabies as well as ticks? I rapped on the pane to shoo the animals off, but they ignored me. Possibly they were smart enough to sense the difference between a real order and a feeble one: Please leave, okay? As I cleared the table, and set the milk carton back in the refrigerator, where there was a heap of squash, four varieties, the phone rang. It was Art, my editor, suggesting that I skip the weekly staff meeting this morning and head to Claire's Collectibles on Barton Road. Over his police band radio, he'd heard that a baby's head was stuck in a pitcher.

Another baby. This one should prove less elusive than the last.

It was before nine and stores weren't open yet. The child must belong to the owner, Claire. Whoever that was. I started to leave by the front door, but the deer were still nibbling and a convention of squirrels had gathered on the lawn. Squirrels did get rabies, and a person bitten by a rabid one didn't always survive the antidote: shots injected into the stomach. A sixth-grade classmate had informed me of this, his eyes bulging excitedly as he whispered behind his earth science book. Exiting by the back instead of the front, I ran down the driveway to my car, jumped in, and slammed the door. Even locked it. I hit the horn several times. This caused the squirrels to scatter and the deer to amble off my property. For a second I felt smart, as if I'd invented a new use for the horn. The honking attracted the attention of my neighbor, Mr. Woffert, who was on a ladder engaged in serious construction. He had removed his clapboards and was stapling on Tyvek, the house-wrap. "Insulating," he had informed me. The task kept him busy from sunup to sundown. I waved and pulled out.

The trip was quick—a scoot three blocks through my residential neighborhood, a left turn onto Route 35, which almost instantly declared a name change to Main Street. In five minutes, I had reached the intersection of Main and Barton. The site of the calamity was obvious. Three squad cars had spun in at odd angles. How dramatic. They'd been summoned while passing and had to make last-second screeching U-turns across the road. I drove past the shop, then turned into the public lot that backed and serviced businesses along both of Sakonnet Bay's commercial streets. After trying the rear entrance to Claire's, which was locked, I hustled down a pedestrian alley to the sidewalk. Flashing my reporter's ID, I squeezed between some gawkers and pushed my way in.

The small gift store was cluttered with glass and china plates, teapots, figurines, and also ruffled velvet throw pillows with gingham bows, mirrors, shelves of soaps and body lotions. Three cops—three-quarters of the on-duty force—huddled at a skirted table, while a plump woman in a flowered dress fluttered around, trying to see over their shoulders.

"Excuse me, I'm Lily Davis from *The Sakonnet Times.* I'm sorry about—"

"Baby." She pressed her hand against her heart. "He gets into everything."

A policeman turned around. "We're taking him to LePater's, Claire. We'll grease him out, don't worry about it. Who are you?" he asked me.

"Lily Davis," I repeated. *"Sakonnet Times."*

"Stay back, out of our way."

"Of course." I read his name tag, Sergeant McKee, and wrote it down on my pad.

He returned to the problem at hand, allowing a viewing instant, and I saw that the baby, Baby, was a dog—a dachshund, to judge from its unmistakable hot-dog shape. A silver pitcher sat upside down on its head. "I should have given him obedience training," wailed Claire. I took notes, as the sergeant scooped him up, supporting his tummy with one hand and the pitcher with the other. We could hear Baby's muffled moans as we moved out of Claire's Collectibles. A small crowd fell in behind for the short walk around the corner to LePater's.

A female officer herded the shoppers into a compact viewing gallery next to a rack of chips. Matt, the cashier, handed over a bottle of Wesson oil. While the third officer held Baby in place on the counter, Sergeant McKee lubricated his hands and began massaging Baby's neck, sneaking his fingers into the pitcher. Onlookers strained with anticipation. Would Baby be pried from the silver jug before he expired from fear? The only sound was the rustle of a paper bag when someone reached in for another doughnut.

Finally McKee managed to ease the pitcher off the dog's head.

Everyone hooted and cheered. Baby barked. His sausage body rippled and twisted. The cop tried to adjust his grip, moving his hands from the animal's haunches to his middle, when Baby squirmed free and fell or leapt about four feet to the floor. He hit the ground on his side, and waved his legs before righting himself. Then he dashed at me and sank his teeth into my ankle.

"Eek." I heard myself utter the tiniest squeal. Baby released my flesh and raced through the fruit section. He skidded a few feet, trying to stop, scrambled in an attempt to move in another direction, and then shot right back. Sergeant McKee seized the dog just before it attacked again.

"Oh my goodness, give me that poor angel." Claire snatched Baby from McKee. "He was only excited, weren't you, my honey?"

I looked down to see if my pants were ripped, and now heard laughter, which made me snap my head up quickly. All I saw was the group of shoppers staring, some slowly chewing. They might have been an audience riveted by an exciting movie but continuing, as if on automatic pilot, to shove snacks into their mouths.

McKee moved in close. "Are you all right?"

"Fine."

"Eek." I heard someone mimic the sound I'd made when I was bitten. Then snickers of laughter. "Eek," someone else peeped. More titters. A wave of amusement swept the crowd.

"Do you want to press charges?" asked McKee.

"I don't give a shit. I don't give a goddamn shit, you idiots." I walked out of the store.

No sooner did I reach the sidewalk than I was horrified. I'd insulted the Sakonnet Bay police. "Idiots," I had said "idiots," hadn't I? And I'd flung "I don't give a shit" at the cops in front of nearly half the town's residents. My ankle hurt, it really hurt. I'm not good at pain. I've cried at the dentist's office, winked tears simply from a novocaine shot, and now my ankle was throbbing. Why hadn't they expected Baby to freak? They should have summoned an animal expert, phoned the SPCA, or taken the dog to the vet. Instead, they oiled it up and yanked it out.

I became aware that I was standing in a throng. People who had been peering in the window were now backing away from me. It was a dog bite. I can't be brought down by a dog bite.

Fixing my eyes on the wall of the building, focusing on dry fragments of flaking paint, I forced myself to walk normally, making sure the heel of my right foot grazed the concrete each time I took a step. The cops might be watching. As well as everyone else. I wasn't going to embarrass myself toe-hopping through the alley and across the public lot.

I sighed into my car as if I had fallen into a safe house.

I sat there not knowing what to do. Suddenly I was hot. Roasting. I fished my keys out of my purse and turned on the ignition so I could roll down the windows. I hit the wrong button and locked the doors first by accident. My eyes were wet. Tears of pain, I hoped, not humiliation. After rubbing them with the back of my hand, I tilted the rearview mirror to assess my face.

I looked like a clown in a sad circus skit. My normally peachy complexion was white, with a watery smear of mascara under each eye. My face, a pleasing oval, had grown mournfully long. Serious gray eyes had a panicky pinpoint intensity. So piteous was the image, it would not have seemed inappropriate if a teardrop had been painted on my cheek. Most alarming, however, was my hair. The burnished red had acquired a garish glint, and short pixyish strands stuck to my forehead and cheeks, while others, on top, torpedoed skyward.

I was beyond repair. I reset the mirror for driving, and forced myself to examine my ankle.

Using both hands, I hoisted my right thigh and gently lay the calf across my left leg. I folded up the hem of my slacks. The back of my tan sock was red.

"I'll have a look at that." Sergeant McKee materialized at the window, a spook, and without asking permission, stuck his head further in, an invasion of my personal space. "I'm going to push the sock down all around, okay?"

I didn't answer, since I would have been talking directly into his hat. Also, I didn't trust myself to speak. Who knew what the simple act of having someone fuss over me might unleash? As I pressed back, trying to merge with the seat so our bodies wouldn't connect, I felt the sock resist separating from the sticky wound.

McKee pulled his head out the window. "It's probably going to swell up a little. You might need a tetanus shot."

"I'm fine."

He folded his arms on the window ledge and drummed his thumb impatiently.

Suppose I became a joke? I just moved here, and already I'm a joke? I could see the sleepless nights ahead. The obsessing. The endless replay of worry. I'd heard those people in the store laughing.

"Let me drive you to the hospital," he said.

"That's not necessary."

"Get out, goddammit, I'm taking you."

"Okay." Capitulating was such a relief that concealing it became paramount. I busied myself, dropping my keys back into my purse, organizing objects there. This must be post-traumatic shock. I was going to either shout insults or sob.

His car was parked behind mine. While I stood, mostly on one foot, he quickly cleaned up the passenger seat, tossing a bag of Fritos and a Rush Limbaugh paperback into the trunk. He must be a conservative, big surprise. This was a Republican town.

"I'm Tom McKee, by the way," he said as we drove out of the lot.

"Lily Davis."

"I remember. Do you have a doctor?"

I shook my head and then, since his eyes were on the road, bleated a short no as well. My doctors were in Manhattan. So was my hairdresser. I wouldn't be caught dead getting a haircut in Sakonnet Bay. I considered whether to mention this, undoubtedly for perverse reasons—having already begun to irritate people today, I now couldn't stop myself. I heard a beep.

"That's my pager," said McKee. "Ignore it. Mynten?"

"Excuse me?" I turned to find that he was offering me a hard candy in a wrapper with a twist at each end.

"What's this?"

"An orange-mint thing. A throat lozenge. My wife buys them wholesale by the gross."

"Thank you." It didn't taste bad, somewhere between medicine and a sweet: even better, sucking it gave me something to do. McKee removed his hat, balanced it on the armrest between our seats, and I got a good look at him for the first time.

He seemed about thirty-two. Five years younger than I. Maybe not. Maybe thirty-four. My obsessing was taking a new turn, compulsive age-guessing. He radiated health, almost glowed with well-being. That's what struck me the most: how robust the sergeant looked, with fair skin and ruddy cheeks, as if he'd just come in for milk and cookies after riding his bike on a cold November day. From the side, he was compelling, mostly owing to an elegant, pronounced jawline. Less impressive from the front, I decided, as he glanced over. Something was out of sync about his features. Thick brows jutted over brown eyes that were possibly too close together, or perhaps the problem was that his nose, while straight, was slightly too wide. No, he was not quite handsome, but boyishly winning.

His dark brown hair was styled for Sunday school: short, side part, front combed up and over into a stiff wave. He might be excessively neat. He might also use mousse. Borrow his wife's. A secret vanity. I imagined him pulsing a bit into his palm, rubbing his hands together, and then, in one motion, coating his hair from front to back. I must have been recovering, or I wouldn't have been speculating about the officer and his hair products.

"Where'd you get those dumb ideas about deer?"

"Excuse me?"

"Deer don't cross the road looking for love. Pumpkins, maybe acorns." He was referring to the article I'd written last week about the increase in car accidents caused by lovesick deer or, depending on one's point of view, the increase in the number of deer killed by careless drivers.

"As a matter of fact, deer do travel farther during mating season, and when they pair off they'll cross the road to get to . . ." I couldn't think how to describe it. "Their love nest, I guess."

"Love doesn't enter into it."

Oh God, was he a hater of hyperbole? A stickler for accuracy? Like, I have to say, my ex-husband. I wasn't going to concede, so I shut up. The beeper went off again.

"Isn't that for you?" I asked.

"I've got a security company, and when I'm on duty my brother's supposed to pick up. Don't know where he is." He looked exasperated by this problem. Did it occur often? He extricated his beeper from his front pants pocket, lifting his rear off the seat to do so. He was chunky around the midsection. "You should write about DUIs instead of Mary Burns." This was a reference to another column I'd written, about a woman who had reported her underpants stolen from a dryer in the laundromat. I hadn't realized until now how carefully my work was read. By everyone? Or just by him?

"DUIs. I'll suggest that to the editor."

"Under-age drinking, too. That's another problem."

I jumped on him. "Are you talking about my son?"

"Sam?"

"Do you know him?"

"Everyone knows him, he's got no hair. Hangs out with Deidre. I wasn't referring to him."

"Oh." Everyone knows Sam? No, everyone knows *of* Sam. Points out the weirdo. Speculates about him. And who was Deidre? Did McKee know more about my child than I did?

He tapped some more numbers into his beeper and studied the response. "How's your ankle doing?" He turned and smiled. This had the effect of a car's brights coming at me on a dark night.

"My ankle's fine." If I didn't move, it didn't hurt. "I'm fine."

"You say that a lot. 'I'm fine.'" He imitated me, catching the cadence of the brave little soldier.

"I'm sorry I was rude to you before. In the market. I truly am sorry." I changed the subject and spoke in what I hoped was an especially bland manner. "Is someone's alarm going off?"

"Yes. I need to take a detour. Five minutes is all."

So he wanted a favor. That gorgeous smile was manipulation, his ace in the hole.

"Are you in pain?" he asked.

"No. Absolutely not." I urged him to go ahead, take his detour, not to think twice about it. I practically slobbered goodwill. It was a way to regain equal footing.

"You can't write about this," he said.

"Of course not." We both knew why. It wasn't police business.

McKee turned left, heading south of Main. He informed Dispatch that he was taking a short break, and we sped through the posh part of town. In less than two minutes we reached Ocean Drive, where residences could house battalions.

Although most of these mansions, spaced football fields apart, were uninhabited in the off-season, the air was alive with electronic buzz. Upkeep. Gardeners, carpenters, contractors—their vans and trucks lined the road. The noisy equipment provided an affectionate reminder of jackhammers in New York City streets. My ears were at home here.

We entered a narrow driveway between two fat round bushes. On an identifying marker, NICHOLAS was spelled out in brass letters on white wood. McKee slowed the car to a crawl.

"I don't hear an alarm."

"It's silent, but in any event, it's not registering on the pager. Probably someone leaving the house tripped it and screwed up a few times before setting it right." His voice was relaxed, but his posture alert, attention shifting left to right. Perhaps someone was lurking behind the stately trees along the gravel drive.

"Why do these people have alarms, anyway?" As a devotee of the police log, I knew that Mary Burns's purloined underpants was about as serious as crime got.

"Who knows." He laughed. "They like to spend money. They like to imagine someone's after their stuff. They like to keep my business going." He snapped open the ashtray; it was jammed with old Mynten wrappers. As we wedged ours in, the shade trees ended, releasing us into a bright sun that illuminated a blanket of pea green. Couture grass. It stretched for what looked like a quarter-mile, interrupted by a few freestanding curved and clipped hedges. On a small upward slope stood a two-story gabled house with weathered gray shingles and white shutters. The white rail on the wooden porch broke for wide shallow steps to the door.

McKee pulled up in front. "Stay here."

"In the car?"

"Yes. And don't take any notes."

"I won't. I told you, I'm not working. I can't even walk."

Craning this way and that, I spotted no life whatsoever—nothing left out that needed to be put back, like lawn furniture or bicycles or a stranded mower. No cars were parked in the driveway or near the garage. This was obviously a false alarm.

After ringing the doorbell repeatedly, McKee began peeking in windows, then disappeared around the porch to the back. I occupied myself by inspecting his vehicle.

Was it a department violation to leave me alone inside? That would make two department violations, doing private work on police time and leaving an unguarded citizen in his cop car. His walkie-talkie hung off the dash; I could transmit false messages. I could completely screw up his life. Why this notion crossed my mind, I have no idea. I consider myself a moral person, the sort who accepts the first invitation and never cancels if a better offer comes along. When a waitress miscalculates a bill in my favor, I point it out. What was in McKee's briefcase? To take my mind off subjects that were none of my affair, I examined my ankle.

Baby had left little doggie teeth marks. The skin around them was rosy pink and puffy. I tapped the wound lightly. This produced a drumbeat of pain, not terrible, even by my standards. There was no serious blood loss. If I washed the cuts, I probably wouldn't have to go to the hospital. All I needed was water. And Bactine. I should definitely apply some antiseptic, and soon.

I opened the car door. The Nicholases must have some form of germ killer. I didn't want to get a massive infection from a dog bite and lose a leg. I could imagine my city friends discussing how ironic it was. Lily moved there to protect her son, and look what happened to *her*. People in the city loved irony, while it didn't seem to be valued at all in Sakonnet Bay. I suspected this was something Sakonnet citizens were right about. I'd find McKee and ask him to let me borrow some Bactine from the medicine cabinet.

I stood outside the car. The quiet was daunting. "Sergeant McKee?" I called softly.

The air was cool, a damp cool, and the breeze chilly. I zipped my jacket and tried to walk. If I pressed only the ball of my right foot on the ground, I could move along briskly. Holding the railing for support, I hopped up the front steps, and then, following McKee's trail, jerked my way across the front porch and around to the back, where I stopped. Everyone knew this was beachfront property, but the contrast between the manicured, civilized front and this wildness behind was startling. Had a kind of truth-telling to it. This is what's really here. This is what's hidden. I half expected to hear *Twilight Zone* music, but the moment passed quickly and then it was only beach. Beach on a gray day. Waves choppy, sand strewn with detritus left by low tide and angry water. Beyond the porch and a tangle of beach plums, I could see tire marks in the wet sand.

A French door in the back stood partly open. "Sergeant McKee? Tom?" I wasn't sure how I was expected to address him, but made my voice sound both inquiring and cheerful. No answer. I stepped in.

The restrained exterior turned out to be a cover for extravagance: overstuffed couches upholstered in richly textured damask, gilt coffee tables and end tables, gold-painted porcelain lamps with silk shades. The living room was large enough for two formal geometric seating areas, one in front of a pink marble fireplace that must have replaced a carved oak original, the other by a picture window offering a splendid ocean view.

I wandered into the foyer, where a chandelier of glass teardrops

descended from the double-height ceiling, and then located the powder room off it. Shiny red walls, brass sconces, and a bowl of scented
soaps next to a sink shaped like a scallop shell. No medicine cabinet.

I didn't see McKee anywhere, not in the dining room on the other
side of the foyer or on the second-floor landing. The Bactine must be
in an upstairs bathroom.

I was beginning to enjoy myself. I loved traipsing along with Jane
to Open Houses. I had occupied a few Saturdays that way, fantasizing
about owning places I couldn't afford. This house was clearly unoc-
cupied. There was no personal scent, no cooking or cleaning smells,
no natural or artificial perfumes. I moved up the stairs slowly, using
the waxed walnut banister as a crutch, and then opened the first door
that presented itself.

The master bedroom. It stretched out to my left in a long rectan-
gle. Directly ahead, across from the door, my eye was drawn to a
beautiful twelve-paned window behind a satin-covered settee. The
glass was old or slightly tinted, and the ocean beyond changed color
as though I were looking through a prism. The window was slightly
open, and white lace curtains billowed inward, caressing the burnt
orange of the satin couch. I heard footsteps behind me, and as I
turned to confront McKee, to explain my presence, I noticed the
canopied bed at the far end of the room. There was a naked woman
on it, asleep. I halted mid-turn and began to retreat, when I sensed
McKee's body behind mine. I stepped on his foot and stifled a whoop
of surprise. He caught me by the shoulders as he saw the young
woman, too. She lay faceup on top of the covers, one arm flung out
dramatically. My eyes landed on her breasts, got stuck there, then
jumped the rest of her body to her toes. Each nail was painted a different color. I was about ten feet away, and as McKee pulled me
backward, her body became topographic—valleys, mountains, undergrowth. I smelled something heady . . . realized it was McKee's
aftershave, felt his warm breath on my neck. I was almost faint while

he steered me out and, with one hand gripping my arm, closed the bedroom door behind us. He had a silken touch, turning the knob quickly, silently.

I twisted away and took the stairs at a clip, but the pain in my ankle erupted with ferocity. So I grabbed the banister and hopped. The plush carpet muffled my thumps like a silencer.

We left by the back, the way we had come in. I limped after McKee, around the porch, down the front steps, and to the car. Following his example, I closed my door gently. He gave the car the barest hit of gas, and we rolled out of the driveway.

I kept my eyes on the road ahead, and assumed he did, too. I had the feeling that I should start laughing, turn the encounter into one big joke, but I kept envisioning that naked body, displayed like some sort of feast. The downy, smooth, coppery skin. The ample breasts sinking comfortably sideways, legs provocatively apart, an arm unfurled. Her waist was tiny, accentuating her curves. My waist was tiny, too, and I always imagined that one day I would meet a man whose hands could circle it. Not a man with big hands, that wasn't part of the fantasy—it was the idea of a lover finding my waist as delicate as the stems of a small bouquet.

McKee suddenly pulled the car over and parked. He plucked a Mynten from his shirt pocket and licked it off the paper.

"Could I have one?"

"You're crazy."

"But my mouth is dry."

"What?"

"I'm asking for one of your Myntens."

He punched open the glove compartment and removed an entire bag. "Take them. What were you doing in that house?"

"I don't need all these."

"What were you doing there?"

"I was looking for some Bactine."

"Bactine." He repeated the brand name as though he had never heard of it.

"I thought I could fix my ankle, you know, I thought they'd have some antiseptic in the medicine cabinet." I could see the nugget nestling inside his cheek.

"You went in that house to write about it."

"I did not."

"Come on."

"I told you, Bactine."

His arms rested on the steering wheel and he twisted the Mynten wrapper, spun it between his fingers. He occupied himself this way while I sat there. "You could have been killed," he said finally.

"Oh, please, by whom?"

"See, you don't take anything seriously."

"What are you talking about? You told me that alarm had been deactivated."

"You never know what's going down."

What's going down? Honestly. This was ridiculous. There was only one thing to say. "I'm sorry." I spoke contritely. I knew what was bugging him. Suppose that woman had awakened to find us? My trespass would have cost him an account. "Who was she?"

He started the car again. "None of your business."

"I just wondered." This whole thing was getting upsetting, what with him so short with me. I was wounded, I had a serious dog bite, thanks to his carelessness. I tried to open the bag of lozenges. The slick paper wouldn't tear. "This is like plastic on a new CD. A person could spend a year trying to strip that off. I always wanted to write a short story in which a woman gets murdered because she can't get the plastic wrapping off in time." My words hung around unanswered, McKee correctly identifying them as nervous babble. I noticed a big blue vein snaking across the back of my hand, which was lying in my lap, clutching the Mynten bag. The woman on the bed didn't have fat bulging veins, I bet. She couldn't have been more than twenty-five.

Now I was feeling unaccountably deflated.

"Cheer up."

"What? What are you talking about?" How did he know?

"Just generally. It's no big deal, right?" He flashed a smile.

"Right." I could see the medical center ahead. What a relief. I would welcome a shot of novocaine. Perhaps directly into my brain.

He kept the car idling while I stuffed the Myntens in my purse. "Thanks for these."

"Do you have someone to come and get you?"

"Yes. Don't worry about it."

"You should drink vinegar tonight. One teaspoon of cider vinegar with a tablespoon of honey."

"Is that a health potion?"

"For your ankle. In case you have a boron deficiency. And take it easy."

"I do."

He laughed, as though it was absolutely clear that I was full of it. "If you ever need help on stories, other stories, call."

"Sure."

"If it's not my shift, leave a message."

"Okay." He must have been buttering me up so I wouldn't betray him.

I put out my hand to shake his. Too formal for what we'd just experienced, and very awkward in the confines of the car. "Take care," he said.

"I will. Thanks for the ride."

THE EMERGENCY room was a fast twenty minutes. Clean, considerate, efficient. After getting a tetanus shot and a butterfly bandage, I took a cab to my car, drove to my house, and decided to stay there. Some days it is a mistake to leave home. I phoned the paper and told Peg, the receptionist, that I wouldn't be in.

I felt peculiar, off-kilter. I had a routine for moments when I felt especially vulnerable, like the time my wallet was lifted on the crosstown bus. Close down. Eat comfort food. In the city I would have ordered takeout, wonton soup and spare ribs. Here I scavenged through the refrigerator, locating one of the many hero sandwiches I kept on standby for Sam. I did not dine at the sink, where I consumed most lunches. Instead, I cut the sandwich into small pieces and placed them on a favorite plate with a border of pansies. I lit a Duraflame log in the living room fireplace so I would feel warm and toasty, and stretched out on the couch under a quilt, with the plate and a cup of chamomile tea nearby on the coffee table.

Chewing slowly (part of the rehabilitation involved proceeding at a leisurely pace), selecting bits of marinated pepper and dropping them onto my tongue, I reviewed events at the summer house. My mind drifted to them and was very happy there, stopping first at the moment of shock when I realized the bedroom was inhabited, and by a nude woman in a state of glorious abandon. Those toenails looked like squares of paint in a watercolor box, a bit of dubious taste on a body that was otherwise exquisite. I remember sensing McKee's stepping in behind me, his body shutting off the flow of air. The prosaic aroma of his aftershave became a fragrance of intoxicating sensuality. Our rush down the stairs. As if we'd bumbled into something ominous. My upper arm still tingled from the pressure of his grasp. I thought about him nervously spinning that Mynten wrapper—his hands, rough, with chunky fingers, incongruously twirling a strip of waxy paper, while he chided me. I *was* out of line, had inadvertently put both his business and his job in jeopardy.

McKee had a trash-compactor grip, that handshake when we parted was brutal—my fingers nearly welded together, then mercifully released. My gold ring, set with the single pearl, had been turned sideways, and I examined the memento of our parting, a round indentation in my pinkie where the flesh was almost punctured.

Time flew by while I was in this reverie. I liked reexperiencing events more than experiencing them, because they were safely over. I was in charge then, mulling, speculating, examining. I could embroider, imagine things that hadn't happened, enjoy the possibility that they might have, and be relieved that they never, ever could. Say, for example, McKee and I, overcome by the unexpected peep-show thrill, retreating to his car and having passionate sex. Clothes and his weapons (as well as reserve, restraint, common sense, even lack of affinity) would be shed as easily as leaves off a tree.

In the short time since I'd moved here, my tendency toward elaborate postmortems had grown. My eyes were not trained to appreciate the outdoors, and spectacular foliage reminded me of the thousand-piece jigsaw puzzles that I used to complete as a child, dense autumn treescapes and me hunched over a folding table trying to find the interlocking match for each piece. Being unfamiliar with nature, living with my taciturn son, having only the ephemeral e-mail connection to my previous city existence had put my brain in overdrive. I was on a mental treadmill, running miles every day.

At four in the afternoon, I was still on the couch, now dozing, when Jane called. "I heard you lost it in the market," she said.

"Who told you?"

"Let's see. I stopped at LePater's to buy cheese, so Matt at checkout and Lionel at the counter. Ginger, at work, heard it from Coral at the café, and then I stopped at the post office to mail food packages to Simon and Carrie, so Leanne there—"

"Okay, enough." I couldn't think how to explain myself. The word "misspoke" did cross my mind, but since I wasn't running for office . . . I admitted it. Blamed it on the pain. On Baby.

"That is a wretched little dog," said Jane. "I've seen him through the window yapping at customers. He acts like he's about to eat their feet."

I heard the front door. "Sam?"

"Yeah." There was a thunk, probably his backpack dropping to the floor.

"Upstairs," he said, not to me.

"Hold on," I told Jane. I lifted myself up on my hands, still treating my ankle as if it had sustained a major injury. Over the couch, I could glimpse the front hall and a slice of person disappearing up the stairs. The tread was almost as heavy as Sam's. Boots, I concluded. "Sam brought someone home."

"I knew he'd make friends," said Jane.

"I just said he brought someone home."

Jane didn't argue. "So you called the cops shits."

I started to correct her, to point out that, in fact, I'd called them idiots, but then I wondered which was preferable—to have called them shits or idiots. Shits, I supposed. More general, less insulting professionally. So I let it stand. If "idiot" was lost as it traveled the grapevine, that was to my advantage. But would McKee forget? He might be someone who collected resentments. Did I care? Momentum was building. For every line of conversation with Jane, there were sixteen with myself.

"Are you going to sue?" she asked.

"Who? Claire? The cops? I'd really sue the cops. That would cement my popularity. Not to mention that I cover them, so if they refused to speak to me, I couldn't work. Of course, they may not be speaking to me already. Besides, I have a butterfly bandage. Don't I need at least one stitch to sue?"

"You could say you had attack-dog nightmares."

"I'm—" I started to say "fine," but finished the sentence with "okay." "Okay" was not really a synonym for fine. It was less spunky.

I have always been worried that I am spunky. Like girl gymnasts. However clumsily they land, flying off that vault, they immediately snap up proudly, arms aloft; toes pivot into a perfect first position. Like them I'm small, only five-one, and although thin and agile, I am completely unathletic. I've always tried to counteract any spunky tendencies by being irritating—slightly grating, often provocative— to keep the cute adjectives at bay. I am resilient, however. Which is a very spunky thing to be. Like girl gymnasts. That's how I ended up in Sakonnet Bay. Believing problems have solutions, which is dreadfully naive.

"How did you get to the hospital?" Jane asked.

This was the opening. The time to spill the secret, the time to turn raconteur. "One of the cops drove me, and I took a cab back to my car afterward."

"You have to rest?"

"Just for a day."

"Call if you need anything."

"Thanks, I will."

I hung up. I had told Jane nothing, and I had no idea why.

From my horizontal position, I called to Sam. I lay there bellowing. No response. His door must be closed.

As I was about to hobble upstairs, my editor phoned to ask what had happened, in a tone that indicated he already knew. Art was solicitous. In his weary, patient voice, he inquired how I was feeling, then announced that he wanted me to write up the incident and be photographed in front of Claire's Collectibles with my ankle bandage showing. It would be the *Sakonnet Times* picture of the week.

I explained that I wasn't inclined to write it, at least my part in it, but I could hear Art's chair clanking.

The office desk chairs, all with swivel seats, had been purchased at a close-out sale. Whenever an employee shifted his or her weight, there was a loud noise and the seat tilted. Art's passive-aggressive method of persuasion was to shift back and forth without saying anything until his victim agreed to whatever Art wanted.

"I'm not the story. Baby's the story." I did not want to be the picture of the week. Last week's had been a basket of newborn rabbits with bows on their ears. He kept clanking, an effective gambit, even over the telephone. "How do you expect me to handle it, exactly?" I asked.

"What?"

"My rudeness to the police."

"You mean that you told them to go fuck themselves?"

"What? I did not say that, who said I said that? That is a lie. My God, who said that?"

"Bernadette."

"Bernadette, the intern? And you believed her? Where did she hear it?"

"At the Muffin Shop."

"I said, 'I don't give a shit.'" I left it at that and he didn't add or correct.

"You should set the record straight," Art said mildly.

"I guess so."

We hung up. Those two calls, Jane and Art, managed to undo the repair work on my state of mind. I tried to conjure up the Nicholas bedroom, the woman's legs enticingly spread, her arm draped across the bed in a flamboyant gesture of surrender. The vision no longer worked its playful magic.

"Sam," I shouted.

Still no answer.

I usually avoided his bedroom. Sam had left his clothes packed. He simply pulled something to wear out of a cardboard box every morning, and threw it back in that general direction every night. I should go up. Be introduced to his classmate. I was curious.

On the way, I stopped at the bookshelf. "Boron: a soft, brown, amorphous nonmetallic element." That told me absolutely nothing. I shut the dictionary and tackled the stairs, swinging my injured limb from step to step like a peg leg.

"Sam?" I knocked.

He peeked out. His face was flushed. "What is it?"

"I wanted to say hi."

He cracked the door a few more inches. His shirt was open and he began buttoning it. "What happened to you?" he asked.

"I was bitten by a dog."

"You look different."

"I do? Different how?"

That stumped him. Recognizing a change in his mom had been a leap; defining it took more observation that he usually committed to. "Are you wearing makeup?"

"I always wear makeup."

"You're brighter."

"I don't know what you're talking about. I'm exactly the same. Is someone here with you?"

He stepped aside and I saw a boy sitting on the bed.

"This is my mom," muttered Sam, as if he'd been dragged by his hair spout into revealing me.

"Nuqneh," said the boy. His arms and legs rearranged themselves like a set of pick-up sticks, as he stood up. He was very, very skinny, and almost as tall as Sam.

"Excuse me?"

"Nuqneh," the boy repeated in a low, gravelly voice.

"Deidre speaks Klingon," said Sam.

I didn't know where to begin with all this information. If this boy was Deidre, then either Deidre was a boy's name and I didn't know it, or this boy was a girl. As for the language—I'd heard of it, but couldn't place it.

I dealt with the easier problem. "What is Klingon?"

"Klingon is the official language of the Klingon Empire. Like English is the language of here."

"Oh, right, *Star Trek*. I didn't realize the Klingons have their own language."

"Yeah. She's teaching it to me."

She. That settled it. I examined her more closely.

Deidre's face was a collection of planes and sharp edges: a square chin, cheekbones like cliffs, blue eyes set so deep they seemed to peer from inside the crevice of a rock. Her skin looked baked, but at a very low heat for a very long time, so it had a flat tone, copper minus the metallic flickers of light, caramel without the mellow richness. Her hair, the eerie white blond of an albino, hung limp—one hank over the forehead, the rest tucked behind the ears with a straight lifeless fringe visible below the lobes. I could not discern the body inside the large man's workshirt with the tails out. I stared at the pockets under which breasts should be. None were visible.

"Wejpuh," said Deidre.

Sam laughed, and so did the girl/boy, revealing a thin straight-lipped smile.

"What does that mean?"

"Charming," said Sam.

"Thank you," I said, feeling I had learned for the first time what being polite was. Sam's worst class was French. After two years he barely knew *Comment allez-vous*, and now he was planning to master Klingon?

"He hangs out with Deidre," McKee had said. I had envisioned some long-haired adorable teenager, who said, "Cool," or "It's a slam." Not—I could hardly bring myself to admit it—a freak. Deidre was a freak. That meant Sam probably was, too. I had to invent a new category to accommodate this twosome: not even vaguely in the normal range (NEVNR) or not in the normal range by a mile (NNRBM). No wonder McKee knew who they were. Freaks were always famous in small towns. Did Deidre speak Klingon everywhere, or just when she wasn't in school? Did she speak pidgin Klingon or fluent Klingon? Maybe she's a genius. That thought actually surfaced, although I quashed it instantly, scorning my own pathetic spunky optimism, the hope-springs-eternal that there could be a saving grace. And . . . I didn't want to consider this . . . but had Sam been necking with this person? His cheeks did have a pinkish hue. If so, psychologically speaking, was he making out with a girl or a boy? Perhaps he was necking with an alien, a creature from his own tribe?

"Do you mind?" Sam asked.

"What?"

"Leaving. We're busy."

"Nice to meet you," I said as he shut the door.

Big City Eyes

BY LILY DAVIS

LAST WEEK I stopped at Jake's Farm Stand. While browsing, I overheard that Charlotte, the niece of the woman buying eggplants, was taking ampicillin for an earache. Perhaps the niece's name wasn't Charlotte. It could have been Charlene and maybe she had strep throat. I purchased a Boston lettuce and plum tomatoes. Then, awed by the beauty and variety of harvest vegetables, I bought three acorn squash, two turban, a butternut, and even a large bluish shapeless hubbard. I like to eat squash occasionally, maybe twice a year.

I opened my refrigerator and noticed these squash, all eighteen meals' worth, last Monday morning just after a mouse had run across my feet and just before several possibly tick-ridden deer breakfasted on my tulip bulbs. These facts don't justify or mitigate my later behavior, but I did leave home in an agitated state to cover Claire Ramsay's 911 call. Her daschund, Baby, had his head stuck in a pitcher.

How this event came to pass is still a mystery. After the incident, Mrs. Ramsay refused to speak to this reporter except to say that the pitcher is 1920s English pewter and sells for $95 at her store, Claire's Collectibles, on Barton Road. According to sources at the Comfort Café, where Mrs. Ramsay buys black coffee to go before work every day, she may sue the police for confiscating Baby and keeping him overnight at the SPCA in Riverhead. According to sources at the Muffin Shop, where Mrs. Ramsay has never been, her baby, whose name they did not know, almost suffocated but is fine now.

Why would a dog poke his head in a pitcher? Was there a treat inside, a trace of spirit or crumb, or was it a whim—one of those moments when an animal does something stupid?

Sergeant Tom McKee of the Sakonnet Bay Police Department ordered me to keep my distance. His exact words were "Stay back, out of our way." I would like to point out that I did exactly that. The sergeant then carried Baby from Claire's Collectibles around the corner to LePater's Grocery. He was accompanied by two other officers, Carl Scott and Denise Woodworth.

Shortly before this incident, Gavin Sturges of East Sakonnet had decided to use his new cell phone, a present from his girlfriend. He grazed a telephone pole, trying to locate the Send button, and ended up in a ditch. I'm sure it was not a whim that caused the police department to dispatch three of its four on-duty cops to rescue a dog but only one to save a human being.

Was it sound police judgment that caused Sergeant McKee to place the dog on the checkout counter at LePater's and grease his neck with Wesson oil? As everyone knows, since word in Sakonnet Bay travels faster than a response to a 911 call, a hyped-up Baby emerged from the pitcher. He went berserk. Wiggling out of the policeman's grasp, he jumped off the counter and bit this reporter's ankle.

I lost it.

Many versions of what I said have been circulating. About this: I would set the record straight, but I don't want to deprive people of the pleasure of repeating and further mangling the mangled tale they've already been told. Gossip is as essential to life here as harvest vegetables. This must be why generation after generation hasn't moved. It's not for love of their beautiful village, or the joy and security of having relatives in shouting distance. It couldn't possibly reflect a failure of imagination, or lack of curiosity or adventure. People in Sakonnet Bay can't bear to lose their places on the grapevine.

Sergeant McKee kindly drove me to the emergency medical center. During this exciting ride, he took the opportunity to criticize my previous column, insisting that deer do not cross the road looking for love, only for acorns and popcorn. These remarks might have provided additional justification for my outburst. Unfortunately, they occurred after.

All I can say about my behavior is that I'm sorry and have no excuse, except perhaps the squash, the mouse, and the deer. It was one of those moments when a person does something stupid.

AT THE Monday-morning editorial meeting a week and a half after publication, Art Lindsay announced that my column had riled many readers and he was thrilled. It was provocative in the perfect way: it upset subscribers but not advertisers. He had received twenty-five letters over the past ten days and at least as many phone calls. Responses were still arriving.

"I'm astonished," I said, which was a bit of a lie. Art broke up laughing. That was a shock. Until now, I'd witnessed only faint chuckles. But his laugh was hearty; the smooth cheeks in his solemn moon-shaped face folded into deep pleats, indicating that sometime in the past (possibly before his marriage, although that assumption may reflect only my prejudice) joy had played a role. "Lily is astonished," he told the staff, and they all laughed with him.

"I didn't exactly expect—"

He waved me off like a pesky fly, and then shambled to the

cooler, as he did many times a day, to down a miniature paper cup of bottled spring water.

The column had poured out of me. My only hesitation was whether to include the word "exciting" in describing our trip to the emergency medical center. I deleted and inserted it several times before letting it remain. A reminder of our detour. But innocuous. Harmless. Like a secret message in a Beatles song. A kind of "Hello, remember me?" I couldn't explain the dig, however—that McKee hadn't used good judgment when he greased up Baby. Or the popcorn business. McKee had actually said that deer like acorns and pumpkins, not acorns and popcorn.

At the time I was typing, I had been distracted by Deidre, who was becoming a permanent fixture. She walked home with Sam after school and stayed until dinner. On the weekend, she remained through the evening. Only once had Sam gone to her house, three blocks away. "Too crowded," he said. I could not adjust to seeing her and recoiled every time I had a sighting.

She reminded me of a character in the Oz books whose arms and legs were sticks tied together at the joints and who, at least as captured in the illustrations, was always in the middle of an awkward, uncoordinated stride. Deidre usually grunted some Klingon at me before escaping to Sam's room.

Always up for a mental leap into disaster, I imagined myself the grandmother of Sam and Deidre's child, born sixty-six inches long, gender unknown, but irresistible nonetheless because heartbreak was guaranteed. Until now, however, I had observed only one instance of physical contact between them. Late on Saturday night, craving some chocolate bits, I'd encountered them side by side in the kitchen, inspecting the open refrigerator. Sam had his head cocked, resting it precariously on the bony shelf that was Deidre's shoulder. He looked peaceful.

When I was writing my column, in the glassed-in porch I'd appropriated as an office, I could see them through the doorway, lounging on the living room couch. Deidre's stilt legs stretched across the coffee table, her gigantic boots hanging over the far side, floating free. They were watching Xena, the Warrior Princess, a long-haired buxom type who did forward flips in a leather gladiator outfit. Deidre's laugh sounded somewhere between a machine gun and a stuttering motor. I looked up from the computer to see them roaring, while they slapped great handfuls of popcorn into their mouths. So I typed "popcorn" instead of "pumpkins" by mistake. And left it.

It crossed my mind that McKee might call to correct me, although it turned out deer did eat popcorn. I had mail to prove it.

Art brought the letters in personally every day. "Dogs, deer, police, you hit all the winners," he said as he dropped a few more on my desk.

The police chief, Ben Blocker, had composed a formal protest, which the newspaper printed. "On behalf of the entire Sakonnet Bay Police Department, I object to the contents and implications in the article, Big City Eyes, October 8th, by Lily Davis." He listed three points.

1. Sergeant McKee took all necessary precautions in rescuing Baby.
2. Any resulting injuries were unfortunate but the consequence of Mrs. Davis's standing in the wrong place at the wrong time.
3. The police responded swiftly and appropriately to the minor accident involving Gavin Sturges. At no time does the police department value animal life over human life.

The chief also registered a less civilized complaint to Art by phone, threatening to bar me from the police log. Art beckoned me into his office so I could observe his end of the conversation. He arched his eyebrows dramatically as he listened, shook his head feigning dismay, made a few disapproving sounds, then reminded the chief that I was from New York City.

Having been the picture of the week, standing in front of Claire's

Collectibles with my foot up on a bench, unobtrusively revealing my butterfly bandage, I was now a minor local celebrity. Occasionally people poked each other when I walked by. While I was buying toothpaste at Bright's Pharmacy, the saleswoman told me that she loved my column, it was really fun. When I was stopped at a light, a man knocked on my car window. I lowered the glass and he said, "Are you a left-winger?"

"What?" I responded, floored not only by the question but by the term, which seemed archaic.

"For your information," he said, butting his face very close to my own, "Tom McKee saved my wife's life when she had a heart attack."

For the next few blocks, I drove without knowing where I was going, right past my destination, *The Sakonnet Times.* I had not expected to be thought of as anti-McKee.

Coral Williams, owner of the Comfort Café and president of Bambi's Friends, a group dedicated to protecting white-tailed deer, refused to accept payment for my morning coffee. She told me that she often fed deer microwave popcorn and had named every doe that visited her lawn.

I received several protests from the anti-deer people, reiterating that deer did not fall in love and that my insistence on anthropomorphizing them was contributing to the community's inability to deal with the serious deer overpopulation problem.

At the editorial meeting, while he gloated about the mail, Art passed around a box of apple crumb muffins, his first complimentary breakfast offering since I'd worked for the paper. This weekly meeting, about as formal as it got there, was held in Art's second-floor office in the small building, which had been someone's house a century ago, and was the most rundown structure on Main and the only one that faced backward, into the parking lot. Whether from being hand-hewn or from enduring decades of damp, salty seaside weather, floors had slanted, walls had buckled. No architectural right angle could be found in the place. In the shabby downstairs foyer, Peg, the receptionist, answered the phone, doubled as a copy editor, and handled subscriptions with relaxed cheerfulness. "I've been here forever," she'd say by way of introduction. Every day she wore the same cardigan sweater over her shoulders and the same bubble-gum-pink wedgies, with or without thin beige socks.

Design and page layout occupied the former dining room, still wallpapered in faded pink roses, and advertising had the living room. The kitchen, unchanged from the forties, had an ancient round-shouldered refrigerator, where Art stored the bag lunch he brought from home. All day, staffers poured themselves coffee from the only modern appliance, an electric drip coffeemaker that sat on the chipped tile counter.

For editorial meetings, the full-time reporting staff—Bernadette the intern, Rob (just out of college), and I—rolled our matching pedestal chairs out of our shared office and through the narrow hallway, bumping over thresholds and banging into walls, to Art's slightly less musty space. We sat around him in a semicircle, notebooks on our laps, mugs of coffee on the floor next to our feet. This morning, we also had our muffins. We held them on little square napkins.

"I want you to keep it up," Art told me.

"Keep what up?"

"Just be irritating."

I didn't argue with that description of myself, since being irritating was a trait I cultivated. Although I was always taken aback when someone remarked on it. As I took a sip of coffee, I noticed that Bernadette was wearing a pullover sweater in a color similar to the burnt orange satin fabric on the Nicholas bedroom couch.

The event, now fourteen days past, had cast a lingering spell. By "the event," I do not mean the dog bite, which had healed, but the brief encounter—the cop, the naked woman, and me. My only comparable experience was fallout from passionate necking sessions with my first boyfriend. After a torrid night with Evan, I would go to high school in a near stupor, attending class after class in a state of obliviousness, reliving every kiss and grope. Twenty years later, here I was with similar daydreams.

Even the chemistry between Sam and Deidre, the palpable connection of alien beings, much as it repulsed me, propelled me back to that moment when I saw the woman and almost simultaneously felt McKee close in behind me.

Sam now greeted me every morning with "Nuqneh." He explained that it meant "What do you want?" There was no word in Klingon for "good morning" or "hello." What was in store for this eccentric child? Was he an accident waiting to happen? I used my sensual daydreams as a distraction to shield myself from worry.

I was unable to formulate the simplest inquiries about Deidre. "Does she have brothers or sisters?" "What do her parents do?" "Tell me about her family." I rehearsed the questions in my head, but as innocent as they sounded, they seemed to reveal their true motives: revulsion and morbid curiosity. I should stop at her house and introduce myself to her mother. Every day, I planned to and put it off. I was sure there was only one parent in Deidre's life, because I believed that every depressed, loner, weirdness tendency in Sam was my fault. I traced the warping back to the day his father, at my request, had left. I couldn't figure out how everything got all mixed up together: McKee and I in that bedroom, Sam and Deidre every day.

One evening at the dinner table, I stared at Sam across a plate of pasta, dreaming about McKee. The grip of his arm on mine, the smell of his neck. At first I had recalled only his entrancing aftershave, but now I imagined an infusion of sweat and brutish masculinity.

Later, behind my locked bedroom door, I'd imitated the naked woman. Although keeping semiclothed, in the extra-large T-shirt I slept in, I laid myself out, supple and willing. The leg arrangement—limbs slightly more than casually separated—felt especially erotic, as if I were extending an invitation. Yet, I couldn't make sense of that right arm. Flung out to the side, it hit the edge of the bed at her elbow, but it couldn't bend down, because she was on her back. This was awkward and uncomfortable. It made my forearm—hanging unsupported in the air—feel like a ten-pound weight. How could she have slept in that position?

I hadn't seen McKee since the event, at least not that I knew. It was difficult to tell one cop from another as they cruised by. I'd visited the dispatch office only once, where I was ignored by Sally, the dispatch officer. She spent most of her time on the phone with her mother, who baby-sat her toddler while Sally worked. They discussed his nap, his diet, what clever thing he was doing. "Hold on, Mom," was what she usually said, before switching to 911 to announce, "Police Emergency," or to handle more routine matters on the regular line. Sally's ignoring me could signify nothing—business as usual— or loyalty to the department in general or McKee in particular. I wondered if he was angry with me. Had I embarrassed him or hurt his feelings by insulting his competence? Most likely I wasn't on his radar screen at all. McKee had a job, a security company on the side, a wife, possibly a family. I had considerably more spare time than he did. I contemplated taking a knitting or patchwork class at the local historical society, and went so far as to phone an inquiry. Curb my lusty thoughts by keeping my hands busy. Wasn't that what nuns did?

"I think I should back off the police," I told Art at the editorial meeting. "I feel really bad."

"If you feel so bad, why did you write that stuff?" asked Rob, the other reporter, taking a large bite of his muffin and sending a shower of crumbs onto his notepad and lap.

"I don't know, it just happened. Like automatic writing. I didn't mean to attack the police, only to tease."

"I hate teasing," said Bernadette. "My boyfriend teases me. We have these big bushes on either side of the front door. They're like cut in a shape so they don't look like a bush."

"Yes," I said, helping her along.

"So he knocks on the front door, and when I open it, no one. I say, 'Hello.' He jumps out from behind the bush, screaming."

"That's scary."

"No it isn't. So then I say, 'Stop teasing me,' and he says, 'I'm not teasing, I'm flirting.'"

Art attempted to get the meeting back on track. "Whatever you were doing in that column, Lily, teasing, flirting—"

"I wasn't flirting."

"Of course not." Art chuckled—the sort of sound you might hear if you placed your ear next to an aquarium and discerned the faintest bubbling of the oxygen pump. "Whatever you were doing, keep it up."

Bernadette raised her hand, waiting to be called on.

"Yes?"

"I don't want to phone Mr. DePosta. He's so mean."

"You have to call Mr. DePosta," said Art. "He's the one who filed the complaint."

"About what?" asked Rob.

"About teenagers hanging out on the sidewalk in front of his store," I said. "I noticed it in the police log."

"I already talked to him once. I won't call him again."

"Reporters make phone calls, Bernadette," I said, not unkindly. "That's what we do."

"Not me, okay? Anyway, you act ways I wouldn't. God, you swore at the police."

"I did not."

"We'll discuss Mr. DePosta later," said Art. "Next week there's a town meeting on the deer problem. Cover it, Lily." He stood up, indicating that we should get to work.

I dragged my chair back through the hall and found several messages and my telephone ringing. "Lily Davis here."

"This is Angela Stubbs. As a twenty-year pet owner—" People

always felt the need to establish their credentials, however dubious. Mrs. Stubbs went on to assert that dogs give unconditional love, unlike children, and the police were wiser to rescue Baby than a joker like Gavin Sturges.

"You're right. Of course, you're absolutely right." I closed her out politely, "Thank you for calling."

"Hey."

I turned to see Bernadette pull a velvet scrunchee out of her ponytail, fluff her long black hair dramatically so it fell around her shoulders like a full skirt, and whisk it right back up again. "You know, your kid does it."

"Does what?"

"Hangs out in front of Mr. DePosta's liquor store." Bernadette sank into her chair as if it were a depressing place to be.

"How do you know?"

"His shaved head. Mr. DePosta complained about it."

"His hairstyle isn't illegal, and neither is his hanging out." I swiveled away from her, my chair seat tilted, and I had to grab the desk to keep from falling over.

I picked up my stack of messages. I flicked the corners, making a little animated flip book, but the image kept repeating instead of progressing. Re: column, re: column, re: column. Except one.

"Hope your ankle's better." No name. I went downstairs.

"Who left this?" I slid the pink slip in front of Peg, who shifted her gaze from a crossword puzzle to my message. She chewed on her bottom lip and took a sip of Lipton's before responding. "Don't know."

"Male or female?"

"Don't remember."

Jane frequently left messages on my home machine, without identifying herself, but she knew my ankle was healed. I heard footsteps on the stairs. Bernadette was coming down fast, tying her orange sweater around her shoulders.

"I love that color, Bernadette."

"Feel it, it's so soft." She batted a sleeve in my direction. I caught it and raised it to my lips, felt an erogenous jolt, and immediately freaked. What in the world was I doing?

"I'm going home for lunch," I said. It wasn't yet noon. "I'm starved. I must be hypoglycemic or something."

"Strange," I heard Bernadette remark, and I didn't know if she was referring to the fact that I had almost kissed her sweater sleeve or announced that my sugar levels had dropped. I didn't look at either Bernadette or Peg, but climbed the narrow steps two at a time to get my purse, and then left the building by the back staircase.

I DID GO home for lunch. I needed to be someplace private, because I felt exposed. That moment of eroticism overtaking me for no reason whatsoever. A Dr. Jekyll and Mr. Hyde thing—the first time the doctor becomes Hyde unintentionally, uninduced, no potion swallowed, and yet the mouth grimaces, teeth protrude, beastlike hair sprouts wildly all over his face. It was a trifling episode—fondling that orange sleeve, raising the soft wool to my face, leaning forward to inhale and caress—but it was not willed.

My street appeared empty except for Mr. Woffert, securing Tyvek to his second story. "Uh-oh," he said as I got out of my car. I assumed he had detected an unforeseen underlying problem like dry rot, and gave him a wave and an encouraging smile. In retrospect I believe he was commenting on my arrival. I entered the house and walked into the kitchen.

Deidre was sitting on the table, naked. Her long legs wrapped Sam's waist and formed an interlocking S twist around his bare behind. Deidre, a few inches shorter than Sam when standing, topped him by a good six inches when sitting on the breakfast table having sex. Her eyes popped wide open, marbly blue martian eyes. Her legs and arms whipped apart and fluttered momentarily.

I backed out in a shot. "Sam, Deidre, get dressed," I yelled from the hall, then retreated further into the living room. Almost immediately I wasn't sure that I had seen what I thought I had seen. If Deidre and Sam had insisted that they had been fully clothed and simply hugging, they might have convinced me. "Get yourselves dressed and come in here," I shouted, while I prayed that the vision be erased from my consciousness, that I be allowed the merciful flipside of trauma—memory loss—the way accident victims cannot recall the moment of impact.

Normal range? Not in the normal range? Who knew?

I heard their feet on the stairs, ascending in a measured way. They didn't have the decency to sprint. They were neither embarrassed nor ashamed. I dug my fingers into my scalp and pulled my hair at the roots. The pain felt good.

A few minutes later, they clomped down and into the living room, flushed but dressed. I pointed to the couch and they sat. Deidre, her boots planted far apart, leaned forward and rested her elbows on her knees, a benched New York Knick waiting to resume play. Sam slumped, his body maintaining all the definition of a potato sack.

"We're speaking English," I said. "Why aren't you in school?"

Before the question was out of my mouth, I knew the answer: Because they wanted to be here, having sex. I rephrased. "How often do you cut school?"

Sam began chewing his thumb. Deidre sent her missile gaze into my own. Two questions, no answer.

I tried to break the ice. "Who are Klingons?"

"They're a weird race of warriors who like to kill people," Sam replied promptly.

"They like to kill people?" No direction was safe.

"They want to die." Sam smirked then caught himself. Deidre emitted one of her motorized laughs.

"Which is it? They want to kill people or they want to die?"

"Both. They want to die gloriously so they can go to Stobcor."

"Stob-o-cor," corrected Deidre.

"Is that heaven?"

Sam nodded.

"Look, I am fed up with both of you. You are too young to be having sex, period." I could hear the inanity of my own words, but I plowed on. "I may have to speak to Sam's father about this."

"Go ahead," said Sam, daring me. He knew my telling Allan would establish my own incompetence.

"I'm taking you both back to school. Deidre, I don't want to see you around here for a while. Sam, I'll discuss your life later."

"Petak," said Deidre.

"What does that mean?"

Sam shrugged.

Deidre's speaking Klingon was like my parents' conversing in French when I was a child so I wouldn't understand. Possibly, I hated her. "Come on, get your backpacks."

Sam rose reluctantly, pulling dead weight into a standing position. Deidre batted at her pale, wilting bangs. It was the first vaguely female move I had seen her make, if I didn't count having sex.

AS SOON AS I delivered Sam and Deidre back to school, I called Jane.

"Are you free?"

She heard my neediness over the phone. "Is dinner tonight soon enough?"

"Absolutely."

"Okay, sweetie. Burgers and Such, seven-thirty."

I arrived before her and parked myself in a booth along the wall so no one would overhear us. This upscale hamburger joint reminded me of my ex-husband, because of the spider plants hanging above the tables beside the front window. Allan had loved spider plants, perhaps he still did. Spider plants produced offshoots, baby clumps of thin green-and-white leaves that he snipped and planted in smaller pots. They never died, and they all reproduced boring replicas that prospered even in the arid atmosphere of our marriage. It occurred to me, staring at those plants, that the most innocuous memories of life with Allan bugged me. I should phone him to discuss Sam. The prospect was demoralizing.

On her way to the table, Jane greeted every single person, or so it seemed. She either had sold each one a house or was planning to someday in the future. She blew kisses to those too far away to address personally, and from Jane this gesture was not an affectation but true affection. We were a perfect pair, she the most popular transplant and I the least.

She leaned down to kiss my cheek, slid into the booth, and took charge. She signaled the waitress, and we ordered. "But first please bring me a frozen margarita. Have one, Lily. Two," she told the waitress, and relieved me of the menu.

Settling in, she smoothed the front of her pink silk blouse and retucked it at the waist. Jane always spruced up before talking and usually offered a self-criticism. "I'm too old for pastels," she said tonight. With suppressed excitement, she added, "So tell me what happened."

As we sipped our drinks, I took her through my story of finding Sam and Deidre, leaving out why I happened to return home at eleven a.m. If Deidre weren't a completely peculiar human being, I pointed out, Sam would just be having sex, which would be sort of in the normal range (SONR) for his age, although there was that other business: When I returned him to school and spoke to the guidance counselor, she told me he was flunking English and French. "He's only been in school six weeks."

"Hold it, one thing at a time," said Jane.

"If Deidre hadn't been bizarre in the extreme, I probably would have sat Sam down and discussed condoms."

"You should discuss condoms anyway."

"I will." My head was spinning. Should I call Deidre's mother? Should my first conversation with her—my first conversation with any parent in this town—be about our children's having sex? "I have to call Deidre's mother." I took such a big gulp of margarita that it dribbled down my chin.

Jane handed me a napkin. "Talk to Sam about condoms first. Eventually you can call her mom. And you don't have to worry about Deidre's cutting school today. It's not your responsibility to inform her mother about that. Believe me, the guidance office has already delivered the news. Oh, good," she said, as her favorite dish, the hot turkey sandwich, was set in front of her. The white meat reminded me of the pale flesh on Sam's bare bottom, and that tan gravy was a near match for the color of Deidre's legs. A new obsession was taking hold. My encounter with McKee in the summer house had been supplanted by the sight of Deidre's pretzel lock around my son's naked behind.

"I'm so glad you could have dinner. So unbelievably grateful. Jonathan didn't mind being left alone?"

Jane licked some salt off her glass. "He probably likes it." She slapped the sentence with a laugh. "You could buy some Trojans and give them to Sam."

"Maybe. Although it is his responsibility."

"Well, you should tell him that if they're going to have intercourse, they should have it in Sam's room and not treat your house like a sex playground."

"Right." I poked around my chef's salad for something I might have the energy to swallow, like a slice of radish. Unfortunately, the radish was white, which also resembled . . . I plucked out a cube of ham.

"Have you ever made love on a table?" I asked Jane.

"No."

"Me, neither." The acknowledgement depressed me. My son's short sexual history eclipsed my own.

"Pretty wild," said Jane. "But probably uncomfortable."

"That's what everyone says."

"Like who?"

"Oh, you know, when you see something like that in a movie, everyone always says, 'It couldn't be very comfortable.' Or, 'Personally, I'd rather do it in bed.' And while they might rather be in bed—"

"What?"

"Being overcome by passion is thrilling. As an idea, anyway."

I wouldn't have taken this detour, academic as it was, if I had not had a margarita. Even one drink tends to unhinge me. I am the walking definition of "can't hold her liquor." Jane had stopped eating. Her knife and fork bordered opposite sides of her plate as if she'd dropped them. I felt guilty noticing this, but stared nonetheless. Our conversation had struck a nerve; it made me wonder. Jane was forty-four, seven years my senior, just old enough to be a fantastic mix of friend and mother. Her two kids were in college. Maybe, after all these years, Jonathan did like her to be out; he had the place to himself. Or perhaps he took her for granted and thought of her as décor, not a lamp exactly, more like a down pillow. I was hardly an expert on long-term relationships. My only long-term was with my son.

I scanned the room to give her some privacy and to settle my tipsiness by attempting journalistic detachment. Burgers and Such was a haven for year-round residents. The blue-checked tablecloths and stumpy red candles supplied low-rent atmosphere; the clunky walnut bar drew customers by being absolutely devoid of intimidating chic. Bernadette was in front, mingling with the other singles. I spotted my cable TV installer planted in front of an iced beer mug. Like many others, he was watching football on TV. I liked the clubhouse atmosphere.

"What are you looking at?" asked Jane, as I saw McKee walk in. He was in uniform.

I swung around. "Nothing. The cop. The one who drove me to the medical center."

"The one you insulted in your column?"

"Never mind. Don't pay attention. He's not looking over here, is he?"

"Well, aren't we grown-up? No, he isn't. He's taken off his hat and he's ordering something, probably a beer. Let's hope he's not on duty."

"So do you know who Deidre is? Have you met her parents?"

"Fine, fine, we'll talk about Deidre. He's cute, though," she said, her eyes veering toward the bar. "It looks like he ordered a Coke."

"Yes, he is cute, and married."

"With three children, as a matter of fact. I just realized I know him," said Jane. "Tom McKee. He's on the school board."

"Deidre's parents." All of a sudden I was sober. "Who are they?"

"I've met the father many times. He owns that restaurant on the wharf, the Clam Bake."

"There's no mother, right?"

"No, there's a mother, too. And four kids altogether. Oddly enough, both parents are short. I handled their sale when they traded up. Needed two extra bedrooms, and I found them a property the bank had repossessed."

McKee had three children. He was a daddy, a devoted daddy who not only was a cop and had a security business, but was on the school board. The school board didn't quite fit with him. It didn't make sense that he would break a rule, check out that house while on duty, if he was on the school board. He was a dangerous type to be a school board member. "Dangerous" was the word that came to mind, but of course it couldn't possibly be right. I must have meant "rakish."

"You're thinking about Sam, aren't you?" said Jane. "I haven't been considerate enough, going on about real estate—big deal that I sold Deidre's parents their home. I know you're a wreck about Sam, distracted and upset."

I agreed, I was agitated about Sam. I pushed my plate away

to clear the deck and my brain of any other subject. Jane looked at me tenderly, and I felt a welling of helplessness. "The thing about Sam—"

"What?"

I held up my hand, damming a flood of anxiety. "Sam seems so lifeless," I said finally.

When I'd left him, he'd been sprawled on his bed, on his back, his arms crossed over his face, blocking everything out, especially me. Pleas of concern, "I'm worried about you," produced no reaction. "Why are you flunking?" made him roll over and face the wall. I was probably asking the wrong questions, but I didn't know what the right ones were. I'd informed him that until I saw significant improvement in his attitude and behavior, he had to come directly home from school and do his homework in my presence, although I wasn't sure that I could be home every afternoon. Were certain words, like "attitude" and "directly," invented by parents for these unpleasant occasions? I didn't feel authentic using them. "Sam, what do you have to say about all this?"

"Why did you come home, anyway? You're never home on Mondays."

That plaint of his had made me nearly insane, as if the entire episode were my fault.

"Lily, honey, he's not entirely lifeless," Jane said pointedly.

"No, with Deidre, actually, he's not."

"That's something. Have you thought about therapy or Prozac?"

"I've been through all that with him already. In New York. He refuses. I think he likes being a slug. I think it feels . . . familiar. I'm not going to cry, I swear."

"Cry your head off. I have Kleenex." She hunted through her gigantic sack of a purse.

"Hello."

"Oh, hello," I said, as I started to reach for the tissue, which Jane released. It wafted through the air like a parachute and landed on my salad. "Whoops." I pinched it off. "I have a cold." I dabbed at my nose. "Jane, do you know Sergeant McKee?"

"Of course."

"What's going on?" It was not a casual question. I must be emitting silent beeps of anxiety, or maybe now he was an expert on me in a freaked-out state. At least my mascara wasn't running.

"Nothing, really." I tried to laugh. "My son's driving me crazy."

"That's rough. I'm sorry." His body inclined slightly toward me and I inclined slightly back. I hadn't noticed before that his eyes were dappled, brown with touches of froggy green.

I heard Jane's compact click open. She took out lipstick and freshened up.

"How's your ankle?" McKee asked. "Or should I write a letter to the editor to find out?"

We both laughed. So he wasn't angry. Or he didn't want to be on the bad side of a columnist. Which? Both? "I'm all healed."

"I'm glad. Good luck with your son." He left, but the smile seemed to linger.

"Nice guy," said Jane.

"Very."

When I returned home, Sam's favorite movie, *Alien*³, was playing on the VCR. I could see it through the living room window as I approached the front door. I was pleased that he'd at least moved downstairs.

He was sound asleep, sprawled on his back, stretched the full length of the couch. His hideous spout of hair lay over the cushioned arm, proudly displayed, the way a hand with a beautiful ring might be offered for admiration. How innocent to show off something so unappealing. His face was blank, not withholding but serene.

"Sam." I touched his shoulder.

He opened his eyes and, upon seeing me, smiled. "Hi, Mom."

"Hi, honey."

And then he was fully awake and our connection was broken. His smile vanished. He seized the remote and upped the sound. His eyes dulled into TV land. He plucked a half-eaten bagel stick from the coffee table and collapsed into a semi-stupor.

Maybe I should watch with him. Maybe if I entered his world, I could bring him back into mine. This was an idea born of total exhaustion, but I sat down, facing the set. Sigourney Weaver was lying in a sleek futuristic coffin. Her head was bald, Sam's minus the spout.

Klingons like to kill people. They want to die.

Klingons like to kill people. I looked over at Sam. He closed his eyes and poked the bagel stick softly against his eyelids. His mouth curled up at the edges and remained there contentedly, then he took another bite. I knew where his mind was—humping his heart out before his mom entered the kitchen and wrecked it all.

Sigourney Weaver was now being lifted out of the coffin and placed in another type of space bed. Her eyes were shut. She was wearing a brief undershirt and bikini underpants, which left an attractive field of skin between her hips and breasts.

"Is she dead?" I asked.

Sam didn't respond. His head rocked gently from side to side while he nibbled his bagel stick.

She couldn't be dead, but when people die are their eyes always open or are they sometimes closed? As I considered this, Sigourney Weaver woke up. Had the naked woman's eyes been open or closed when McKee and I intruded? Closed, I was quite sure. So, like Sigourney Weaver, she was probably sleeping. Or was she dead? Sleeping, definitely. This fantasy of mine was as absurd as *Alien*³. Ridiculous.

"Did you want me?" Sam's nasal drone interrupted my thoughts.

"No, nothing, never mind."

I didn't want to ask Sam about dead bodies. I didn't want to discover that he knew all about them or that it was one of Deidre's areas of arcane knowledge. I would have to ask McKee. That woman's arm flung out, off the bed, was peculiar. No one slept like that. If she wasn't dead, perhaps she'd been drugged. I would call McKee tomorrow. I had an obligation, a moral responsibility even. Suppose we had stumbled on something nefarious.

THE BEACH was bleak. Gray clouds shading to black, and a biting wind off the water. It was my idea to meet here. No one would see or overhear us. The tide would take care of our footprints, as surely as it had erased the tire marks behind the Nicholas house.

I could feel the damp through my thin cotton socks and the canvas of my white Keds. It was cold. I hugged myself, rubbing warmth into my arms. Too revved to sit on the driftwood log that had conveniently washed up near the Town Beach parking lot, I started pacing in hillocks of sand, but that took too much energy. He was ten minutes late. Was his lack of promptness a character trait or a rarity? And what did that matter, anyway? What about him was incidental, and what was constant? That was the sort of speculation I indulged in about men I was going to date. I settled for working off my nervousness by rocking on my feet, burying them so I now had the unpleasant sensation of sand in my shoes. I wasn't even sure why I was nervous, except that I was aware there was something infelicitous about our meeting at the beach. What would he think I wanted?

A FedEx truck pulled in. Then Wilson's Plumbing. So much for privacy. Neither driver removed himself from his vehicle. As far as I could tell, they were both whiling away the time, watching the Atlantic. The FedEx driver rolled down his window, stuck his hand out and shook liquid off a lid. He must be drinking coffee.

Now a big black four-by-four arrived. A Jimmy, according to the lettering on the side. Not until the driver got out and started toward me did I realize it was McKee. He was not in uniform.

I hadn't expected him to show up off-duty. When I had spoken to him at the police station and he had suggested this hour in the early afternoon, I imagined he would be on break. Not that it mattered. So what that he arrived as a civilian, wasn't that the term?

He walked with the casual, relaxed gait of an athlete, even across dry sand, which, for me, required a plowing force. His faded jeans and thin gray sweatshirt hung gracefully and naturally. His true uniform was not policeman's blues. He was taller than I had thought. And hadn't he been chunky? This was confusing. The equipment that a cop attaches to his belt—gun, handcuffs, ammunition clip—must have created an illusion of chubbiness. In any event, he was underdressed. Immune to cold, I supposed, like all tough guys. Or he might disdain jackets because he knew he looked sexier this way.

I waved broadly and called at the same time, "How are you?"

"Good." He glanced up and down the shore. He wore slick sunglasses with reflector lenses.

"Do you always do that?"

"What?"

"Check out the place?"

"Sure, it's habit. You know cops always sit facing the door." He spoke rapidly. "I don't have much time. I'm due somewhere."

"Oh, sure, of course." I pointed toward the driftwood log. "Should we sit down?"

He waited for me to get situated. Then he placed himself carefully, allowing enough space for a person, possibly a person-and-a-half, to sit between us. Companionable but aloof.

"Mynten?" I offered him one from my pocket, having planned this moment ahead, to soften him up so he would be more receptive. "The pack you gave me," I explained. "I carry them in the glove compartment, I've nearly finished them. I've even tried some other flavors—cherry, honey." I stopped chattering.

"Thanks. So what's the problem?" he asked.

"It's not a problem, well, it is a problem—" I popped a Mynten in my mouth and stashed it in my cheek. "Remember the day at the Nicholas house?"

"Yes." His voice was noncommittal.

"I know you'll think this is completely crazy, but—"

He waited.

"Is it possible that woman was dead?"

"No." He dismissed the question as if I were inquiring about parking regulations.

"I'm serious. I keep remembering her arm. She was lying on her back and her arm was hanging off the bed." I demonstrated, throwing my arm out, with the inside of my elbow facing skyward, a limb rendition of sunny-side up. My hand drooped from the wrist, the way hers had, fingers softly curled. I checked my arm to be sure the imitation was accurate, then looked to see if this rang a bell with McKee. Who could tell what was going on behind those sunglasses? From the slant of his head and a lack of motion around the mouth, he seemed at least to be paying attention. Then his tongue snaked along his upper lip. I let my arm drop. "I experimented at home," I said, feeling self-conscious.

"Experimented?" Now his voice sounded amused.

"Yes." I sat straighter, trying to maintain a serious demeanor. I even sucked in my stomach because I had once observed that good posture gave me confidence. "I got on my bed and lay on my back. When you stretch your arm out horizontally, half hanging off the mattress"—I extended my arm again, in the most precise and specimen-like way—"believe me, you cannot sleep."

He said nothing, and I had a flash. He didn't remember. He was so fixated on that *Playboy*-centerfold body, the arm had escaped him altogether. "You remember, right?"

"Sure."

"So it doesn't make sense, right?"

"Well—" he said vaguely.

"And who lies naked in a room like that?"

The second I uttered those words, I wanted to retract them. "Who lies naked?" If I could pose the question, the answer was mortifyingly self-evident: Obviously not me. I saw him start to grin, then stop. "Some people," he remarked. "It was a nice day."

"No." This was something I had given thought to. In spite of my planning and the fact that I was doing most of the talking, it was the first moment the ball was in my court. "It was chilly. I remember zipping my jacket."

"Look." He spoke kindly but firmly, as if he had decided to end my foolishness. "When a person dies, the blood pools. She would have had deep color in her buttocks, her back . . ."

"Not if she had just died."

"And her eyes would have been open."

"What if she'd been drugged, and died in her sleep?"

"Sometimes your lids roll up anyway."

"They do?"

"Yes."

"That's creepy."

He laughed. He'd been resting his elbows on his legs, and most of his contact with me had been occasional sideways glances. But now, as he laughed, he flexed backward, sitting up. He took my measure in a friendly way, and the space between us altered, becoming finite.

"So how many dead bodies do you see in a year?" I asked.

"Four or five in car accidents, about the same in heart attacks, strokes, that sort of thing."

"And their eyes always flip back open?"

"Not always."

"See?" I was getting excited.

"My grandmother's eyes did that, though. I'll never forget it. She had these amazing eyes—"

I interrupted, anxious. "Don't you have to leave? I mean, how soon do you have to be somewhere?"

"Don't worry about it." He pushed up his sleeve. Spying his bare arm, I was gripped with the urge to run my finger along it, grazing the hairs lightly and ending in the crook of his elbow, which appeared exceptionally tender. Do men have secret vanities, and if so, were McKee's his beautiful tapered forearms, with their ideal density of body hair, suggesting man not bear? Apparently unaware of my fixation—although he did adjust his sleeves higher—he continued talking. "My grandmother's eyes were pale blue, the color of ocean sky on a hazy day."

He also commented, apropos of nothing, that his grandmother was a tiny thing who weighed ninety pounds with a rock in her pocket. I dragged my focus from his arms to his sunglasses. All I saw there was my own reflection, and the clutter of detail visible behind: the ribbon of wire fencing, a metal sign, beach grass waving. My face looked little and lonely.

"My granny could scare the truth out of me. No," he amended, "no one could scare the truth out of me. I was a world-champion liar, but when she aimed those blue lasers in my direction, I always thought she knew the score."

"You lied a lot?" I watched my mouth move.

"Sure, about where I'd been and where I was going and what I drank. We're talking sixteen here. And after. I was bad." He confessed this with nostalgia. "My mom hadn't heard from her in a whole day—which in my family is a long time—so she called me. Tom the cop. That's who they call when they're worried about anything."

"I'm always worried."

"I can tell."

"What do you mean, you can tell? How can you tell?"

"I don't know, you're jittery. With your little notebook, always scribbling, it seems like—"

"What?"

"Your brain's working double time."

He had noticed that? He saw things in me I didn't intend for him to see? How was that possible? I was the designated observer. I was *paid* to observe. There was something humiliating but also impressive in his exposing me offhandedly and then breezing on with his own story. "I found my granny on her bed. Dressed, wearing an apron. I guess she'd gone up to nap."

"How could you tell she was dead?" I was determined not to be sidetracked, even by the revelation that my interior life was visible to someone who was practically a passing stranger and that, perversely, I found it seductive.

"I felt her pulse, but I knew."

"How?"

"There was an awesome quiet." He gave a majesty to this phrasing, dwelling on "awesome." We both stared toward the ocean; the metaphor for the depth of this silence lay at our feet. "Anyway," said McKee, "I closed her eyes, and her lids scrolled right back up again. It was like she was saying, 'I may be dead, but you'll still never get anything past me.'" I heard him crunch, demolishing the last of his Mynten. Like a chain-smoker, he took a couple more out of his pocket. I accepted one, and we both unwrapped and popped—

partners in a shuffle-and-slide routine. "Where'd you get this crazy idea?" he asked.

No way was I going to reply, *"Alien³."* I just swished my lozenge from one cheek to the other.

"There was no weapon, nothing was disturbed, she wasn't disturbed."

Was he positive about that? Was the world-champion liar deluding himself? I bet he couldn't describe one thing about that woman that wasn't between her neck and knees.

"Also, her hair wasn't messed up," said Tom. "Like she'd just combed it."

"Her hair—" I was about to comment when I realized I had nothing to say. I couldn't remember much about it. Was her hair light brown, maybe blond, curly, or simply wavy, perhaps straight? And how long was it? And what color were her eyes? Oh, right, they were closed, but what about her face? Angular, oval, round? I searched for an end to the sentence I'd started. "—was pretty. Her hair was pretty."

"It was peaceful in that room," McKee declared conclusively. "Harmonious." He rolled the word out with pride.

I would have to disabuse him, but I would do it as to a doctor, the way I might discuss something embarrassing like gas as a medical phenomenon. "Actually, it wasn't peaceful," I said. "It was sexually charged." There I'd said it. No big deal. My mouth felt dry. I swallowed, and the Mynten slipped into my throat.

I started to smile but horror took over. I gagged. I tried to cough, then to swallow again, but found no way in or out. The nugget was permanently, stubbornly lodged. I jumped up and bent over, heaving compulsively. I'm going to die. No thought more original than that, I chided myself—even while choking I clung to irony—as McKee's arm circled my shoulders. He jabbed me under my ribs, once, twice, and the little Mynten shot into the air, making a graceful arc before plopping soundlessly into the sand.

McKee turned me toward him and into his arms. I sagged against his chest, feeling the warm cotton sweatshirt against my cheek and even recognizing the scent of softener with which his wife had sweet-ened the wash. "Are you all right?" It was as if he'd added "darling," I could hear the worry in his tone. "Lie down," he said. "Just lie in the sand."

Obediently, I went limp, letting my legs crumple. He lowered me into a sitting position, then squatted in front. "Those suckers are dangerous," he observed, smiling. Dangerous, yes. I had barely the energy to lift a teacup, but was seized with a desire to throw myself at McKee and knock him backward into the sand, where we would writhe amorously.

"Come on, do as I say, lie down."

I stretched out on my side, the least exposed of the possibilities. "That was scary," was all I could manage.

He nodded. "Look at the sky."

I didn't want to. Several months of tears, maybe a few years of them, were about to burst forth. I needed to board up my eyes, ham-mer crisscrossed two-by-fours over them, or I might drown in a flash flood.

"Roll onto your back and look at the sky."

I did as I was told. "It's all sooty," I said, taking emotional cover in my usual disinclination to appreciate nature.

He leaned close. I felt his breath against my cheek. "Rain clouds," he whispered. "Big black rain clouds."

"Sooty," I said. "Like the kind of grime you wash off your face after a long walk on a windy day in New York City."

"You miss that place?"

"I ache for it."

"So move back."

"I can't. My son."

While I confided about Sam, McKee sat down next to me. He consumed three Myntens, twisted the paper into skinny swizzle sticks, and used them to draw aimless lines and loops in the sand. It was cold, and the wind echoed the crash of the waves. There was something brave, even daring, about lying in the sand in threatening weather and pouring out my heart.

He listened. On that afternoon on Town Beach, I found out how sexy listening was. I was used to asking the questions, to drawing men out, but I had no idea that listening could be a form of tenderness. I remembered things long forgotten. Not that I spilled them all. I didn't reveal what had upset me the most, couldn't bring myself to, and I wasn't quite that needy. I only insisted to McKee and myself that Sam had been the happiest baby, a joy bug, as images, like recovered memory, flitted in and out of my consciousness: Sam in his Sesame Street pajamas marching in circles on his bed, Sam galloping through the apartment to throw himself into my arms, Sam squealing, "Again!" after Allan and I kissed him simultaneously, one on each cheek. "Don't ever get divorced," I told McKee, recollecting the night after Allan left. Sam, five, was playing with a twistable plastic toy, ignoring me, intently converting it from robot to truck and back as I tucked him into bed. No marching around, no flopping down, his bangs and forehead damp with excitement.

"I kept telling myself he'd get past it. Like grief. Work it through."

McKee didn't argue that Sam couldn't be shut down solely from the divorce. I was grateful because I knew I was right.

"Divorce is the destruction of childhood." I couldn't recall the first time that thought came and clonked me, the first bedtime Sam turned away to face the wall and seemed to squeeze his eyes shut rather than close them. From then on, it arrived regularly, a night visitor, to make me heartsick. Later, as I aimlessly channel-surfed or flipped through magazines, this crushing guilt would be nudged aside by a different feeling: relief giving way to happiness, even exuberance that there wasn't a whiff of Allan anywhere. He was gone. As a mother, perhaps I was not in the normal range. How could my sadness be kicked out of bed so easily, even by a dam-bursting sense of liberation?

"Why did you split up?" McKee asked, startling me.

I answered another question—a trick journalists were always on the lookout for—intentionally misunderstanding what had been asked. "His father's in Massachusetts, lives in Newton, has a chain of pizza parlors along the East Coast." I loaded on details to deflect McKee further. "He inherited them. An okay guy—he's responsible financially and he loves Sam. Technically, we have joint custody."

"Big-city lives."

"Isn't it the same everywhere? I'm just here because . . . no clubs, no heavy-duty drugs for Sam to buy. Less temptation. So much less temptation."

"Is there?" He brushed my bangs lightly to the side.

I shuddered, an involuntary temblor.

McKee stood up. Scrambling to match his move, I got up, too. He collected the sunglasses he had discarded on the beach, and put them back on. I busied myself beating the clammy sand off my arms and legs. "So tell me," I strained to speak naturally, "was that woman in the beach house Mrs. Nicholas?"

"There is no Mrs. Nicholas."

"Who was she, one of the owner's girlfriends?"

McKee checked his watch. "I've got to get going." He started back to the car.

"Tom?" I used his first name without thinking. "Who was it? Come on."

"None of your business." He tugged a cell phone from his pocket and tapped in a number as he kept walking. I trudged after him. "Sorry, Billy, I got held up. . . . Be there in five, bye."

"Whoever she was, she wasn't from here."

"Why do you say that?" he asked. I tweaked his sleeve, and he swung around. I expected the return of his bold flirty smile. Although if I could have decreed it, I would have erased that smile from his lips and stripped off his horrible reflector lenses so I could take one last dive into his absolving eyes. Instead I saw the cop. He folded his arms across his chest and boasted the backing of the entire police force as he inquired, "What information do you have, exactly?"

"None. Just speculation. Never mind. Thanks for—" I couldn't figure out how to finish the sentence. I could write an entire column about my tendency to thank people when I felt hurt or wanted to kick them. Maybe I *would* write a column about it. "Thank you for taking time," I said finally.

"No big deal. Good-bye."

He opened the door of his heavy-duty Jimmy. I walked across the lot to my Honda.

"I still think you should call Mr. Nicholas." I couldn't resist lobbing a last directive his way, some offhand bossiness to show that in fact nothing had happened on that beach in the way of intimacy. Although . . . I could also write a column about my inability to let things rest. "You should call."

"I did," said McKee.

I sprinted to his car and rapped on his window until he lowered it. "Who was it? Tell me."

"Mr. Nicholas did not authorize any visitors to the residence." McKee spoke as if he were logging a report. "Pursuant to my call, he came out last weekend to ascertain if anything had been taken, and it hadn't. I'll see you." He started the engine.

"Wait. Let me get this straight and then I'll leave you alone."

"Is that a promise?"

I ignored the question. "If Nicholas is telling the truth, the woman broke in. No—" My mind was crackling with what I now considered "the case." "No, the alarm was deactivated, so she or whoever she was with knew the code. An assignation. I bet we arrived in the aftermath of an assignation. That would explain the sexual tension."

"Would it?" asked McKee.

"Of course. So who had the keys, who knew the alarm code? Omigod"—I restrained myself from shrieking—"I saw tire tracks in the sand."

"A trespass with nothing missing does not merit an investigation. We changed the locks and the alarm. Mr. Nicholas wants the entire matter dropped. In situations like this, the police comply."

This barrage of police-speak was making me cranky. "Did you notice her toenails?" I asked.

"What?"

"Each nail was painted a different bizarre color—black, blue, green, silver. She could have been a hooker."

"That's why you suspect the woman wasn't from Sakonnet Bay?"

"No," I said, though it was one reason.

McKee did not respond. He appeared to be watching the waves through the windshield, and I wished I could disown my toenail/hooker theory. I had been on a roll, only to blow it with that inanity. McKee scratched his neck.

"When my daughter was about seven," he said, "all she did was color nails. She lugged around a shoe box packed with polish. She painted her brothers', her dolls', her mother's." He burst out laughing.

In cataloguing his responses—and I was becoming an expert—I'd noticed a mocking, amused laugh, which was short and abrupt, and a deep appreciative laugh, a rarer thing. But this particular laughter was wholehearted and spontaneous, as if it had bubbled up from an underground spring. "Alicia's a real case," he said, still chuckling. "She even painted the fingers and toes of this statue of Jesus my mother-in-law gave us."

"So are you saying this woman might have been a seven-year-old?" I was furious and possibly something else—jealous.

"I'm saying that, in this instance, she might have had a sister or a niece." He was serious now, reinstating formality. "Why else is it your opinion that she wasn't from here?"

I rushed on to get it out before I thought about it. "Her pubic hair—" Why, at the age of thirty-seven, did I still find the word "pubic" embarrassing? "It was trimmed in a triangle. I used to see this in locker rooms in Manhattan gyms all the time. But I use that gym behind the candle shop, and I've never seen it in the locker room there."

Now that I was getting down to describing that naked body, I was relieved that McKee was manifesting all the animation of a traffic cop. His woodenness bolstered my confidence. I opined, to no particular end, that the woman's breasts were real. I didn't say that they sagged comfortably sideways like beanbags, but I did mention that they didn't have the pumped-up look of basketball breasts on late-night cable TV. This, I admitted, might undermine my high-class-hooker theory. But it might not. With this final pronouncement, I ran out of steam.

I waited, longing for an argument. Hoping to delay him another hour.

"A trespass with nothing missing does not merit an investigation," he repeated.

"What about a trespass with a dead body? Or a drugged body? Don't forget that arm. That arm was weird."

He released his emergency brake, prepared to depart.

"The question is"—I imitated his cop formality—"what person with access to the house possesses a car that is capable of being driven on the beach?"

"Me." The smile that knew its own power broke out once again.

"What about your brother? Does he drive one?"

McKee raised the window.

I felt the wet smack of a raindrop on my cheek. Another landed on my head with a splat. It was going to be a drenching rain that began with single bloated drops landing here and there. I glanced down at my sand-coated sneakers; dirty wet spots began to muddy them. I heard the crunch of big wheels on gravel. The lumbering family car pulled back past me. I didn't bother to watch, only heard the insult of its leaving me behind in the lot.

THAT EVENING the wind threw torrents of rain against the house. Shortly after six, the electricity blew, so Sam and I dined by candlelight. I preferred not to consider the irony. As I was not in a mood to engage in futile attempts to amuse, I turned on Jane's handy housewarming gift, the transistor radio. It filled the void with local news about the nor'easter and the power outage.

Sam leaned on his elbow as he shoveled in a few bites of stir-fry before leaving his plate on the counter, a half-moon of it jutting off precariously. I didn't point this out, just accepted his carelessness as a further burden. He navigated his way up the stairs with a flashlight.

I had a supply of votive candles, also thanks to Jane, and turned the house into an Italian church, offerings burning from one end to the other. Amid the flickering flames, I settled under my quilt on the living room couch. It was perfect obsessing weather: a stormy night, no lights, and two teenagers having sex above my head.

Deidre had arrived around eight, paying a rare school-night visit. I assumed her parents were strict about studying, though without electricity, there was no way to do homework. I hadn't heard a knock, but my son came down from his room with astonishing swiftness. How had he known she was there? Were they linked by an extrasensory connection? In the dim light, I saw him bound across the foyer—love having raised his energy and spirits—and open the door to an enormous yellow slicker with a hood that left only a rectangular opening to see through. The rain-slicker killer, I found myself thinking, as the huge shiny ensemble followed Sam up the stairs.

Sam had ignored my banishing Deidre, and I had let the matter drop. It wasn't that I was helpless in controlling my son, although perhaps I was, and it wasn't that I reneged out of guilt, although I was consumed by it. I couldn't separate Sam from his only friend. I had raised the subject of condoms, of course, made an impassioned speech about them, and handed over a paper bag containing several packets. He accepted them, and I tried to find that reassuring, since I was sharing my house with insatiable lovers, to judge from the amount of time they spent in Sam's room.

In dread of overhearing any orgasmic yelps, I raised the sound on the radio. I considered phoning Jane and telling her the entire McKee saga from dog bite on, then mentally thumbed through my New York friends. The telephone was one of the few activities available. But I would not confide, even considering it was pretense. I didn't want to reveal my own complicity, my provocativeness, my foolishness. Besides, my attraction to McKee was solely physical. A product of my own dislocation and loneliness.

What had put it all in perspective was the statue of Jesus.

I had a bias against religion, inherited from my father. "Most wars were caused by religion," he used to mutter with some frequency. One of my jobs, self-appointed, was to retrieve his asides and lob them in my mother's direction, hoping to stimulate her interest, yearning for them to connect. "Really, Daddy, most wars?" I wasn't subtle, and she wasn't interested. My father died of a heart attack when I was fifteen, before I knew that blaming religion for war was not particularly original. This didn't matter, because he had said it, and I, caretaker of his words, observed it as a sacred canon of a faith of my own.

Since my divorce, I had dated often and had several tepid affairs. None of the men had been more than casually observant—Jews who attended temple only on High Holidays, Protestants and Catholics who went to church on Easter Sunday or Christmas Eve. I had never, knowingly, even had a drink with a guy whose decor included religious artifacts.

Was McKee's statue large, a big stone object occupying a corner of his living room, or had it been consigned to the garden, a shrine next to the swing set? Maybe it stood on the mantel, an image in plastic or plaster of Paris. It couldn't possibly be a crucifix hanging over his marriage bed—that vision appeared only in Catholic hospitals and Italian movies. To think of McKee sleeping under a crucifix amused me. In an iron bed, the plain gray kind. I saw it clearly—the line of thick metal poles forming a headboard with all the charm of jail. My fantasies kept getting away from me, beginning in spite and ending in perverse enjoyment. Maybe McKee didn't want the icon, displayed it only to humor his mother-in-law, a religious fanatic? That was the most favorable interpretation of the whole statue-of-Jesus business, and I discounted it immediately.

I was not going to consider anything that made him more appealing. My anger, after all, was about being humiliated. Seeing him leap to his feet after my inadvertent frisson. Seeing him repelled. Just thinking about it made me cringe. And his snide remark after I had pathetically pledged not to bother him again if he would answer one measly question. "Is that a promise?" he had said. That was cruel. I hadn't asked him to touch my hair, to smooth my bangs.

If he went to confession, he ought to confess that slick, seductive move.

Being attracted to McKee was ludicrous. N-I-C. Nothing in common. I hugged my legs—a sad consolation, having only my own limbs to cozy up to. And then there was a knock on the door and I stiffened so suddenly my back cracked. I felt my spine, it was still there in one piece, and as the rapping grew more insistent, I sprang off the couch.

I checked to see if something should be cleared, removed, prepared. I looked down at my dismal sweatpants, paused to regret my outfit, then, untangling the quilt from my ankles, grabbed the flashlight. I had trouble turning it on, jamming the button in the wrong direction. I would send McKee away. Not even let him in the front hall, although he had braved a virtual hurricane to see me, although it couldn't possibly be he, because at this moment he was reading *Goodnight Moon* to one of his many children, conceived because he didn't believe in birth control. Fears and wishes tumbled over each other as I opened the front door and aimed the light aggressively into the face of whoever was there.

"I hit a deer," said Jane.

I pulled her inside, and she began to sob, apologizing over and over, berating herself for crying, and sobbing harder. She was a mess, in a trench coat so soaked that it clung to her in patches, and a silly plastic rain hat that tied under her chin. I hugged her and immediately needed to be hung out to dry myself.

"Now we're both drenched. My God." I failed to elicit a smile as I began to extricate Jane from her coat. I undid the belt, then the buttons, a teacher creating calm around a child who has gone to pieces. "Tequila?" was all she could say. I peeled off the sopping garment.

"No, but I have vodka. Did you kill it?"

She shook her head and continued to weep helplessly. I untied the strings under her chin and took off her hat.

"This way, please"—I nudged her into the living room to wrap her in the quilt, then steered her into the kitchen. She sat at the table, sniffling. The quilt fell slack, unnoticed, while she followed my orders to replace her wet shoes and knee-hi's with a pair of my thick socks.

I poured two inches of vodka into a juice glass and set it in front of her. "What happened?"

The words did not come out in logical order. Between gulps of vodka, Jane recalled seeing a large object pass in front of the car, only she wasn't sure it had, because the wipers provided only a split second of visibility between blasts of rain.

I heard a thunk above our heads, and ignored it, hoping she would, too. "Why on earth were you driving in this?" I asked.

She ran a hand through her hair. "Coming to see you."

Had I invited her and forgotten? I didn't think so. "So you missed the deer? I'm confused."

"Missed it, that one, but then another—" She wilted further. Her mouth crumpled up, she blinked rapidly. Another thunk. This time the ceiling vibrated. She jerked up, stunned.

"The kids," I explained. "Sam and Deidre."

"They're there now?"

The ceiling shook again.

"Good grief," said Jane.

"I know. It's like living in occupied territory. I have to talk to him about it." I wondered if I would.

We both gazed at the ceiling, waiting for another rumble.

"Could we sit someplace else?" she asked weakly.

We toted the vodka, my diet Coke, and a box of Kleenex into the living room, away from the sounds of aerobic sex. Jane snuggled into one corner of the couch, and I occupied the other, my legs curled under me. "So then what happened?" I asked.

"I hit that second one. Smacked it. The back of the car scooted sideways and then swung back. I got out and was wandering around in this total downpour. I couldn't see anything, I don't know."

"How terrifying."

She nodded.

"Did you walk here from the accident?"

"No, I drove. The car's smashed in front, I think, but it's working." Having told the story, Jane sighed, her head listed slowly toward the back of the couch and touched down there, a safe landing. Her eyes closed.

I reached over to squeeze her shoulder. "You're having an attack of the Bambis." Jane's eyes popped open, and I was inches away from a look so desolate, from pain so stark as to be unmistakable. "You know, it must have felt like you hit Bambi," I babbled, plumping the patient's pillows with my voice. "That's why you're upset. There are too many deer, and they're all worked up into a mating frenzy."

"I think Jonathan's leaving me." She was dry-eyed now, and flat.

"What? How do you know?"

"He has a girlfriend."

"Who?"

"I don't know."

"Did he say?"

"No."

"The ponytail."

"Yes.

It had been in front of my face, niggling at me, actually. When I first met Jonathan, the day Sam and I put up the hammock, I had been struck by that ponytail. Jonathan was a tall, thin, sleepy-eyed guy. The way he dressed and carried himself suggested he had only a passing acquaintance with his own body. Narrow shoulders hid in plaid shirts, khaki pants bagged over a flat behind. He had a sweet face—soft round eyes with heavy lids, and a hesitant smile. As a couple they made sense: Jane all vigor and pep, Jonathan a quiet comfort. I was a little thrown by his glasses—brash angular black frames—but the real incongruity was his hair. Graying brown and wavy, it had receded to leave a smooth oval, a lagoon on the top front of his head. In the back he'd grown it out and fashioned it into a small ponytail. About four inches then, who knew what it was now. I was too preoccupied with my son's invention in the hair department to keep track of anyone else's. I had assumed Jonathan was compensating for the baldness on top, the way women of a certain age wear short skirts to show off their legs in the hope of distracting from the lines in their faces. My ruthless mother had pointed this out. "After fifty," she said, "a woman with good legs should walk on her hands." Jonathan's ponytail was like that, a version of holding on to youth. "When did he start wearing his hair that way?" I asked.

"Last winter," said Jane.

So it was fairly recent, and I'd underestimated its significance. How unusual, when leaping to conclusions was my stock-in-trade.

Jane laid out the evidence coolly, as if Jonathan were somebody else's husband. His golfing hours had changed, from early morning to late afternoon. But not always, which was the strange part for someone so orderly. Occasionally, for the first time in twenty-one years of marriage, he went out to lunch or disappeared for a few hours in the afternoon. And, Jane threw in the final proof, this man who never used to leave home except to golf, who spent hours isolated in his den hooked up to his modem, playing the stock market, remarked that he needed fresh air.

"Oh, he offered an excuse for leaving, when you didn't ask."

"Exactly," said Jane. "And then"—her cheek twitched, leaking tension—"I made a joke about gambas and he didn't laugh."

"Gambas?"

"'Shrimp' in Spanish." Jane smashed a tissue into her face in an apparent struggle not to wail.

"Are you okay?"

She shook her head. "I'm so scared," she said, after blowing her nose.

"I know, honey."

We smiled at each other. If Jonathan left, we'd end up together on Saturday nights, having cozy talks in front of the fire. Accompanied by vodka, I noted, as Jane finished her drink and poured another. She had an ease with liquor. She never held it in her mouth before committing to it, as I often did. Nor did she savor it. She just polished it off. Was this new? A subtle seismic shift in behavior?

Jane pressed the cool glass against her forehead, then her cheeks. "We went to Barcelona ten years ago. We ate all these gambas. Gambas galore. They make the most delicious grilled shrimp in Barcelona. Have you ever been?"

"No."

"Then we'd go back to the room and make love in the Roman bath. It was a gorgeous tiled sunken tub with steps. Do you mind my telling you this?"

"Of course not," I said. This was not true. Details about other people's sex lives made me squeamish. The sounds of lovemaking upstairs might now be accompanied by a torrid narrative downstairs. I was in danger of being trapped in X-rated surround sound.

"One night while we were in Spain, I had a dream about losing my underpants—only in the dream, my underpants were called gambas. It became our joke. 'How are your gambas?' 'I lost my gambas.' 'What's for dinner, gambas?'"

"It's a good word," I said, realizing why I'd hated that story about the statue of Jesus. Because McKee and his wife had laughed about it together. The statue was their gambas.

Jane ranted on, picking up speed. "So last night we rented *My Cousin Vinny*—that's another thing, now whenever I ask him what he wants, from the video store, for dinner, anything, he says he doesn't care—but we were watching, and I wasn't really concentrating, because all I think about is how he doesn't want me anymore, and that fills up all the space in my head. Anyway, this is so silly, but the movie's about this car, and how to identify it, and I said, 'By its gambas.' Jonathan didn't react, no smile, nothing."

Allan and I never had a gambas. The closest we ever came was my senior year at Barnard when we told my mother I was pregnant. He traveled home with me for spring break, and we were eating hummus, sitting on the low couches around her coffee table, a large brass Chinese tray balanced on squat wooden legs. My mother had gone through a big hummus-and-pita phase, and also a Middle-and-Far-Eastern-everything phase. The Chinese tray, curry, hummus, embroidered Indian pillows, kimonos—it was all one culture to her. One big bazaar. But hummus? I never could figure out how my mother, whose idea of providing comfort was to hold out a box of tissues for me to pull one for myself, could enjoy such an earthy food. "Didn't you use birth control?" she'd asked.

"No."

"It was a concession to aesthetics," Allan added. This was a joke we'd already cracked to each other, and once again we laughed as if it had been so clever of us to end up in this predicament. My mother waited for us to get past our amusement, her eyes, hard as pebbles, peering at us over half-glasses. "How stupid," she said. Allan threw me an anxious glance, and I jumped in, explaining that we really wanted to get married anyway. My mother, who practiced the art of well-chosen silence, managed to convey the idea that this remark was not even worth responding to.

So at twenty-two, when my friends began living the histrionic lives of single New Yorkers, something unexpected happened to me. I fell in love. With Sam. He passed through my ironic armor with ghostly ease. My tenderness for him felt almost illegal, born as I was into a family of non-connectors. On one of her rare visits to New York, my mother saw me leap from a park bench to protect Sam's head from an errant swing. She informed me that I was fused with him. This infuriated me. My feelings were not twisted, just deep. What I felt for Allan was, in comparison, trifling. I had assumed that he was my match because of his attributes—the right Jewish boy with the right IQ, from the right family. He was no soul mate, but proper casting for the part. Besides, I was pregnant, and that had fueled my need to think him right. We came undone fairly quickly. At twenty-seven, with a five-year-old, I reentered single life as my former classmates were tying the knot right and left. I was doomed to spend my life out of step and over my head.

"So that's how you know Jonathan's having an affair? He didn't laugh at a shrimp joke?"

"Plus no sex for ages, the ponytail, the so-called lunches."

"You connected the dots."

"Yes."

"I'm good at that, too."

We shared a silence, acknowledging the bittersweet fruit of our brilliant intuitive powers. And then Jane dropped the bombshell.

"I went to the bank today and discovered he'd cleared out our savings account."

"What?" Even I was aware that my "whats" were remarkable. An utter capitulation to disbelief and astonishment. Very satisfying to the person at whom they were directed, I'm sure. Jane responded with a wan smile as Sam's bedroom door banged open, and his and Deidre's threatening procession downstairs commenced.

"Oh God, no, bad timing." I rose to greet them, but in almost perfect synchronization they lapped their bodies around the newel post at the bottom of the banister in order to make it into the kitchen without being accosted.

"Good, a reprieve." I flopped down again. "Now go on, whisper, they'll never hear."

"No, I don't want to discuss it." Jane folded the quilt and

rearranged herself, smoothing her pants, crossing her legs. "I want to have a normal conversation. I want to pretend my life's okay."

"Maybe he made a bad investment, and he's disappearing daily to brood."

"You don't believe that, do you?"

"No."

I heard the kids bumping around, cabinets opening and closing.

"Let's not talk about it," said Jane. "Tell me what you did today."

I considered before answering. "Nothing much," I said. "I didn't feel like working, so I took a walk on Ocean Avenue, sneaked down driveways, checked out the mansions, it was fun." So now I had lied to my close friend. Not only that, the lie came easily. I hoped this wasn't the beginning of a descent into an underworld of intrigue and murder. Feeling a rush of competence, possibly excitement, I moved on to worm information out of her. "Do you know the Nicholas house? It's beautiful."

"Yes. Lovely. He gutted it."

"He?"

"George Nicholas. Bought it two years ago, around the time Jonathan and I got our new place and Simon had just left for college. It's strange to wish for a time before, isn't it? I pine for before."

"I think it's clear we can't talk about anything else."

"Yes, we can. Ask me a question."

"No."

"Please."

"Well . . ." I pretended to think. "Who is George Nicholas?"

"Mid-thirties. In direct mail, whatever that means."

"That means rich. You know, Jane, if you owned one of those big four-by-four cars, hitting that deer would have been like swatting a fly. You wouldn't have even known it happened. I saw a dark green SUV in the Nicholas driveway." The lies were piling up. "Was that his?"

"Maybe. Not sure. I think he drives something German. Lives in Manhattan, has an accent. Could be English, could be affected."

"His taste is affected," I said, then realized with horror that, so gifted was I at sleuthing, I'd given myself away. How would I know his taste unless I'd been inside his house?

But Jane wasn't paying attention. "That shit," she said. She was not speaking of George Nicholas.

"It must take major bucks to service those mansions. I wonder how many people have keys to that house."

"The housekeeper, the caretaker if there is one, the contractor if the house is undergoing renovation." Jane ticked them off. "Not the gardener or the pool man, but the security company."

"If the house has an alarm." Was my pretending not to know lying or simply being evasive?

"I look terrible, don't I?" demanded Jane.

"No, just sad. I wonder who Jonathan's girlfriend is. Do you have any idea?"

"I don't want to know. I haven't decided what I want to say or do. Until then I'm going to act as if I know nothing."

"How cold-blooded," I remarked with some admiration. So Jane would go about her life, being cheerful, which she was awfully good at, while she contemplated her dreadful options. She might be coping with Jonathan by imagining him a tiresome client and chatting about the scarcity of parking spaces (a big Sakonnet Bay topic) or beach erosion or the advantages of gas heat over electric. "He's planning to run away with her," I said. "It's obvious. He's cleared out the account."

"My last four commissions."

"He's going to split with that money, and you're going to have a hell of a time nailing him legally, because he can play the market from wherever. All he needs is a computer. You better get a lawyer."

Now we heard some cupboards banging.

"Sam? Sam, come and say hello to me," called Jane.

Silence. Possibly a huddle was taking place. Then feet pounded, and Sam and his giantess appeared in the doorway.

"Hey." He bobbed his head at Jane. He was carrying a bag of popcorn.

"Hi, Sam," said Jane.

"This is Deidre Hall," I said. "Deidre, Jane Atkins."

Deidre sliced the air with her hand, presumably a hello. She looked particularly ragged, in baggy jeans whose waistband floated somewhere in the neighborhood of her hips. A brief dirty white T-shirt left her belly button exposed, a tiny piece of her body that I had not had the good fortune to witness the other day. My life is like *Appointment in Samarra*. I fled death in New York City only to find it waiting for me in Sakonnet Bay. Deidre had to be the only person in town with a belly-button ring.

"I hit a deer," said Jane.

"Majqa," said Deidre.

I explained that Deidre spoke Klingon, and Jane feigned ignorance.

"What does 'majqa' mean?" I inquired.

Sam scratched his cheek. "'Good.'"

Good that Jane hit a deer? Perhaps he hadn't translated accurately.

"It happened just before the turn to your street," said Jane.

Sam and Deidre exhibited all the interest of posterboard, which for some reason made me more determined to have a normal-range conversation. "There are too many deer. I'm covering a town meeting next week about it. Coral Williams, that woman who owns the Comfort Café, is head of Bambi's Friends. She wants to institute a birth control program, do you believe that?" The words "birth control" echoed like some grotesque Freudian slip. Not that it embarrassed Sam and Deidre, but I lost the power of speech, and Jane came to the rescue.

"My husband's head of the relocation group," said Jane. "They want to load the deer in a truck and ship them upstate to a farm."

"They should shoot them," said Deidre. Speaking her first English words in my presence, she adopted the electronic, expressionless voice of a robot.

"Show no mercy," Sam hooted. Deidre let loose a volley of machine-gun laughter.

I didn't dare exchange a look with Jane. The conversation had just sailed so far out of normal range it had docked in China.

"They should shoot my husband," said Jane. "Show no mercy." She let out a hoot of her own.

Sam and Deidre's levity ceased abruptly. Sam scratched his head. He really was like a big dog. Possibly he had fleas. Deidre rolled her eyes in Jane's direction, a smirk hovering, held back only by a bit of puzzlement visible in her shady gaze. At the same time her hand ventured into the bag of popcorn.

"I'm kidding," said Jane. "In fact, my husband agrees with you guys. He's championing this ship-the-deer-out plan as a compromise. You know, Deidre"—this version of Jane could coax charms off a bracelet—"I met you once, when I was showing your parents' old house, before your family moved. They weren't home, so I let myself in. You were about eight and you looked so adorable in a Brownie uniform. You were watching—I think it was that wonderful show on Nickelodeon, *Clarissa*." Deidre apparently did not appreciate being reminded of her normal childhood. She blinked a few times, that was all.

Jane got up off the couch. "I guess I'll go." Deflated, she moved to the window and stared into the darkness.

"You don't have to. Stay as late as you want. Live here, it's fine."

"No." She walked past me, colliding with a footstool, before locating the path to the kitchen. I followed, and watched as she opened the refrigerator, poured herself a glass of milk, and chugged it.

"Thanks to having no electricity, that milk's probably not even cold," I said.

She chewed a hunk of Jarlsberg and downed another glass. "I am now officially sober," she announced. I trailed her to the hall closet, careful not to dislodge or tread on a candle. Sam and Deidre were as we'd left them at the entrance to the living room: Deidre inserting popcorn into her mouth kernel by kernel; Sam on the floor, stroking the top of her bare foot.

"Deidre, don't you have to get home? When are you being picked up? It's late, it's a school night." I broke into a streak of mother-speak, bringing the evening to an official close. "Where's your slicker, dear?" The "dear" shocked even me, and Sam paused in his stroking and glanced up to curl his lip disgustedly. I looked down and noticed Deidre's feet.

"Is that black polish or red, I can't tell in this light."

She didn't answer.

"There's no word for it," said Sam. "It's black."

"Did you buy it in town?" I was now forced to play twenty questions with a Klingon.

"Ghobe."

"No," Sam translated.

"Perhaps Jane can drive you home."

"Of course. Go get your coat, sweetie, and I'll drop you." Jane's speaking matter-of-factly, as to a regular person, reminded me of the way some people address babies as if they understood everything. This had a promising effect. Deidre thumped her way upstairs. Sam followed halfway. I hadn't lit the route, so I could barely discern his form now slumped on a middle stair, but just as a good painter can convey shape and emotion in a few strokes, Sam managed to transmit his own self-portrait: I will die, I could die without her. Did I imagine this, or was I perceiving clearly? I should ask Jane. No. She was proving she could reassemble—fastening her damp trench coat with a one-handed twist of each button into its hole, giving the belt a sharp yank. "Still wet and squishy," she commented, as she put her shoes on.

"I'm here if you need me, Jane. Call me any hour."

"I'll be fine." She tucked her hair efficiently into her rain hat. "Come on, Miss Deidre."

At that moment, the lights went on. I had to shade my eyes, which gave me a second of grace before the shock of viewing life without the filter of candlelight. Jane's red nose and cloudy eyes. Sam's pallid complexion and, visible even ten feet away, a startling hickey gnawed into his neck. The living room and foyer with pretty braided rugs, nubby soft fabrics and patchworky things that were supposed to make the place home, and in which three souls stood unmoored.

Now Deidre reappeared on the landing, mercifully camouflaged in yellow, and she seemed so innocent. Just a very tall child dressed for rain.

Big City Eyes

BY LILY DAVIS

LAST SATURDAY MORNING, Deborah Cooke, owner of Deborah's Hair and Nails on Main Street, opened her beauty salon door and discovered a pile of trash that appeared to have been stuffed through the mail slot. The garbage included cigarette butts, several crusts of pizza, a broken bottle of Hello Kitty children's perfume, and a hank of pale orange hair. Because of the dime-store scent splattered about, the shop smelled putrid. "Like vase water after flowers have sat in it for a month," remarked Mrs. Cooke, whose ten-year-old son once attempted a science experiment involving dead flowers.

"This is not random vandalism," said Detective Maureen Mooney, whose long sandy-blond hair is pulled back in a twist and secured with a tortoiseshell comb. Her nails are coated with clear polish that she applies herself. "Most likely the incident was an act of revenge by an unhappy employee or client."

No one recognized the pale orange hair.

Not Mrs. Cooke, whose bouffant coiffure, a vision of symmetrical perfection, is so rigid that it is somewhat unexpected to see that, when she turns her head, her hair rotates, too. Not the only other stylist, Becky Ray, who rubs Frizz-Ease into her curly hair every morning before blow-drying it straight, and sports "French nails," a beige tone on the pink part and a whitener for the tips. There were no unhappy clients, they insisted. No one had recently complained or asked for a refund.

At the regular Wednesday 9:00 a.m. press briefing, Police Chief Ben Blocker backed off the revenge theory. "That place is one big happy family," he said, pointing out that Becky has worked years for Deborah, as have Rita, the part-time manicurist, and Angela, who cleans. "Furthermore," he said, "that clump of orange hair didn't ring a bell. Nobody recognized it." The hair has not been analyzed—animal versus human, natural or dyed. To do so, the police would have to ship the sample to the Suffolk County laboratories in Riverhead.

"Suppose Goldilocks escaped after sleeping on a bed in an Ocean Drive house?" I asked him. "Could the three bears confirm her identity only by sending her fingerprints and strands of hair to Riverhead?"

"That's correct," said Chief Blocker.

He did not say, "Why do you ask?" If he had, I would have answered, "That's another incident I intend to get to the bottom of."

Instead, he mentioned that all the clients for the past two weeks at Deborah's Hair and Nails had left tips. Citing that as proof of customer satisfaction, and noting that Mrs. Cooke wanted the matter dropped, he announced that the department was not planning to proceed further.

I had a bad haircut once, from a woman named Cecile, and the experience was distressing. Like buying something ghastly that you can't return and then being forced to wear it daily. I became obsessed with my awful haircut, stopping at every mirror and at every pane of glass. Was it really as bad as I thought? I then worsened my plight by going to another stylist for a correction. My hair ended up approximately a quarter-inch long.

I continually brought up the subject of my hideous hair. I needed to mention the outrage so my friends didn't think they knew something about me I didn't. The situation became a torture. All I saw around me were haircuts. People on the street were simply a collection of better hairdos I didn't have.

But here's the strange thing: I knew the cut was going to be terrible as it took place. I sat in that beauty salon chair with the towel around my neck, unable to stop it. Could not bring myself to speak up. Could not bolt with my hair parted and clipped, my head mapped like farmlands for planting. I let the haircut happen, and then thanked Cecile and tipped her.

Sometimes I do this—thank people when I really want to kick them, apologize when I'm actually furious. I behaved that way last week in the Town Beach parking lot. A man treated me coldly, and in return, I acted grateful and even threw in an apology. I suppose I do the opposite of what I feel either because I don't know what I feel at the time or because my feelings are so hurt that I don't want to face them. If the police had consulted me, I could have tipped them to this weakness of certain highly sensitive women. I could have helped them solve the crime.

But my loyalties are with the vandal. A bad haircut is an injustice, even if it's not illegal. Just because your hair hasn't been stolen doesn't mean you haven't been robbed of your looks. Somewhere in Sakonnet Bay is an upset woman with a bad haircut. She is looking in mirrors nonstop and beginning every conversation with "I hate my hair." She's angry now, so watch out. Believe me, once she's been mistreated in this manner, there is no way she is going to shut up.

WAITING to make a left turn into the Town Hall parking lot, I was trapped in a long line of cars, and relishing it. A traffic jam. I imagined that I was not driving, but sitting in the backseat of a cab listening to the driver complain that Yasser Arafat was in Manhattan and really screwing things up. All access to Sixth Avenue was blocked. This fantasy was more gratifying than the memory of Deborah Cooke at the newspaper office, berating me for having implied that she had any unhappy customers. "You are cruel and thoughtless," she had shrieked. I suspect she was peeved mostly by my description of her stiff hair. It was a cheap shot. I had enjoyed writing it, but shouldn't have. In the pleasure of the moment, it's easy to forget that your subject is a person. Deborah's body, thick and wide, called to mind a mattress. She might employ it as a weapon—fall forward and flatten me wafer-thin. She had the right to complain. I resented only Bernadette's excited face peeping over Deborah's military shoulder, almost getting whacked by Deborah's green leather pocketbook, which swung back and forth as she made dramatically threatening gestures.

"Maybe she'll sue." Bernadette flapped her arms at the thought after Art had led Deborah into his office. He calmed her down—an activity at which he was becoming experienced—pointing out that the newspaper had received fifteen letters attesting to her skill. The paper would print them all, the equivalent of a full-page endorsement.

"She has no grounds to sue," I informed Bernadette.

"That doesn't stop anyone. Now like two people don't speak to you for sure."

"What two?"

"The lady in the antiques store and Deborah. She's been cutting my mom's hair since forever, so maybe my mom isn't speaking to you, either, and a whole bunch of other people. My mom says you're hyper."

"I am," I said, although in fact I was depressed, but that was none of Bernadette's business. A person wishing to be caught in a traffic jam caused by the head of the PLO could not be feeling too thrilled about her life.

"Mr. DePosta's thinking of arresting Sam."

"My Sam?"

"Who else?"

"For hanging out on the sidewalk? I don't think so. Besides, he can't arrest Sam, he's not a cop. Don't you have anything to do?"

"Are you getting your period or something?"

"What? Bernadette, for God's sake."

"Sorry, I'm just trying to talk and you're so weird."

Finally she loped off on some assignment or other. I took the opportunity to browse through several sourcebooks on detection and criminal behavior. There was a catalogue I'd borrowed from Chief Blocker. In exchange—though he didn't know this—I'd omitted a phrase in my column that compared his gray hair to the fuzz on a new tennis ball. Under evidence collection, page 155, I contemplated the Bluemaxx Illumination System, a krypton lamp that made finger-prints visible at a crime scene. $149.99. Too much money. The fin-gerprinting kit was cheaper, $105. Still, I couldn't imagine dusting the entire Nicholas house. Then I read an old pamphlet I'd purchased at the used bookstore. *Secret Hiding Places,* it was called. I was cer-tain that drugs had something to do with that woman in the Nicholas house, and this was a how-to on concealment. Many techniques, like false fronts and bottoms, involved the use of Velcro. I had to get back into that house. Perhaps at this upcoming deer meeting, which promised to be a sizable event, I could make the acquaintance of Tom's brother, Billy. He might be less honorable than Tom, although how ethical was the world-champion liar? I had that feeling, that un-erring-intuition, that Billy was a slacker. He hadn't responded when that alarm went off, and I bet it wasn't the first time. Where had he been?

A high school student waved me into the lot, and another, armed with a flashlight, routed me onto the field behind, which was being utilized for overflow.

Getting out, I bumped my door against an adjacent car. The driver caught his wife's eye and inclined his head in my direction. I'd been made. Perhaps his wife was part of Deborah Cooke's loyal clien-tele. I didn't wait for the dirty look or to be accosted, but strode across the field. Tall, dense weeds scratched my pants. In the fading light, I couldn't see the ground. Strange live things lurked there, as they did beneath the waves. Walk quickly. Do not scream and run.

A steady stream poured in. Everyone in town was gathering on a Monday evening to debate deer. Tom was probably here, on duty or off. Maybe his wife.

Sakonnet Bay Town Hall and Courthouse, a gray stone structure, bore a passing resemblance to a church because of its oversized arched wooden doors, both of which were thrown open tonight, and its imposing elongated tower. The building stood on a flat, broad expanse of grass. No trees or other landscaping softened its grim appearance, romantic in a kind of medieval way.

Inside, the place had been renovated and chopped up, ceilings lowered and covered with white acoustic panels. No haven for gothic intrigue, just offices for the pedestrian business of civic life. Along the left side of the hallway, a series of cubicles housed the mayor, city planning office, and traffic violations bureau, and on the right side, two sets of doors led into the courtroom, which doubled as the town hall. Here neighbors came to yell at each other.

The atmosphere was noisy, but not festive. Not festive, because there was too much aggressive bonding. People entered the hall and immediately tried to spot their friends and co-conspirators. The room was rapidly filling to capacity.

Coral Williams, owner of the Comfort Café and tonight, more significant, head of Bambi's Friends, signaled for me to join her. Her group had nabbed the orchestra section. I declined, preferring not to sit. Standing in the back, I would have the best view not only of the proceedings but of the audience.

A hand on my shoulder. Forcing a countenance of politeness and calm, I turned, expecting to be rebuked or attacked, and stared into the face of Jane's husband.

"Jonathan, hello." I stopped myself from recoiling from his kiss. It grazed my cheek. "Where's Jane?"

"At home." He licked his lips. Was it nervousness, or were they just dry?

"But she said she would be here. I spoke to her this morning."

"She's coming down with a cold." Jonathan pushed up his black-framed glasses, wiped both eyes, and carefully rested the frames back on his nose.

"I suppose you're speaking tonight?"

"Well, I have to present the case for shipping the poor devils upstate. I'm afraid it won't be pleasant." His whispery voice, which I had always taken for shy, now seemed obsequious. "I liked your column very much."

"Not me," said a woman walking by.

"Just ignore her," he advised. That was infuriating—to be patronized by a deceiving little shit. "Maybe you'll discover the bad haircut at this meeting."

"Maybe."

"Would you like to sit with me?"

"No, thank you. Since I'm working, I think I'll be better off here."

"I'll tell Jane I saw you."

"Yes."

I coordinated that last yes with a hunt through my purse for my notepad and pen, a defensive move to prevent any departing pecks on the cheek. I watched his scrap of a ponytail go down the aisle, his head bobbing and his hand gently rising to acknowledge hellos. He was dressed slightly sharper than when I had seen him last month at his own house, for a potluck supper. Tonight he wore a flannel shirt with rolled-up cuffs, cords with pleats instead of shapeless khakis. Still, he had an unsexy way of carrying his overcoat, over his arm, as if it were a large napkin and he a waiter about to take an order for drinks.

I was considering ducking into the hall to phone Jane to see if she was all right, when Mayor Ray Dorley banged his gavel. He tried to call the meeting to order but couldn't because of the speaker system. It sounded like a load of sand had been dumped inside. "Is that better?" asked the mayor, an erect and proper gentleman with a trim white beard.

"No," everyone shouted, and laughed. This, I jotted on my pad, would probably be the last friendly moment of the evening.

The walls were decorated with Halloween crayon drawings on construction paper—ghosts, jack-o'-lanterns, and witches, made by the third-grade class at the elementary school. The mayor sat at a table in the front of the room. Behind him hung the American flag, and next to that the Sakonnet Bay standard—white background, two horizontal blue stripes, and a sailboat perched on two orange curlicues meant to represent ocean. The audience seating consisted of linked wooden chairs. Several hundred people were here. I spotted Deborah Cooke, whose broad back and heavily sprayed puffball hair were unmistakable. Deidre was present, too, how surprising. Third row from the back. Perhaps she'd make a speech in Klingon. That would knock everyone for a loop. Be a good lead for my story as well, although Sam might object. The woman next to her whispered something and Deidre turned to grin. Perhaps it was the same mirthless smile she gave me, but from my angle, it appeared remarkably un-sinister. Was this her mother? Did Deidre have a good relationship with her mother? What a defeating thought.

"Is it better now?" the mayor asked.

Now it was, so he called the meeting to order and efficiently laid out the facts. An estimated six hundred deer lived within a four-mile radius of the town center, and that was about five hundred deer too many, it was generally agreed.

"Generally agreed not by me," shouted Coral Williams, and all of Bambi's Friends clapped and stamped their feet.

"I was almost killed last week." A man in a neck brace waved his hand. "The antlers busted my windshield and damn near poked out my eye."

"Sit down, Richard, and shut up," Coral boomed over consider-able hissing and booing.

"Deer are rats with hooves," shouted another man.

Mayor Dorley banged and lectured. "Richard, settle down, and the same goes for Coral and all of Bambi's Friends. Everyone will get a turn." He continued with his speech, explaining statistically the damage caused by deer: Loss of money in ruined shrubbery and car accidents. Injuries to humans and loss of life from crazed deer leaping across roads. The added frenzy during the mating season. He joked about how deer are not faithful and how they abandon their lovers once they've impregnated them.

"Loss of alimony and child support," someone yelled.

Mayor Dorley slammed his gavel again. He pointed to a metal folding table containing show-and-tell—deer darts for tranquilizing and immunization, information pamphlets on entrapment and disposal methods, accident statistics, and Lyme disease. Then he ran through the agenda, introducing speakers who would be making the case for various solutions: Coral Williams for birth control; Fred Till, an expert marksman and authority on other methods of extermination; Chief Blocker, who would discuss nuisance permits in case a person wanted to eliminate a deer himself; and Jonathan Atkins, who would cover trap and transport—the option of shipping deer upstate in cattle cars. Later the floor would be open to anyone who wanted to be heard, and Dorley hoped that everyone would be respectful. The evening would begin with a short film, a segment from *60 Minutes*, a useful summary.

While a screen on his left was raised and a man fiddled with a video machine, I perused the room again. This time my sights landed on McKee, who, like me, had opted to stand. I eyed him frankly, testing his effect—would my heart quicken, my palms grow sweaty, would there be any other telltale signs of sexual attraction, even at this distance? None. His head was cocked, listening while a man jabbered in his ear.

Was this Billy? His age was in the vicinity of Tom's; they had similar complexion and hair color. But this was a big, sloppy fellow, with a round face, juicy plump cheeks, and an ample girth, cinched by a narrow black belt that forced flab to spill over.

No woman was by Tom's side. His wife must be home with the kids. The sergeant was enjoying his brother's chatter—it must be his brother, something about their exchange was snug. I detected the faintest curl of a smile before McKee straightened up, hooked his thumbs into his jeans pockets, and traded the coziness with his brother for a bold gaze at me. He'd known all along that I'd been watching.

I quickly began scribbling, filling my notebook with details for my article, such as a description of the sandwich boards worn by several of Coral Williams's compatriots. They were plastered with photos of deer, their names gracefully scripted underneath in black marker: Strawberry, Squeakie, Uncle Joe. Then, the way one cannot resist poking one's tongue into a tooth to see if an ache is still there, I checked to see what he was up to. His eyes remained fixed, awaiting my return. I succumbed, felt my shoulders slump, my will turn to mush. I was pinned in place, a helpless butterfly. Oddly relaxing, the sense of having no choice whatsoever. Similar to hypnosis, a state for which I have always been certain I am completely unsuited.

After a few moments, maybe minutes, months in dog years, of being linked to McKee with mesmerizing intensity, I moved backward, and then sideways to the door, skirting the standing-room crowd. I was no longer looking at him, and had no sense of seeing or hearing anything. I was responding only to an overwhelming desire to leave, which I did. In the hallway the spell mercifully evaporated under the harsh, unforgiving fluorescent lights and the institutional flatness of beige linoleum, dead-white walls, and the smell of disinfectant. My head throbbed, and I went to the drinking fountain. I tucked my notebook under my arm, and was patting cold water on my neck when McKee came into the hall as well.

"Hi," I said, as if we had bumped into each other by chance, and I had not been ordered by some higher force to attend this rendezvous.

"There's a staircase behind you."

"So?"

"Lily, for God's sake."

I opened the door at the end of the hall to find narrow, uneven stone steps winding upward. The hidden gothic remains. It made me nervous to have McKee following me, I would have preferred the reverse. The staircase was a confining swirl, and I kept climbing until I arrived at the tower. A small unlit space. I felt the wall, stone, cold and rough. A large open window on one side framed a massive square of black sky awash with stars. A perfect place to knock me off, like that girl in *Vertigo*. Kim Novak. Falling right out of a church steeple before some nun or Jimmy Stewart could catch her. There was just enough starlight to perceive McKee as a solid. The gingerbread man minus the identifying sugar sprinkles.

"I wish you'd never come here." He sounded wild, a little crazy.

"Why?"

"You know why."

"I should never have gone into that house."

"Right."

"I'm in danger?"

"Yes. Don't be dense."

What I saw there . . . that girl. How foolish to have alluded to that event in my column, to have vented my frustration at McKee's refusal to take me seriously. It was madness to announce that I was going to get to the bottom of things.

"Tom?"

"Hush."

His hand was now against my cheek. In the dark I didn't see it move there, but found myself biting it. Shifted my head barely, and gnawed his palm. And then he kissed me, an experience I can liken only to being knocked down and run over. A spectacular collision from which I ended up not demolished, but the opposite: so whole and so fine, but just as out of it. Only vaguely did I hear the sirens, getting louder. We broke apart. My head was swimming.

I realized he was at the tower window, nearly cantilevered. I uttered a slight sound, a swallow intended as an inquiry, What do you see?

"I've got to go down there."

"My God."

"Exactly."

He left, and I pulled myself together enough to venture a dizzying look. Three patrol cars had whizzed in, sirens blasting and spinning, red lights atop the roofs.

I should go down, too. This simple directive took a second to sink in, and then I attempted to renegotiate the stairs. The way down seemed especially perilous. Baby steps. Palms braced against the wall, I proceeded tentatively, and didn't remember until I struck bottom that I was supposed to be covering this event and had absolutely no idea what had taken place that had necessitated the arrival of the Sakonnet Bay police.

Where was my notebook? I had dropped it during that clinch. Somehow, I was still clutching a pen.

The corridor was jammed, and filled with a jumble of noises that couldn't penetrate the fog around my head. I attempted one feeble, croaking *"Sakonnet Times."* Would the sea part for me? I didn't care. My face was pressed against the back of some tall man's Gore-Tex jacket. Did tears roll off as easily as raindrops? Did it offer refuge from steam heat as well as snow? I was too light and too short—could hardly squeeze out the door from my stairway to heaven. I would have to jump to see anything. I couldn't jump, too weak-kneed. I could sit, that was possible. Passing out was also possible. Where was McKee? I didn't have the energy or inclination to find out anything.

Time passed, I had no idea how much. The crowd thinned and I followed the flow outside. Apparently the meeting had been cut short. I saw an ambulance pull away, escorted by patrol cars. I stumbled through the parking lot to the meadow behind, wondering what had happened to me in the tower, when I should have been wondering what had occurred downstairs at the meeting. Had I engaged or simply acquiesced? As I recalled, I had participated enthusiastically. Where was my car?

Waiting for it to reveal itself, standing dumbly as vehicles departed, I saw a wild bird: Bernadette galumphing toward me, her jacket ballooning, catching the wind. "Thought that was you, give me a ride, okay? That was bonkers, wasn't that completely bonkers?"

"Yes."

"Why are you standing here? Where's your car?"

I looked around. Fortunately, I spied it. "Over there." We started walking.

"Are we going to put out a special edition?"

Omigod, it was that serious. "I didn't know Art ever did that. Is it even possible? Don't we rent the presses for only a certain hour every week?"

"What presses?"

"Forget it, never mind." We got in the car. "Where do you live?"

"Extra, extra, read all about it. I live on Wilton off Branch, you know where that is, behind the Little League field, near Jake's Farm Stand. You weren't there."

"What do you mean?"

"I saw you leave the meeting."

"I didn't leave. I got a drink of water, Bernadette, and came right back."

"Hey, Timmy." Bernadette shouted at someone driving by in the other direction. "Wonder where he's going? Uh, where's my lipstick?" She began searching her purse.

There ought to be a psychiatric term for Bernadette's mental gifts, like narcissistic perceptivity: the state of being really perceptive but being so preoccupied with oneself that one doesn't notice one's own insights. "Has Art ever put out a special edition that you can remember?" I asked again.

"Nope. Not even when an airplane crashed in the bay and an arm floated onshore."

I would not under any circumstances ask her what had taken place at Town Hall. Too humiliating. There ought to be a psychiatric term for my behavior, like narcissistic self-destruction: the state of preferring to lose one's job rather than be perceived as human.

"Then I guess I don't have to write tonight."

"Yeah, don't you hate it?"

"No, I love it. Bernadette, why do you intern at the paper, anyway?"

"My nail polish chipped." She proceeded to scrape more of the red off her thumb. "I didn't go to college."

"I'm not following." I wasn't sure whether it was her addled logic or my addled state.

"My brother married Art's niece, and my mom said reporting would be a good thing to train for since I'm not trained for anything, so she called Art."

"You hate to write. You hate making phone calls."

"It might change. I've only been working for three months."

"It's unusual to decide to be a reporter if you didn't enjoy journalism or English class. What gave your mother the idea—?"

"Life isn't perfect, Lily, like you don't get to do everything you want. That's what my mom said. But I wasn't good at school. A dolt, sort of."

"I'm sure you weren't a dolt."

"Thanks." She popped across the seat and kissed my cheek. "Good grief, you're burning. Wasn't Coral Williams just nuts?"

So what happened this evening had something to do with Coral. "Yeah. What's her story?"

"She's got the biggest butt in town," said Bernadette. "From being plopped behind that cash register in the Comfort Café day in and day out, it stretched. My mom said that when she got married her butt was small, but then it spread like batter on a hot griddle." Bernadette giggled. "What do you call it when you did it but it's not your fault because you're crazy?"

"Not guilty by reason of insanity."

"That's my house, stop. Where's the door handle?"

I reached across and opened the door for her.

"Bye, Lily. You're really nice."

After staring blankly at the illuminated dashboard, continuing to experience post-necking torpor, I forced myself to consider my options. I could go home. I could go to the hospital. I should go to the hospital and find out who was injured and how. McKee might be there. Another reason not to go. Where was the hospital? What hospital? I could stop by the police station and find out where everyone was and what had happened. I didn't want to go to the police station. I didn't want to be exposed; some officer, aside from McKee, might have noticed more than Bernadette had. I could remain in my car and be still. I could daydream about New York City on a glorious spring day when people jostled for space and sunlight. The choices there were so simple. Whether to change at Fifty-ninth Street, or stay on the Number 1 train and walk an extra block. What a lovely problem. McKee was married. A rogue. This situation was unacceptable. I was in a mess. A complete mess. Perhaps I could persuade Sam to give me one of my own dopey lectures. McKee told me I was in danger. Oh my God. I wasn't going to sit on this dark, empty street. Besides, I was working. Tonight I was reporting. I needed some baseline knowledge about what had happened this evening, and there was only one logical place to get it.

The problem was that now I was nervous. My eyes darted back and forth from the street ahead to my rearview mirror, expecting to see big bold headlights closing in. To have thrown that Nicholas house into my column about haircuts—that was definitive proof of how off-center I was. And what about that last paragraph . . . Watch out . . . Once mistreated, she wouldn't shut up. Whatever I had written—my nerves were too frayed to remember precisely—I had been so pleased with it.

On the main drag, I changed lanes several times and pulled over once, which, in retrospect, seemed especially muddled. My block was deserted. What I wouldn't give for Mr. Woffert to be stapling Tyvek in the middle of the night. Although what did I know about Mr. Woffert? Was it normal for a person to spend his life encasing his house in padded synthetic fiber?

I dashed from the car to the house and went up to Sam's bedroom. "Sam?"

"What?"

"Can I come in?"

He grunted, and I opened the door to find the person I wanted. "Deidre, when did you get here?"

The usual alien stare, but not as intimidating, because I knew something. I'd seen her smile at her mother, so I prattled on. "No words for it in Klingon, I suppose. No words for 'My mother dropped me off.' Was that your mother with you at the meeting?"

Deidre remained silent, sprawled on her back on the floor, her long legs wrapped up and over the bed, dusty boots plonked in the middle of formerly cleanish blue sheets. "I need your help. Desperately. It's very important for my job."

Sam said something like "Blah chug qua."

"I hope that means, 'Tell my mom what she needs to know.'"

"It means, 'If you say the wrong thing, I'll kill you.'" This produced a harsh bark of a laugh from his girlfriend.

"Please."

Deidre's head rocked back and forth. I assumed she was considering my plea.

"How would you guys like some cocoa?"

Cocoa is powerful, very powerful stuff. Luckily I also had minimarshmallows in the cabinet, because I sometimes sit in my room late at night and eat them. It makes me feel that living without a man is fun. Cocoa with marshmallows invokes simultaneously the childhood you had and the childhood you wish you'd had. Deidre could not be immune. Cocoa would produce normal-range behavior.

"What happened at the meeting?" I asked Deidre, explaining

that I had stepped out to the bathroom at the crucial time. I pushed a hot mug in her direction across the breakfast table, and she dropped in a few marshmallows from a fairly high altitude. Her manners were normal range but barely (NRBB).

"Coral Williams stabbed Mayor Dorley with an immunization dart." When she conversed in English, her voice remained uncommonly low but not unpleasant. She was quite serious. She compartmentalized, all amusement and bizarreness the province of her Klingon persona. For our interview, she was unnervingly efficient. Not exactly adult in her speech, but devoid of teenage slang. And immobile—Jell-O that had been left in the refrigerator for weeks and stiffened. Thank goodness, she had excellent recall. Coral Williams had charged the stage when the film showed Fred Till igniting a blast in which deer bodies flew into the air and were trapped in a net. She barreled toward Till with Bambi's Friends in her wake. No one knew she had a dart. Deidre detoured momentarily, informing Sam that these darts, injected with either tranquilizer or birth control medication, were generally shot from a blowgun. They looked like pushpins, she said, except that the steel part was about half an inch longer and the point had a fishhook snare.

"Cool," said Sam.

They shared a moment of appreciation for the design of the weapon.

"How do you know that?" I asked.

"The movie had a close-up," said Deidre. "It showed the dart under a magnifying glass. But someone knocked over the display. The darts rolled every which way, and probably some tranquilizer or birth control fluid leaked out, because the floor was wet." She went on to report that Till ducked, and Coral jabbed Mayor Dorley by accident. First Coral screamed. Then, when the mayor collapsed, she cried. A woman wearing a sandwich board and an antler beanie put her arms around her. "Lonnie Webster—"

"Who is that?"

"A friend of Glenn's."

"Who's Glenn?"

"My mother. Lonnie was sitting next to us and she said, 'Now Mayor Dorley can't have any more fawns.'" I smiled, but Deidre did not. "Afterward, when Lonnie found out that he'd had a heart attack, she told Glenn and me that she felt awful." Deidre added that Coral insisted deer only know flight, that's all they know. "Deer only know flight," she repeated somberly.

"What was that about, when did she say that?"

"Earlier. The film showed deer being herded into cattle cars to go to a farm. She said that even if they were sedated, they would try to flee the car, and go crazy crashing into walls."

"So she first got upset during the movie?"

"Yes," said Deidre.

It was not clear whether our talk marked the beginning of a new relationship or merely an interlude.

I drove Deidre home, taking Sam in the car with me. I felt safer with company.

I AWOKE the next morning, my arms hugging my pillow, my head nestled in soft down. I lay there viewing my shaded bedroom sideways, then sat up. The place appeared so mundane. The usual messy stack of magazines on the side table, my flats kicked off near the closet, last night's clothes tossed onto my wicker rocker. How could I, Lily Davis, a person with a broken clock radio and a half-drunk bottle of Evian, possibly be in danger?

I must have overreacted.

As I took a shower and got dressed, it crossed my mind that the danger was McKee. That's why he wanted me to leave town. We were trouble. Our attraction. Yes, that's what he was talking about. Things had been so deranging the night before. I ticked off the reasons. First of all, it had been night; night is always distorting. Second, I had been trapped in an eerie starlit tower. Third, I was reeling, initially from his presence, then from his embrace. In fact, in spite of this display of logic, my head was still logy, a hangover from the astonishing kiss.

I hadn't seen anything in that summer house anyway, only a naked woman whose face I couldn't recall. I threw on a robe, went out back and retrieved the previous week's *Sakonnet Times* from the recycling bin. Rereading my column would reassure me. My words may have upset Deborah Cooke, but not anyone else. There was nothing in print except a lot of noise about haircuts.

As I sipped tea and skimmed the piece, I wasn't entirely reassured. My attitude had been provocative.

Over the next few days, my mood and opinion seesawed. One minute I was relaxed—a problem with McKee was at least not life-threatening. The next, I became panicky, sure that my initial intuition had been correct. Something unscrupulous was going on in the Nicholas house, and someone out there thought I knew about it. After considerable debate with myself, I left a message for McKee at the police station. I had to get a proper fix on my situation. He did not return my call.

One evening, lounging on the couch, I became nearly paralyzed with anxiety. Hoots and caws, whistling, rustlings outside the window—were these sounds animal or human? I forced myself to take a soothing bath, then rushed the soap from one end of my body to the other. I didn't like being naked. Too vulnerable. I left my bedroom TV on all night, and considered wearing my cross-trainers to sleep.

All deer business was postponed until the mayor recovered. Coral Williams had been booked for assault, but the charges were dropped at Dorley's insistence. "I forgive her," he had proclaimed from his hospital bed. I had been there to witness it, and Art heralded the mayor's words in a banner headline. "This town has pity," my editor pointed out, and advised me to write a column on the subject. I may, if I'm alive.

He assigned me to cover the town's annual Oktoberfest. I agreed before realizing that this was Sam's weekend to spend at his father's. I should have trumped up an excuse to visit Manhattan. Instead I would be stuck here alone.

On Saturday, after another choppy, fitful night of sleep, I arose early to cart my son to the Islip airport, forty minutes away, for the eight-o'clock flight to Boston. He set off the alarm at the security check. They made him strip off his black boots with silver studs, as well as his gift from Deidre, a metal necklace resembling a chain-link fence.

On the way to the festival that afternoon, I stopped to see Jane. She'd come down with the flu, caused, in my opinion, by a crushing depression.

Jonathan answered the door. It was odd to feel a queasy trepidation, then to have him appear so ordinary. "Hi, Lily," he said cheerfully. He looked out into the day. "Chilly."

"A bit." I bounded up the stairs. "I know the way."

Jane lay flat in bed, all covered up, seemingly disembodied. Only her sad face was making an appearance. She sneaked a finger out from under the covers to point to the door, indicating that I should close it.

Jane needed me to stroke her head, push her unwashed hair off her face, hold her hand. But I am shy, uncomfortable expressing physical affection. Sam is the only person I have ever cuddled and hugged with abandon. All I could manage was to bring my chair close so we could whisper, and to give her a little present, a selection of herb teas. I offered to brew some, but she declined.

"Where is he?" Her voice was hoarse.

"Downstairs, I think, in his study."

"He hasn't been going anywhere," she whispered.

"Maybe his whatever, affair, is over."

"Or she's off somewhere waiting for him."

"Is he being nice?"

"Sort of. I guess. But you know how . . . at least I've read that when a person is about to commit suicide, he can seem all pulled together and content. Everyone in the family thinks he's fine, but really he isn't fine. He's just decided once and for all to do it. That's what Jonathan's like. He's decided once and for all to split." Jane began coughing uncontrollably. She sat up and I patted her back. When she was finished, I held out a Mynten.

"What's that?"

"An orange-mint thing." I untwisted the paper and handed her the treat.

She sucked a minute and her voice became less scratchy. "I've seen these in the drugstore, they're good."

"So you think that's what it is. He's around, he's nice, because he's ready to abscond?"

"Yes."

A sudden roar. I jumped up.

"What's wrong?" asked Jane.

"Nothing. That noise—what is it?"

"The leaf blower. Aren't they loathsome? I've told Mr. Poltry—the lawn man—I've told him, they're loud, disruptive machines."

"Terrifying."

"Yes," said Jane dully, then tried to muster some enthusiasm. "So what's new?"

I was bursting to tell her. I needed to get into bed beside her and confide my own chaos and madness. Instead I told her about Deidre. I made it a funny story, about going to the ladies' room at exactly the wrong moment during the deer meeting and then being forced to get my facts from a Klingon. I was almost talking about McKee, near, in the vicinity of, and I kept thinking that at any moment I would nudge the conversation there or it would somehow nudge itself, and before I knew it—bam—but this did not happen. I controlled myself. I did get Jane to smile, even to laugh once, but she was a tough audience.

"I have big bags under my eyes." Jane poked her fingers into her cheeks and pulled the skin toward her ears. "Better, huh?"

"You always look beautiful."

"I'm so tired at night, but I can't sleep."

"Of course, you're upset."

"I want to suffocate him."

"What?"

"Last night he was sleeping soundly and I was wide awake, and I was thinking I could press a pillow over his face and end my agony."

"Jane, that doesn't make sense. You're terrified Jonathan's going to leave you, so you fantasize knocking him off? That doesn't make any sense."

"It doesn't?" She picked up an emery board and began brisk, intense filing. I watched her work her way across three fingers, moving with the speed of a buzz saw, before she threw the emery board down.

"Jane, honey?"

"What?"

"I think you're wrong. I think he made a bad investment and blew your savings out the window and that's it, that's the whole awful story. You'd find out if you would just ask." Jonathan's black-framed specs had been splotchy this morning, and no one but a wife could stand a man with lenses resembling a bug-spattered windshield. "And he's not been paying attention to you lately because he's preoccupied with the disaster. Wait a minute, how come he's sleeping so well?"

"Tylenol PM. He's taken it for years."

"You should take it, too. In fact, I'm going to take it."

"So you think that's all it is, a money screwup?" She sounded hopeful.

"Yes. Absolutely." My confidence was a stretch, a white lie. Still,

Jane's suspicions could be unfounded. I had noticed that sometimes we see our mates as desirable to others, because it justifies our choices. I had projected that numerous women were hot for Allan— hostesses in restaurants, a cute clerk in a video store. Also, this "he's cheating" business could be Jane's subconscious wish that someone would run away with Jonathan and take him off her hands. I didn't get into any of that, though, because the phone rang. It was Jane's daughter, Carrie, from college. As they chatted, I signaled that I was leaving. Jonathan held the front door open for me. He smiled in his usual tentative way.

"Thanks, Lily."

"For what?"

He responded as if the answer were self-evident. "For cheering up my wife."

By the time I arrived at the fair, around one-thirty, I was worn out, thanks to five nights of spotty sleep, that early drive to Is- lip, and my visit with Jane. Once I'd taken Demerol for a medical test, and this feeling was similar: a sense of sweet oblivion. I was making my dazed way past a giant corn roaster when I spied McKee at the barbecue.

He was spearing chicken and sausages with a large fork, serving lines of people five deep. To keep him in my line of vision, I had to keep shifting, which was difficult in my groggy state.

"Why didn't you return my call?" I demanded loudly across people calling out orders. Exhaustion had a freeing effect. I might say anything that came into my soft head.

"I got back last night from a police convention in Atlantic City. White or dark, Winston?" he asked the next customer.

"White. Are we going to fire this principal, too?" the man asked.

McKee laughed, and they discussed how disruptive it was to have three principals in three years. A woman named Sarah interrupted to inquire whether Tom would please have a talk with her neighbor, because he was siphoning her water supply. McKee promised to take care of it the next day.

Someone bumped my shoulder. A woman in a baseball cap. She tapped her brim by way of a hello. I nodded and moved away, out to the crowd's periphery. "I'd like to interview you," I shouted to McKee, knowing he would go along with the ruse.

"By the big pumpkin. In an hour. What can I get for you, Mrs. Whitley?"

He continued serving, didn't miss a friendly beat, and I wandered off to do my job, among the makeshift plywood stands decorated with crepe paper. McKee's wife could be volunteering in one of them. I meandered past the ring toss, the win-a-goldfish booth, and the fortune-teller. Teenagers knocked into me, hurrying by in noisy clusters. A terrible country-rock group wailed from a portable stage. I drank a Coke, pumping in sugar and caffeine to spark the energy to collect some quotes, carefully selecting people who did not turn away when I made eye contact: kids happy to show off their newly won fish or stuffed animals; small children tugging their parents along to spin-art or the makeup booth; fairgoers with lips dyed red from cherry Sno-Kones, and wisps of cotton candy stuck in their hair. I enjoyed it. I always enjoy collecting data. Only one mother rejected me, hoisting her toddler and brushing past with a curt, "We're late." The hour did not pass quickly. Twice that woman in a baseball cap turned up where I was. First she was hanging around the hook-and-ladder truck. It had been backed from the street onto the Little League field, and four- and five-year-olds were scrambling all over it. She showed up again at the booth where kids knocked down wooden pins with a softball. Was I being tailed, I wondered, then kicked myself for having such a ridiculously paranoid thought. Across the park, where the green grass evanesced into woods, two does, munching rhododendrons, basked in what might be their last protected days on earth.

Eventually I drifted over to the enormous misshapen pumpkin, a sideshow specimen on which these words were painted: GUESS MY WEIGHT. People paid a quarter to drop their answers into a huge fish bowl in hopes of winning an eighteen-speed bike.

McKee was no longer barbecuing. I surveyed the area, expecting to locate him easily in the throng because his charm and vitality would pop. Sure enough, I picked him out—his hands on the shoulders of a young girl, steering her forward. It was impossible not to recognize that this was his daughter, from the trust with which she allowed him to navigate her. They stopped at a snack stand, she confided her preference, and he relayed it. As they continued on, she bounced along, alternately licking her blue Popsicle and throwing a torrent of words and energy back at him. He glanced at his watch. From a distance, I understood the whole interchange. As he fixed her barrette, pulling her hair to the side and pinning it off her face, he said something, something like he had business to attend to. She drooped before rebounding, yelling and waving to friends, two giggling girls who were trying to lean on each other as they walked. As Alicia tore up, one of the girls shook a paper skeleton at her. They all shrieked and sprinted off.

When I couldn't see them anymore, and assumed he couldn't, either, McKee walked rapidly in my direction, greeting a few people along the way. He picked up a popcorn box and a soda can, and tossed them in the garbage, just as the woman in the baseball cap was entering the Guess My Weight competition.

"Hello," I said to him, sounding breathless, even though there was no reason for it.

"Are you hungry? Can I get you something?"

"No, thanks. Let's sit over there." I pointed to the bleachers.

We started across the Little League field, leaving the crowds and carnival behind. The earth was damp from a drizzling rain the night before, and I kept my eyes down, watching my shoes sink into the damp ground as we trekked across the diamond. "The fair's lovely," I said in a bright, ordinary voice, then hissing like a ventriloquist, added, "Why am I in danger? You have to tell me."

He halted, puzzled. "Who said you were in danger?"

"You."

"Me?" I could see this struck him as nothing short of incredible.

He resumed his pace. "We were in the tower," I reminded him, "and you—"

"Lily, hold it, slow down."

I followed him docilely to the risers. He waited for me to sit and then climbed one bench higher, so I had to swing around and straddle the bench.

"I said that I wished you'd never come here," he noted slowly. "*You* asked if you were in danger."

"Oh," I was thinking back. Was that correct? I asked? I assumed? But hadn't he agreed?

"What danger could you be in?" he inquired.

"The naked woman. I wrote about it. What I saw. I threatened to figure it out."

"My God, you really are a madwoman." This broke the ice, his appreciation of my lunacy. Furthermore, I could see that he found me irresistible, because he smiled in a most affectionate way.

"So I'm not in any danger?"

"Only from me."

"Oh." I heard myself swallow. So that guess had been the correct one.

He moved down next to me. "We'd better discuss the mess we can't get into."

"Okay."

"We're not going to be friends," he said.

"No?"

"We're not even going to be friends because it's not possible."

I flipped open my notebook. "Not friends," I wrote, and showed it to him. "I paraphrased, but that's the gist, right?"

He nodded.

I looked out across left field. Beyond it, the pint-sized Ferris wheel circled 'round and 'round, legs dangling from every seat. "I got so crazy with worry, so freaked out, I almost wore my big fat rubber-soled cross-trainers to sleep," I told Tom.

"You go at things full tilt," he said with admiration.

"How was Atlantic City?"

"I loved it. Had a great time. Played two-hand blackjack. Have you ever done that, played two hands at once?" He took a Mynten from his shirt pocket.

"God, no, I'm terrible at math. I could never keep two hands straight."

He laughed. "I'd like to see your crazy brain playing cards."

"No, you wouldn't."

"I would. I stunk at math, too. Hated it. But I'm a devil at poker and blackjack. Deal the cards and I—"

"What?"

"Nothing. Never mind." He put the Mynten back in his pocket.

I jumped in to be the first to say it. "I guess I'll see you around."

"Absolutely." He stood up. "Bye, Lily."

I jabbed a spunky fist into the air. "Have fun, Tom."

Before he was halfway across the baseball field, I succumbed to exhaustion. I lay on my back, my narrow body balanced on the narrower strip of board, and let the warmth of the sun swaddle me. I had been in danger, but only from him. I wouldn't have to spend my life looking over my shoulder, sleeping in sneakers, maybe taking baths in them, my feet bobbing like buoys. I was relieved to be safe, happy to have been desired, even in such an unsatisfactory manner. I fell asleep.

I opened my eyes to the sight of the baseball cap bending over me. I scrambled to sit up, and the woman moved back so that she no longer loomed, a specter. "What is it?" I said.

"Lily Davis?"

"Yes, that's me."

She lifted her cap.

THE PROBLEM was that I wanted to tell Tom. He would enjoy hearing my blow-by-blow, the saga of my interrupted siesta. This was the moment when I understood that our aborted relationship would not be so easy to dismiss. The kiss and whisking of bangs had faded, but the pleasure of talk was fresh. Being appreciated and appreciating is such a basic need, like protein. I hadn't experienced that with my ex-husband. Allan's mind was as interesting as the dollars in his wallet that he arranged according to denomination in ascending order. He had corrected my every exaggeration. "We were driving around sixty," I would dive in, relating an adventure. "Forty-five," he would interject. He was a teacher with a switch, flicking my wrist when I spoke out of line. Here's one very handy thing about having an ex-husband: It's a place to dump all your anger. I should mention this advantage to Jane. It might give her something to look forward to.

"You go at things full tilt," Tom had said. I could love him for that alone.

I wasn't allowed to write about what happened, either. The woman in the baseball cap had insisted that our encounter be off the record. For the time being, it had to remain secret.

It felt like a luxury to return home and not have to search every closet before sitting down to a cup of tea. I blasted a CD. Sam was not here to groan at Van Morrison, but once a certain amount of dancing and singing along was accomplished, I deflated anyway. I was thirty-seven and would probably be single forever. The "single forever" fear—almost as upsetting as worrying about, say, death. Oh, right, what an overstatement. Yes, but it is comparable only because the thought causes an identical reaction: a sudden clamping, a cold hand squeezing the heart. Whenever "single forever" plagued me, I would take action, find an activity so that I could move quickly and leave the fear in my wake. Tonight I would go to the movies.

I didn't check the backseat of my car before getting into the front, nor did I scour the road via rearview and side mirrors. No outrageous fantasies, like being garroted from behind, plagued me while I watched the film. And on the way home I had enough peace of mind to miss the action of the city. In-betweens—walking, riding the bus or subway—often yielded great sights, chance encounters, vicarious thrills. Life in New York tended to be continuous rather than intermittent, I was thinking. I barely heard the sirens. Four police vehicles, one more than had visited Claire's Collectibles to rescue Baby, screamed past. I followed the answer to my prayers, something exciting that would delay my having to be lonely in my bed. Perhaps a resident had keeled over from drinking too many martinis (that had been in the log last week), or maybe the police had nabbed the woman in a headscarf who had lifted a hand-tooled belt from Strictly Suede (also a log item). Mr. DePosta might have engineered a roundup of naughty teenagers, yanking them out of a Saturday-night party. Fortunately,

Sam was away, not that he would have been invited. The swiveling lights on police car roofs threw reflections onto the trees. I could follow the sirens and flashes of red more easily than I could the black-and-whites. They sped far ahead.

I drove into an unfamiliar area, near the beach, undeveloped. Thickets scraped my car as I approached at a slow roll. No street-lights or other signs of civilization—this must be swampland or a bird-watching preserve. I turned on my brights, which illuminated parts of the picture. Wide horizontal yellow stripes that moved about morphed into men in oversized black rubber topcoats banded with yellow for safety. Stationary blocks of white turned out to be the doors of cop cars parked every which way. Their red roof lights continued to whir. Beams flipped one way, then another, as officers aimed their flashlights. Then flares brightened the road, giving visual definition to the area, but no explanation of the circumstances. Gradually the random dance of lights became choreographed as officers advanced, all flashlights now pointing in one direction, into heavy bramble. It must be an accident—an accident with a deer. Deer must really love to hang out in this wilderness.

I left the car, and cold still air zapped my bones. The sky recalled my one visit to the Hayden Planetarium, a fantastic trip through the galaxy with every star available for observation. A heart-stopping sight evoking, in comparison, my own puniness. The vegetation grew low here, a wicked impenetrable tangle. Despite the police invasion, this seemed a place of true isolation.

Amid the rustling, the relayed orders, and the gibberish on walkie-talkies, I discerned the bark of his voice. This was not quite as hard as selecting one particular violin out of a symphony orches-tra. He was with the men securing the area with yellow tape. Which of these guys shrouded in black was Tom—that was anybody's guess. I didn't see any smashed vehicles, so the commotion did not have to do with a car accident. A bike was abandoned at the side of the road, and a thin, nervous fellow, shifting from one foot to the other, spoke quietly to a policeman. Day-Glo bands wrapped his ankles.

"So what's happening?" I slipped over to an officer, who glanced at me but didn't respond. I corralled another, who answered, "Dead body."

"Who is it?"

"Move back," he said. "You're contaminating the crime scene."

Crime scene? This had to be a stroke or heart attack victim, a jogger. Being someone who fears the worst, I went into complete denial when faced with it. "You must be mistaken," I actually replied.

Two more headlights were coming this way, and everyone turned, awaiting Chief Blocker. His car door slammed and all conversation stopped. The crowd parted to create a slender path to the wilderness. I took the opportunity to scoot behind the chief, alert to the flashlights directing his eyes. They swung across the undergrowth—wet murky soil, thorny branches, bushes of needled twigs—and landed on two bare feet sticking out. Ten toes with at least six beams on them showed very clearly the different colors of polish, one per toe.

"What are you doing here?" McKee's voice was behind me.

I spun around. "It's her," I whispered.

"Who?" He was in police drill, and there was no way to imagine this was anything but an interrogation.

"The girl in the Nicholas house. I told you she was dead."

He gripped my arm and pulled me across the road. "How do you know?"

"I recognize her feet. Her toes, remember the nail polish? You didn't listen to me."

"What are you doing here?"

"What am I doing here? Nothing. I was driving home from the movies."

"And you're so sure it's her."

"I'll be happy to identify her breasts if you like."

I calculated roughly back to the afternoon when she obviously, oh so obviously took a drug overdose, possibly self-inflicted, possibly not. "She's been dead almost a month."

"It's not clear."

"It *is* clear."

"We're waiting for the county medical examiner. He'll do an autopsy."

"So someone took her from the house and dumped her."

"Buried her," said McKee. "Did a half-assed job of it. Animals smelled her and dug her up."

And then the sergeant left, called to the huddle of men in black.

She was dead. The shock of being right. The triumph of being right. The sadness of being right. That was somebody's daughter and somebody's friend. But I *was* right. I know a weird arm when I see it. I cornered the bike rider, bled him for information. He'd been pedaling along and smelled gas, like a stove gas leak but stronger. He'd reported it to the police, who sent a truck from Suffolk Gas and Electric to check the main. This was bad luck for whoever ditched the body. The main turned out to be right next to those bare feet poking onto the road as though thumbing a ride—a ride to the coroner's. His truck arrived a few minutes later, and my last view of the young woman was of a lump zipped into a bag.

Of course I wanted to talk to McKee again, was dying to, we had so much to discuss. I got in my car, with the lights and heater on, and waited while the police completed their business. As everyone else was driving away, he finally came over. "Did you see her face?" I asked.

"What was left of it. Some beast, probably a raccoon, feasted on her."

I went limp. The import struck with that grisly tidbit. "We have to go back to that house."

By way of response, all McKee did was poke his tongue into his cheek.

"We should go tonight. We'll find something. Evidence. I swear. We saw her, we have an obligation."

"Lily, go home."

"Listen, when I was in the bedroom, I saw . . . I didn't realize it at the time, but you know how elegant the place was, pretty fancy for a beach house . . . well, later I remembered that there was no plate over the electric outlet."

"What are you talking about?"

I was lying, but I was on a roll. I had to lie to hook him, and it wasn't going to be easy. His manner was professionally impersonal, which was fine. I appreciated that. This was business. This had nothing to do with our former extracurricular activities. They were over. "In two places, plates were missing. Downstairs in the living room, and upstairs in the bedroom by the couch. I read this book about concealment"—this at least was true—"it was very informative. One of the prime places to hide drugs and jewels is behind electric plates. I think that woman had taken drugs, don't you? Look, I'm not saying there's something hidden, but you really didn't do a serious search, either. It makes no sense, in that perfectly appointed place, for socket plates to be gone. If you take me, I'll show you where. And besides, we were there together. If I go back with you, I might see something different from what you see, or remember something different. My brain could get jogged in a helpful way."

For a very long minute, McKee appeared to consider my request. "I can't go in there unless I have a phone call."

"A phone call?"

"Yes."

"From whom?"

"I can't go unless I have an anonymous call from a pay phone, reporting some lights or activity in the Nicholas house. I need a reason to enter and investigate."

"I see."

He extracted a business card from his wallet and handed it to me.

I held it by the dashboard light to read his name, Sakonnet Bay Security, and a beeper number.

"Thank you."

He stashed his rubber coat in the trunk of his car so he was no long masquerading as a member of a toxic cleanup committee. With no further discussion, we proceeded to collaborate as if born to it. I trailed him to the station, where he signed off, and then he followed me, waiting a half-block away while I left a message on his beeper from the pay phone at a Shell station. I put my hand over the receiver—this was very exciting, to disguise my voice. After pulling into my driveway, I entered the house, found a screwdriver (in case we needed to remove any electrical plates), and exited the side door, a stealthy move that seemed brilliant. The ever-vigilant Mr. Woffert would have no hint of my nighttime excursion. I rendezvoused with McKee at the corner.

Climbing into his SUV was no smooth move for a short person. A red wool scarf lay on the passenger seat. He tossed it into the back. Scattered on the floor were an empty apple juice can, a child's sneaker, several toy airplanes, and a large mottled autumn leaf. He picked it up and laid it carefully on the dash.

"Alicia's," he said.

Rife with souvenirs of family life, the car functioned as a sort of chaperon.

The curious thing about returning to the Nicholas home was that, regardless of whatever might have taken place there, the sense of foreboding that had infected our previous visit was gone. No alarm had been triggered, and I hadn't suffered a destabilizing dog bite. And in spite of any uncontrollable flirtatious thoughts, I believed, as much as he, that our personal involvement should go no further. Those erotic memories had been replaced by something more powerful—the sight of him at the carnival, a captain steering his precious cargo through the crowd. Her enthusiasm. Her innocent joy. Sam could be like that, he had been like that. McKee and I donned professional personalities, took refuge in them perhaps. The two people who returned to the summer house were a reporter and a cop.

Even the residence, in the glare of spotlights fastened under the eaves, appeared less formidable on second viewing, simply an overblown version of a beach house. We closed the car doors gently, but only because, in the quiet, every sound was amplified. "You can forget the screwdriver," he said. "I hope you didn't think I bought that bullshit about socket plates."

As we walked up the steps to the porch, McKee mentioned that no one had stayed in the place since we'd been there. He must have had this information because his security business was kept informed of the comings and goings in the off-season. He deactivated the alarm, and clicked on his flashlight, and we entered.

"Where's the light switch?" I whispered, although we were the only ones there.

"No lights." I heard his voice behind me and the sound of the door closing.

"How come?"

"Because we don't want an anonymous call. Another one. A real one."

"Oh. Of course." I was obviously not gifted at deception. Having embarked on a game plan, I had forgotten about it.

With his flashlight, McKee made a wide sweep from one end of the living room to the other, then investigated in sections, moving the beam from top to bottom. Outside the bright pool of light, the room remained dark. I couldn't see even a speck of him, although his sleeve brushed mine, sending a prickle up my arm despite several layers of clothing between us.

"Someone came and cleaned."

"Yes," he answered as the flashlight revealed plumped cushions on the couches and coffee table books arranged just so. "The housekeeper," he added, and his voice was not next to me any longer. I hurried to catch up with it and bumped into a hassock. "What happened?" He shined the light my way.

"I tripped."

His hand grasped mine, leading me into the kitchen, where he released it.

"These folks are loaded," I said as we viewed the gleaming top-of-the-line appliances on the granite counter. He worked with precision, whipping open cabinets and drawers, hunting through a maid's room off the kitchen as well as the dining room. Here and there I frisked objects that turned up in the light—I was utilizing information gleaned from my criminal guide pamphlet. Did the aerosol can have a false bottom? Were the moldings mismatched?

"Wait, I smell something. What's that?" I asked. "Someone's perfume?"

"Not unless they're wearing Pine-Sol," said Tom.

With my eyes now adjusted to the darkness, I followed him into the hallway. The flashlight beam shot upward, revealing the staircase and the bedroom door at the top. "Ever been in the Variety Shop?" he asked.

"That store on Main? No." I noticed the banister was freshly polished. I didn't touch it.

"It's a clothing store with a lunch counter. My wife picked up a pair of jeans for me there. I swear they smell of hamburger grease." He stopped and I crashed into him. Because I was on the step below, my head banged into his behind, and his billy club hit my chest.

"Are you okay?"

"I'm fine, I mean, yes, okay." I moved next to him. "Did you hear something?"

His hand smacked flat against my breast. I think he was putting up a stop sign, indicating that I should be silent, but didn't realize my proximity. We both pretended this grope hadn't happened. McKee continued to listen, I assumed, since he didn't respond immediately.

Then he uttered a slow "No," and we moved onto the landing and he aimed the light toward the bedroom. He turned the knob and let the door swing in. We entered and our heads swiveled the same way, to the left. The bed. No one was in it. But a light was on—the reading lamp on the right side-table. No other fixture illuminated, but here in the master bedroom, a silk shade on a Chinese lamp cast an inviting peachy glow over the duvet. We approached and looked down. I expected to see the imprint of a body, a soft indentation on a pillow, but the spread was ironing-board smooth, and the pillows, three deep, perky in organdy jackets.

"The housekeeper could have left it on."

"Was it lit when we were here before?"

Neither of us knew the answer to this question. I recalled a curtain billowing inward, the softening of daylight by the tempered glass, but once my eyes had landed on the naked woman, I wasn't noticing lamps.

"My wife's going to be wondering where I am," said McKee.

That was out of the blue, or maybe not. His wife. Good.

"What's her name?"

"Ann."

A simple, stalwart name.

"Most likely scenario," said McKee, having stirred himself into action by reminding himself that he was married, "she died of a drug overdose. A tryst involving uppers or heroin or something." He moved into the bathroom, where there was no bloated dead woman slumped in the luxurious circular tub, large enough for two as a matter of fact, with Jacuzzi sprays. Nothing out of order here, although McKee gave me a moment of fright when he opened the shower door.

"People are always discovered dead in the shower or bath," I blathered, as he walked past me. "You know, in movies, the house looks deserted, and then they move into the bathroom and there's a bloody arm hanging over the side of the tub." McKee now scanned the surfaces, turning three hundred sixty degrees, trying to find something of interest, something that wasn't perfectly appointed, something that didn't belong in a hotel room awaiting guests.

I opened the closet door and we both stared into the organized abundance of clothing in the walk-in vault.

"The parts that weren't eaten were pretty much intact. Don't imagine that she was in that brier patch very long."

I didn't argue that, even though he was a cop, he'd probably had no more experience with the decomposition rate of murder victims than I had. "She was dead here. I saw her arm." I was tugging at the two-inch strip of wood trim along the base of the settee. A niche for dope could have been hollowed out under it. "You never believe anything I say."

"Never?" His eyes softened as he contemplated me crouched on the floor. "I haven't known you long enough for 'never.'"

His words unsettled me. As I got up, my legs felt wobbly. He offered a hand, and in a moment that took forever and was over in a blink, I found myself in his arms. I didn't know how our passion could erupt so suddenly. It turned out that I am a desperate, even thrashing lover, but also utterly pliant. I think Tom picked me up, and I was dead weight; he could have mailed me, without protest, UPS. Anyway, my feet were definitely off the ground for a while, and then we were both horizontal: Tom, a master of timing and nuance, and I, his wild consort. I was not a virgin, obviously, of course, yet, thanks to irony—my constant companion, my invisible shield—I was intact emotionally. I cried throughout the entire event. I realized this only in the afterglow, when Tom touched my wet cheek with his fingers, then tasted them. "Tears," he said.

It is not easy for a cop to undress, I can attest to that. His belt had taken a while to discard, between the buckle and the attached equipment. Lying skin to skin, with our stuff strewn about, this room we had visited for clues now felt as if it belonged to us: our hideaway, with beautiful linens carelessly rumpled, and light just low enough to obscure consequences. I would have bet my life that, no matter how passionate I was, I could never have made love on a bed where a dead woman had lain. I would have been wrong.

"Do you hear something?" Tom asked.

"No. Yes, oh my God."

I leapt off the bed, grabbing for my clothes, flailing about stark naked, sensuality blown to bits by panic. One shoe was upside down on top of the settee; I had no idea how it had gotten there. I snatched my shirt with one hand, pants with another. They trailed the ground, I almost tripped over one pant leg as, hugging my belongings, I dashed for the bathroom, where I fell against the door to hold it shut. I dispensed with underwear, threw on only outer garments, shoving my bra and underpants into my pocket.

"Jesus," I heard Tom say as I was coping with a shoe. Then the murmur of someone responding softly. Should I stay here or go out? How far had Tom managed to put himself together before meeting the intruder?

Probably I should have remained in the bathroom. Probably, in retrospect, but I am a hysteric and have no logic or clarity. I pushed my hair around, splashed my face with cold water. Noticed my chin— chin burn. A giveaway. I flushed the toilet, having at least the presence of mind to provide a pretext for being in the bathroom, and then exited.

"My brother," said Tom. "Billy, this is Lily Davis." Tom was un- making the bed. He had stripped off the spread and was throwing back the top sheet. Why was he doing that?

"Hello." I extended my hand.

"She's covering it for the paper," said Tom. Then he regaled his brother with the details of the dead woman—her exact location, how her feet had been poking out from under an inkberry bush, where ex- actly he had been when the call came. All this talk smothered any possibility that Billy and I would connect past his mumbled "Nice to meet you" and a handshake, in which he engaged only after wiping his palm on his pants.

As I'd figured, Billy was the fellow who'd been hanging out with Tom at the deer meeting. Tonight he wore the official company windbreaker, gray nylon with "Sakonnet Bay Security" printed in an arc of yellow letters on the left upper sleeve. The jacket barely zipped up, girdling the solid mound of his belly.

"There's nothing here." Tom began remaking the bed. "You know, Billy, I thought since she was lying here that day, there might be something." Oh, I see, the picture was coming into focus. Tom was disguising our crime scene as hers.

"How'd you hear about her death?" I asked Billy.

"His radio," Tom answered. "Not a clue how she died." He was mostly reassembled and completely self-possessed. Awesomely so. Only a few visuals were askew. His official police uniform was unbuttoned to mid-chest, although he had a white T-shirt under it, and he was capless, his hair spiky. That could be construed as postwork casualness, I suppose, if one were into self-deception. At the moment, God knows, I was.

Billy screwed up his face, his eyes nearly disappearing into swells of chubby flesh.

"What?" Tom identified the look as confusion.

Billy took a moment to figure out what was bothering him. "Why'd *you* get the call?"

"What call?"

"That something might be going on here tonight. I was on duty."

"Who knows? I give my card to everyone and his uncle. And it's got my personal beeper number on it, not the company emergency. I was lucky to get the call. It gave me a legal reason to search."

"I was interviewing him when his beeper went off." Why did I volunteer that? Billy hadn't asked, and why else would I be here? I reached into my purse for my notebook, relieved that I was able to produce it, although I did not possess a pen.

"I was just driving by, checking out the place." Now Billy sounded apologetic, and aimed his comment at Tom.

"You thought we were robbers?" I laughed.

"Saw his wheels."

"Oh, right." I forgot, everyone knows everyone else's car, and brothers do for sure. "And this is the first suspicious death since when?"

Billy's eyes skittered my way. Could he see my underwear bulging in my pocket? "I better get," he said.

"Since a bar brawl two years ago." Tom answered my question, tossing me my jacket, which lay on the floor. "Don't forget this. Summer people. College kids. Remember it, Bill?"

Billy didn't answer, just thrust his hands deep into his pants pockets and rocked. He acted indifferent to tonight's news. I would have expected some slobbering, for him to beg his brother for the skinny. Maybe the unexpected shocking discovery was my being here with Tom. My presence had trumped a dead woman.

"Were you here that day when your brother saw her?"

Billy shook his head. "I kind of better be going . . . I better . . ."

"Sergeant McKee mentioned tire tracks in the sand. Who do you think that could have been?"

"Huh?"

"A four-wheel-drive car. Some kind of SUV. Not yours?"

"No. N-O." As he spelled it out, he looked at his brother, who laughed.

"She thinks she's a detective," said Tom. This remark hurt my feelings, sort of, but then he winked, or did I imagine it? One eye closed while the other didn't—that must have been a sign to me that we were together, playing along. He pushed his brother toward the door. "Let's go, there's nothing here, that cleaning lady's a fanatic. You could use her, Billy."

"Oh yes, is that right? Are you messy?" I asked.

Tom commenced some friendly joshing about Billy's place being the town dump.

As we trooped out, I caught a glimpse of myself in the gilt-framed mirror, which I hadn't noticed, since it was to the right of the door and we were always focused left, bedward. My eyes were dewy; my cheeks flushed with thrill. No wonder Billy kept trying to excuse himself. Just because he could hardly string together a three-word sentence didn't mean he couldn't spot the obvious: I looked as though I'd just been laid.

We spent some minutes alone on the landing while Tom investigated the two other bedrooms. Billy kept his flashlight pointed at our feet, so our faces remained in shadow, a relief to me. I felt less exposed, and wondered if he did as well. "It's eerie," I said, "knowing she was here."

He chuckled—a reaction I found odd.

"Your brother's been really helpful. I was coming home from the movies when the police whizzed by. I followed. I'd like to interview you, too."

"I got nothing to say." Peculiar inflection here—he wasn't denying that he had specific knowledge, but that he had any knowledge whatsoever. Astonished he was that anyone would think he had. Not that I jump to conclusions, but Billy McKee's self-esteem was not in the normal range. Low. Say, basement level.

"We could talk about your job. Get publicity for your company."

"Don't know."

In the bedroom, Tom had answered almost every question for him. I wanted Billy to myself. "How about Monday?"

"What?"

"An interview. It's fun. You'll enjoy it." Why hadn't he answered that alarm? Where had he been? Perhaps he was bringing girls out to these fancy houses, showing off. He might need to inflate his bitty ego in this grandiose way. I could pump him without having his brother along to throw out a life preserver. "About two. At the Comfort Café."

"Can't."

"When are you free?"

"Four."

"Fine. Four o'clock."

Abruptly he flashed his light in my face, blinding me, then dropped it again. That shut me up. We stood in silence, and I became aware of how bulky he was. With a push down the stairs, I'd be history. Allan, my ex, had once been mugged. He'd been entering the subway station, reading *The New York Review of Books*, his version of showing off, when an arm circled his throat from behind, choking off circulation. He tumbled six steps and broke his ankle. He could have broken his back.

Tom rejoined us, announcing that the place was spotless enough to perform open-heart surgery in.

"Maybe somebody in addition to the housekeeper turned the place out. Somebody especially careful," I said.

"Could be." Tom pointed his flash down the stairs, indicating that I should proceed. I demurred. I wasn't going to descend the staircase ahead of Billy.

Tom would probably cover for his brother. He'd covered for him the day of the dog bite, speeding us over here. Wouldn't he cover again if Billy eliminated me because I guessed that one of his rendezvous had gone awry? Unless Tom loved me, in which case he'd be torn asunder trying to reconcile my death with his brother's guilt.

The naked woman would be Billy's first victim; I'd be the next. Multiple murders. "Got out of hand," said Billy McKee to whoever interviewed him on Monday at four because I was too dead to do it. "Got out of hand." I could see this guy rising to the occasion with an explanation that psychologically perceptive.

But he did not kill me on the way out of the house. He burped once, making me wonder if he'd been drinking beer on the job, and

when we were outdoors in the prosaic world of timer lights, he mentioned that Mrs. Stockley, a client, would throw a fit if she didn't see
their security company car pass every twenty minutes. He and Tom
laughed about it. "So how'd she die?" he asked.

"I told you, I don't know yet," said Tom.

Billy played with the zipper on his windbreaker.

"Pretty insane," said Tom.

Billy continued to zip, up and down, up and down, as he backed
toward his car.

"Nice to meet you," I called.

"Uh-huh." At least that's what I thought I heard him reply, as he
climbed in.

WE WATCHED as Billy's taillights receded into the night.

"Did he suspect?"

Tom shrugged. "It doesn't matter."

"No?"

We got into the car, and traveled upright and well-behaved back to my block, our clasped hands hidden by the dashboard.

"I'm crazy about you," said Tom.

Blissful words.

"I solved the crime at Deborah's Hair and Nails," I told him.

"Janet Rosco."

"How did you know?"

"Curls tight enough to lay a mattress on," he said.

And so we resumed our post-lovemaking intimacy, cozy specu-lation on how the hideous permanent had come to pass, hideous even by the woolly-lamb standards of Sakonnet Bay. All the while our hands joined and rejoined, fingers intertwining, thumb adjustments that sent electricity along with oxygen through my bloodstream. Deborah had miscalculated the proportions when she mixed the goo, or hadn't set the timer, so Janet Rosco's hair had overcooked. Perhaps the box of hair dye had had an expiration date long past.

"Like old milk," said Tom, letting go of me only long enough to open the glove compartment and distribute Myntens, lemon-mint this time, as we compared our moments of discovery. I told him about awakening from a nap on the bleachers to the awesome sight, the cap lifted, the hair revealed. He'd solved the case while barbecuing. "Chicken," she'd requested, "be sure it's done." When he'd handed over a paper plate containing a leg and a thigh (from his lips, even poultry parts were a turn-on), the plate buckled, the chicken slid. As Janet Rosco had bent to save her lunch, her cap tumbled onto the barbecue. McKee had spiked it before it charred, and upon returning it to her, could not help noticing her permanent.

We were parked on my corner now. "The hair through the mail slot wasn't gray or curly," said McKee. "Wonder whose hair she snipped."

"Her daughter's?"

"Doesn't have one."

Sitting here we were courting discovery. "I'd better go," I said, not moving. "Does she have a dog?"

"I think so."

"I knew it. What kind?"

Tom kissed his hand and placed it over my mouth. "I'm crazy about you," he said again.

I pushed against the door, the handle poking into my back, providing the equivalent of electrical grounding. I had to be able to stand upright. It was essential that my legs maintain the strength to convey me from this corner to home.

"Tell me what breed."

"Golden retriever," he acknowledged, as his hand traveled along my neck. Now a lone finger heading south.

"Whose coat is a brownish orange, the exact color of the strands on the beauty salon floor. You see, you should listen to me. I'm good."

"Good night, sweet Lily, I'll call you tomorrow."

He didn't drive off until I reached the driveway of my house, a moment before I saw a bushy beast the size of a backpack underneath my car. An opossum or a raccoon. I sprinted to the front door, expecting the animal to dash after me and attack my feet. I fumbled getting my key in the lock, desperate for a table to leap onto, when I felt a soft touch on my shoulder.

I could not have screamed louder.

"God, you're nuts—take it easy."

"Bernadette?"

"Don't let anyone see me." Bernadette ducked behind a bush as Mr. Woffert opened his front door. He was wearing a plaid flannel bathrobe and carrying a rifle.

"Oh, hello, Mr. Woffert."

"You got a problem?"

"No, I just saw an animal or something. I'm very sorry, it scared me."

"It scared you?" He didn't seem to believe me.

"I'm fine," I yelled to my neighbors across the street, their porch lights glowing, front doors ajar. "Fine" was beginning to plague me. "Really," I told Mr. Woffert, who had noticed that the paint on his porch post was peeling. He chipped at it with his free hand, while the other still gripped the gun. "I'm sorry I woke you."

His wife turned up now, pink quilted robe buttoned to the neck. "What's that, your gun?" She relieved him of it.

"My sincere apologies for waking you," I said to her. "I'm not used to country sights."

"No trouble here, never been any," said Mr. Woffert.

"Good night," I called, "I'm very sorry."

"This isn't the country," Mrs. Woffert insisted, and he answered, "To her it is, I guess," as I closed my door and waited for Bernadette's inevitable knock. She'd be really screwed if Woffert decided to repair his porch then and there, producing a putty knife that he probably carried everywhere, even to bed. She might be stuck in the shrubbery for days. But a few seconds later I heard her rap.

"Where were you, I was waiting for ages." She assessed her options, then headed into the living room and flopped into a chair. She stuck her legs out, and bopped her toes together a few times. "Where's your kid?"

"Sam's away for the weekend."

"My boyfriend's after me."

"The same one who hid in the bushes?"

"Who else? Don't you love fleece?" She sprang up and over to me, raising her arm so that I could stroke her fluffy jacket.

"Yes. Fleece is nice. What do you mean he's after you?"

"This house is cool. You have good taste."

"Thank you."

"God, where were you, anyway? I thought you'd never come home. With some guy? Were you in that car at the corner? Who was that?"

"I don't know what you're talking about."

"You're seeing someone who doesn't even take you home? That's a bummer. My mom has a quilt like that. Is it worth a lot?"

"I have no idea."

"Please, Lily." Tears welled up with impressive speed. "You've got to let me stay here." She threw her arms around me and rubbed her damp eyes against my neck.

"You must have friends you can stay with, Bernadette."

"He knows my friends, he knows everyone, nobody knows you." She sniffled a few times.

"If he's a threat to your safety, you should call the police." I pushed her away and moved toward the kitchen. She stayed at my heels.

"He's not a threat. God, he wouldn't hurt a flea. He doesn't want me to break up, and he's just bothering me to death. Wherever I go, he's going to bug me, but he'll never find me here."

I took down a can of peanuts, and before I'd even unlocked the vacuum seal, Bernadette held out cupped hands, awaiting her portion.

All I wanted was privacy, the one thing that now seemed unattainable. I needed time for some processing and for the sexual thrall to subside, but Bernadette was relentless. I settled her for the night on the living room couch; but with my bedroom door closed, I could hear her rattling kitchen cabinets, helping herself to God knows what, raising the TV volume, flipping channels. She was a noisy, fidgeting presence, incapable of doing anything unobtrusively. The next morning she appeared early, that was irritating, complaining that there were no shades on the windows and, besides, she couldn't sleep in a strange place. "Your bed's big, could I sleep with you?"

"No." Did that request mean she planned to remain another night?

I had tiptoed past her into the kitchen for coffee, and when she came in yawning and grousing, I was contemplating the telephone, worrying that Tom might call and she might answer, worrying that while I was at the airport getting Sam, she might answer, and worrying that when Sam came home, he might answer. Or even Deidre might pick up: Deidre had smarts enough and an attention span long enough to put two and two together.

Concealment was going to be a full-time job.

And the phone wires were sizzling. News of the dead woman had traveled around town, and every time the phone rang, I leapt for it, stretched for it, raced for it, with athleticism I didn't know I possessed. "I can answer, you know," said Bernadette as I practically catapulted over the kitchen table to seize the phone from under her nail-bitten fingers. These lunges were like sliding into home plate. Safe, the umpire shouted, as I grasped the receiver.

"You can't answer the phone," I told her, "or people will know you're here."

"Oh, right." This seemed to depress her.

She hung around, listening to my end of a conversation with Jane. "Why didn't you tell me last night?" asked Bernadette.

"Why didn't you call me?" said Jane, virtually simultaneously.

"It was late."

"I'm going to the bank tomorrow to separate my money from Jonathan's, what's left of it."

"Oh, dear. Have you talked to him yet?"

"Who?" asked Bernadette.

I ignored her. "No," said Jane. "Meet me at Suffolk Bank, would you? At one? I need propping up."

"Of course."

As soon as I disconnected, Bernadette grilled me: What was it like on that deserted road? The dead woman's skin, was it blue and bloated? Had I seen her face? I mentioned that she'd been nibbled at. It was stupid to nourish Bernadette's ghoulish interest or cheapen the tragedy, but I couldn't resist watching the pop and widening of her eyes.

Art called, wanting me to write up my experience, a column as well as a standard news piece. I shouldn't forget a story on the Oktoberfest as well. "Big day," he said.

I received a call from the receptionist. Peg had heard I was there when the body was discovered, as had Coral Williams from the Comfort Café, and Rob, the other reporter, who lamented the fact that I'd gotten my claws into the story first. I repeated my tale again and again, the drive home, the sirens, the feet poking out of the brambles.

I persuaded Bernadette to keep me company when I drove to the airport. I left the phone machine off, a fact she pointed out, and I replied gaily, "Who cares." As we drove through town, we saw people standing in clusters. Dead-body talk. LePater's, on this Sunday morning, was packed to capacity. News like this meant doughnut-eating time.

Sam returned with a letter from his father, complaining again about the hair spout and suggesting that Sam might be better off living with him. This was typical of exchanges between Allan and me. We were both remarkably polite during any phone calls that might be overheard, but disparaged each other's parenting skills in secret whenever possible. Allan clung to a certainty that whatever went wrong at my house would never have taken place at his. I despaired of my own inadequacies even as I refused to admit them.

A most curious thing to greet my son, the strangest mix of elation and depression, the taste of sweet and sour on the tongue at once. He had invented a hug that kept me at arm's length by holding his body in a posture so concave that it prevented any meeting in the middle. He acknowledged Bernadette with only the merest flick of his eyes. She hefted his overloaded dirty backpack—he was dragging it along the floor—and announced, "What a ton." She informed him that she was our houseguest. "But I'm not staying in your room, don't worry," she added graciously.

"So your mom's got a boyfriend," she said as we drove home.

"Huh?" said Sam.

"What are you talking about?" I asked.

"Just kidding," said Bernadette. "She got home late because of the"—she dangled over the front seat between Sam and me to throw in the last piece of information—"dead body." Then, without stopping for breath, she told him every particular before collapsing into the back.

"Did Deidre call?" Sam spoke a whole sentence. How encouraging.

"No," I said, "but I've been on the phone a lot myself."

"The dead body," Bernadette intoned again. "Is Deidre your girl-friend? She's thin. I wish I was thin, but my hair's great." In the rearview mirror, I saw her flip a lock in front of her eyes to reassure herself.

"How'd she die?" asked Sam.

"No one knows."

He smiled.

"Why are you smiling?" I asked.

He shrugged.

"Well, that's inappropriate." Bernadette giggled. "You must get it from your mom."

"Excuse me?"

"You smile all the time, like on the way to the airport, you were grinning. Just driving along with this dumb grin on your face. Turn on KRCU, *Swap Meet* is on. I once traded my mom's crocheted shawl for a ceramic dog bowl. She was pissed."

Deidre was folded up on our front doorstep, waiting for Sam, skinny arms wrapped around her pole legs, chin resting on bony knees. "Nuqneh," she said.

"What's that?" asked Bernadette.

"Klingon."

"Oh, cool, I've heard she speaks that. But *Star Trek* is over, you know. It's kind of a dead galaxy. Nice to meet you, Deidre, wonk, wonk."

"Wonk?" said Sam.

"I just made that up," said Bernadette.

Dinner was interrupted continually by trick-or-treaters. I answered the front door, admired the costumes, and distributed candy, while Bernadette, Sam, and Deidre ignored them. They preferred to recap plots of sci-fi shows, delighting especially in one bad guy who had his head reprogrammed. Deidre scratched her arm incessantly. Bernadette finally seized it, examined the red blotches, diagnosed,

"Poison ivy, what bushes have you been hiding in?" before returning to a discussion of messages written in blood that oozed out of a wall.

The phone rang. "I'll get it," I said.

"Maybe that's my boyfriend."

"Did you tell him you were here?"

"No," said Bernadette.

I picked up the receiver. "Hello."

"Hello." Tom's voice, and a noisy background. He must be out somewhere.

Bernadette was watching me. "It's for me," I told her. "I've got a full house," I said to Tom.

"Okay. Meet me in the parking lot behind Bright's. I'll be on regular patrol tomorrow, passing by around twelve-thirty."

Perfect. I could meet him before my bank visit with Jane. "Sounds good to me." I hung up.

"Who was that?" asked Bernadette.

"Are you the nosiest person in the world or what? Who wants dessert?"

Deidre pressed her rash against Sam's bare arm, then slid her eyes up to lock with his.

"That's so romantic," said Bernadette.

Oddly, it was.

OVERNIGHT the temperature dropped. In the morning people were sporting knitted caps and gloves, down parkas, and especially fleece, the fabric du jour. "An unseasonable dip," the radio reported. "February knocks in early November." Parked in the public lot, I was holed up in my car with the heater blasting.

In my childhood, before something new or exciting, I was always seized with hunger. This accounts for why I was devouring a large bag of sour-cream-flavored potato chips on Monday at 12:20 p.m. in the parking lot behind Bright's Pharmacy. I adjusted the rearview mirror to examine my reflection, and indelicately poked a nail between teeth to dislodge embedded chips, trying to remain spiffy for my encounter with Tom. A driver honked—was I about to back out? I waved him on. Another honked. I waved again, and shoveled in another handful.

The chips were my only nourishment since coffee and yogurt at breakfast, when Bernadette had asked if Sam belonged to Aryan Nation.

"He's not a neo-Nazi, he simply has a similar haircut. It's more samurai," I responded.

Sam remained mute, constructing a sandwich out of an English muffin, slabs of butter, and jam. I had been considering whether I should get his cholesterol checked when the word "samurai" issued from my mouth, and I realized that, unknown to my conscious self, I had been searching for a relatively benign explanation for his appearance.

"Where's the milk, aren't you kind of fancy?" Bernadette was commenting on my attempt to look slightly prettier than usual: eyeliner, a hint of sage-colored shadow, and one of my more sparkly lipsticks, in addition to the usual mascara and blush. "God, you're wearing a ton of makeup."

"Hardly."

Bernadette wrinkled her nose. She was big on facial contortions to accent her remarks. For disgust, she might stick out her tongue; nose wrinkling indicated disapproval. "Can I ride with you to work? What kind of mustard is this?" She removed a jar of Grey Poupon from the refrigerator.

"It's called Dijon mustard. The milk's on the table. Where the hell is your car, anyway?"

No matter how waspishly I spoke to Bernadette, she roared on— tasting the mustard, informing me that her car's plugs were shot. "My boyfriend's supposed to replace them, only he's not my boyfriend. Sam, you're a pig."

Sam actually laughed.

In the car, I requested peace and quiet, but she droned on about how everything in her mom's vegetable garden always died.

"Can't your boyfriend waylay you at the paper?" I asked.

"He would never. Besides, he crews on a boat that leaves at the crack of dawn. He respects my professional life."

"Really. That's nice."

"Yeah," said Bernadette, as if she did not think so. She leaned over. "What's this? A wrapper." She snatched another off the floor, smoothing it to read the print. "'Mynten.' Well, you're a slob, dropping garbage all over the car."

In a scattershot way, Bernadette's intrusiveness put me at risk of exposure. As a protective measure, I censored both expressions and thoughts. I didn't revisit my night of rapture, didn't recall my favorite moment, when he kissed my eyes to open them, ruffling my heart with his lips. Tom had a light, almost ticklish touch, but I had better not dwell on that. A lustful grin might overtake me. Having surrendered myself wholeheartedly, I was denied the tiniest journey back. Life is cruel, although it is also occasionally ironic, even after irony has been tossed overboard.

At the morning editorial meeting, Art polled us for ideas. He wanted to cover every inch of newsprint with the dead woman. "I noticed a line to get into the hardware store," I told him. "What's that about?"

"Locks," Bernadette answered. "There's a maniac loose. I could write something about that, how everyone's installing more protection, couldn't I?" She seemed amazed to have floated an idea.

"Sure you can," Art replied.

"Doors *and* windows?"

"Absolutely."

She noted this, then kept her pen poised above her pad as if another great notion might alight at any minute.

"Talk to Len at the hardware store and to Sakonnet Bay Security. Their business has undoubtedly picked up," Art advised. Bernadette wrote madly. "Who else?" he asked. It was more a test question than an actual question.

"Just folks," said Bernadette. "To discuss their fears."

"Right."

She beamed.

"There was no foul play," I piped up, aware that it would only irritate Art to be deprived of his felony. "The death was an accident, a drug overdose from extensive frolicking of some sort, somewhere, that's all."

"How do you know?" Art asked.

"Intuition." I trotted out my smuggest smile.

After that we adjourned, and I spent the rest of the morning interviewing the young man who'd stumbled on the body. Then came my hunger attack, when I purchased the potato chips and repaired to my car.

Twelve-thirty. I brushed the salt from my hands and left the Honda. As I sauntered toward our assignation, a police car entered the lot and traveled the same way.

"Lily! Lily, over here."

Jane? Where was she? Oh, on the steps of the *Times* office, where she'd obviously been hunting me down. She was early, a whole half-hour. We weren't suppose to meet at the bank until one.

She beckoned me over, but I stubbornly persisted in tacking toward McKee and pointed to the pharmacy as if I had urgent business at the shampoo rack or a desperate need for antihistamines.

"Watch out," she called. I was so busy transmitting hand signals I didn't realize that I was about to slam into McKee's car, which was stopped, awaiting my arrival.

"Hi," I said to him, somewhat shocked to find the car looming, a sudden wall.

"Lily, take care," he said.

"Don't worry." I glanced around to see if anyone was noticing us. Jane, still a distance off, was weaving in our direction through a maze of autos. "I can be secretive."

He shook his head. "Not that. You're such a scrambled egg.

I mean, don't get hurt. Don't get so nervous that you have an accident."

How had I lived so long without someone who worried for my safety?

"How are you?" Tom could charge the most ordinary pleasantry with intimacy.

"I'm great," I said.

"You look beautiful."

"Really?"

The littlest things could make me cry now. I had to guard against this, let in the joy inch by inch.

"Hello, Sergeant McKee." Jane came up behind me. "What's the news on that poor girl? How'd she die?"

"My lips are sealed," said Tom.

"And I'm a gossip," said Jane.

So here we were, having a sunny conversation, each of us with something covert on our minds.

"There are no autopsy results, are there?" I asked.

"I heard we might have them by tonight, by the time I get off. Nine o'clock."

"That late?"

"Nine tonight," he repeated, hesitating a dramatic instant before adding, "But maybe not, maybe not until the end of the week."

"How exciting, I can't wait." I was getting mixed up, displacing my thrill at receiving a secret message—a date tonight at nine—onto autopsy findings. I endeavored to speak more soberly. "I'll phone you with the details, Jane, as soon as I hear."

Jane was facing me, but there was no other evidence that my words had penetrated. She had drifted, possibly to the worrying business to come, our bank visit to separate her money from her husband's.

"I'll call you, Jane, as soon as I hear about the autopsy." I spoke louder.

"Oh, okay."

"You must be hungry. She's always distracted when she's hungry," I told Tom. "See you around."

"Likewise."

"Bye," added Jane, a bit late.

And then he was gone, off to patrol, perhaps to cite a jaywalker.

"Should we go to the bank or have lunch first?" I asked.

"The bank."

"Okay." I towed her along. "Let's get it over with."

We dodged a few cars before taking an alley shortcut.

"Where do you think Jonathan got together with his girlfriend?" I asked her.

This problem interested me for a personal reason. Where could I rendezvous with Tom? In Sakonnet Bay, privacy was more elusive than neon. Consider Bernadette—she was compelled to hide out with me of all people. Every car was known, not just by model and year, but by dents and bruises. The beach was only marginally private. Shore parking lots were a favorite for in-car lunching, as I had noticed during my meeting with Tom. I'm sure cops regularly prowled them at night, and occasionally napped in them.

"An out-of-town motel on the road past the bay, or maybe those dilapidated stops along Route 12." She'd given this some thought.

"Nobody would spot you?"

"It's less trafficked."

"Jane, you could figure out something by checking Jonathan's odometer. See what it registers in the morning, then read it when he returns home." This was a depressing but clever notion. I might be more suited to being the betrayed than the betrayer. I might be better at being Jane. Or Ann. Her name is Ann, I reminded myself. Tom's wife is real, a person. Although I was clearly ruthless and uncaring, having just pumped my dear friend, distraught over her husband's infidelity, for ideas on how I could conduct my own. How could I account for this level of duplicity? How was I able to detest Jonathan, but adore Tom?

Jane balked. "My legs won't walk."

"Yes, they will." I tugged her on. "There's Coral Williams, say hello."

"Suppose Jonathan turns up," she whispered.

"He won't. I promise. Hold it, don't cross yet, the light's red." The bank was now directly across the street. We had to reach the fort before the ambush. "Tell me what you're planning."

Jane's hand took up residency in front of her mouth. She spoke into her palm. "I'm going to take most of what's left out of our joint savings, only about two thousand dollars, and transfer it. Then I have a commission check to deposit, it's really all I have left."

"Come on, the light's green."

"He raided my earnings. That weasel."

"Jane, cross. We'll open an account for you, and then you won't have to worry."

"Right." Her voice had all the animation of defeat.

There was one place for Tom and me to meet, I realized. Only one. I wasn't stopping this affair. I could scold myself, berate, condemn, but my heart was mapping a plan with the efficiency of a brain. The problem was as simple as this: A nut once cracked open could not be put back together.

As Jane moved across the street, I could feel her trembling. I clamped my hand around her arm and guided her into the bank.

Every commercial establishment in Sakonnet Bay seemed ambivalent about whether it was a home or a business. The bank was no exception. Both vice presidents sat behind desks decorated with pictures of their children; one displayed a china family of miniature painted spaniels. Teller lines were lively with conversation and people shouted across the echoing space to weigh in on matters that had nothing to do with them. I steered Jane to the VP who did not have miniature dogs. His name plate read "F. Pritchard." I was reassured by his solid geometric shape: square head, square shoulders— a box of a person, with a trim set of bristles above his upper lip. Reliability and order were what Jane needed.

"Could you please help us?"

"Hi, Frank." Jane kicked into gear, pulled out a chair, sat on her purse, then wrenched it out from under herself. "Do you know Lily Davis?"

"From the paper?"

"That's right." I sat, too.

"I heard you were attacked last Saturday."

"Excuse me?"

"Right after that girl was found strangled."

Several customers in line swiveled our way.

"Who told you that?"

"Rose Bacon."

"I don't know Rose Bacon."

"Her brother lives across the street from you. Heard you scream."

"I wasn't attacked. Someone surprised me at my door, that's all. Good grief, what an insane rumor."

"Oh." I thought I detected disappointment. Frank wiped a large red handkerchief over his face. "That's not what I heard."

"And that girl wasn't strangled." I turned to address the viewing gallery. "She wasn't strangled."

The VP at the next desk rolled her chair closer. "What happened to her?"

"I don't know. The cause of death wasn't apparent."

"You certain about that?" asked Frank.

"Positive."

"Well, well," Frank clucked sadly. "I'd better tell my wife. Now what is it you wanted?"

"Not me. Jane."

He turned to Jane, whose lips parted, but no sound emerged.

"She wants to open a new account."

"Checking or savings?"

"Fine," said Jane.

"Which?"

She looked to me for an answer. "Savings," I suggested.

He thumbed through some forms, extracted one, and passed it over. Routine to him. "How's Jonathan?" he asked.

"Fine," said Jane again.

Fine. Everybody used this word when they meant the opposite. Although perhaps Jonathan was fine. Perhaps, like me, he was better than fine.

I chatted more with Frank about the dead woman. He used to go bird-watching where she was found. Jane pressed the pen down so hard she tore the paper. He handed her another form.

"I've forgotten my Social Security number," she said.

He pecked a few computer keys and reeled off the number. "Anything you need, I've got."

"What are the current balances in my joint checking and savings?" she asked.

"Do you want to transfer money from there?"

"Yes."

He consulted the computer, wrote down the amounts, and passed the paper across the desk. I smiled encouragingly at Jane, and kept up a breezy conversation with him about identifying fowl by the Peterson method. "Every bird has a unique marking that is visible from a distance," he told me.

"Like a walk or a hat?" Or a spout, although I didn't say that.

"How recent are these balances?" inquired Jane.

"Close of last business day."

"I've changed my mind," she said. "I really don't think I need to do this."

"What?" I squawked. I sounded like something Frank Pritchard might spot and mark off his life list.

"I'll just deposit this check into our joint savings."

"Whatever you want," said Frank.

I smacked my hand on the form before he could discard it. "Wait a minute. Don't you need an account of your own? Because of your will?" This rationale was all I could come up with.

"No, I don't," Jane said. "I'm going to deposit this into our joint savings." She endorsed her commission check.

"Do you want me to take care of that?" asked Frank. "I can make out the deposit slip."

"Would you? That is so kind. Thank you." She stood up, smiling widely. "I hope I didn't waste your time."

"Of course not. Always a pleasure, Jane. Nice to meet you, Lily." He shook my hand.

"Same here."

She sailed toward the door and I hurried after. "What happened?"

She didn't respond until we hit the street. "It's back."

"What?"

"The money. It's all back in. Oh my God, I feel—"

"It's all back in?"

"Yes. All our money is in the account."

"But that's impossible."

"It's not impossible, it's there. Let's go celebrate, I'm starving. Lily, it's not happening." She threw her arms around me.

"Impossible."

"No, I imagined everything. Oh God, I am crazy, I really am a crazy person. I want a hamburger with onion and Russian dressing."

She gesticulated as she walked, waving and calling to people on the other side of the street, even hailing folks as they drove by. She'd metamorphosed from a depressed, barely ambulatory wreck into the town mayor on parade.

"You didn't make it up, the money was gone."

"It could have been an investment thing—you know, Jonathan's quite brilliant, how do you think he could retire so young? He was probably moving money around. Didn't you suggest that?"

I had suggested it, but I hadn't believed it. "What about the ponytail, his coldness?"

"Preoccupied, I guess. Look, Lily, you weren't married very long, so you have no idea. A husband and wife can go through long periods when they don't connect." Now she linked her arm in mine. "You always see the worst."

"What are you talking about?"

"Oh, please, don't act coy. You're the all-time doom-and-gloomer."

I supposed she was right, but to hear it announced so bluntly was wounding.

I trailed her into Burgers and Such, where she loudly declared to the hostess that she was famished.

"I'm buying," she said as we sat down. "What do you want?"

"Just a diet Coke with lemon."

"And I'll have an iced tea, a steakburger medium-rare, onion, Russian dressing, fries crisp, that's it. Thanks, Toni," she told the waitress. "Lily, my life has been given back to me." She opened her compact, bared her teeth and ran her tongue across them. "My teeth are too big. Just a little. Thank goodness I didn't start smoking again, I was on the verge. If I'd started smoking and didn't get divorced, I'd have to kick a nicotine habit." She dropped the compact in her purse. "Look at me, I'm making jokes."

"It's wonderful."

"Yes."

We observed a moment of almost religious silence in gratitude for this development.

"Gambas," I said.

"What about them?"

"Was it Jonathan or you that started all that crazy gambas this and gambas that?"

"Jonathan." She smiled. "He can be so silly."

I suppose I should have taken the gambas into account before jumping to conclusions about Jonathan. Gambas were sweet.

"I'm sorry I dragged you through this." Jane reached across the table to turn my collar down properly. How swiftly her motherly nature reasserted itself once she had her equilibrium back. Hearing her soothing voice, I couldn't believe she'd ever been distraught. Her deranged self might be something I'd fantasized rather than experienced. "You cannot imagine how horrible it is to think that someone you love is betraying you. If you've been married forever, as I have, Lily, it's beyond bearing."

Our drinks arrived, fortunately, and I had an activity: squeezing lemon into mine. Looking at Jane was not an option. Seeing her calm face, the anxiety washed away, was a hideous rebuke to my own behavior. The bridge she was standing on wasn't burning, after all. I wished she would stop confiding in me, sneaky fire-setter that I was, cease recalling her emotional ordeal, yet she seemed compelled to expunge it, even relished recounting it. Her restless nights. Her inability to eat. Her dreams, utterly real, in which she and Jonathan made love, followed by dreadful mornings when she awoke to her shattered reality.

"Believing I was deceived, Lily, that was the worst."

I wanted to bolt, scrambled to invent a reason, a sudden migraine, but I couldn't bring myself to speak up.

"Believing that every day he looked me right in the eye and fibbed. Even worse, suppose he said in some momentous way, 'I have to talk to you.' I kept expecting him to do that, to sit me down and reveal the truth: 'I love someone else.' I dreaded that the most.

"I couldn't envision life without him. I couldn't conceive of putting one foot in front of the other."

"Even though you thought he stole all your money?"

"Yes, isn't that awful? Even then."

Jane took pleasure in unfolding the cloth napkin, fastidiously arranging it in her lap when her food arrived—a burger obscene enough to satisfy Bluto, with gobs of pink Russian dressing and a thick slab of onion on a lettuce leaf, both of which she stacked inside the bun. "And now I don't have to diet. If I were single, I'd have to be thin."

"YOU LOOK like a load of cement landed on your head." Bernadette delivered her greeting buoyantly, before I had closed the front door. She must have observed me slogging up the walk, the stuffing unwittingly punched from my body by Jane.

It's amazing how powerful attraction creates a need that can be satisfied only by more. I have to shut down. Be sensible and honorable. But what about my undernourished libido, not to mention my parched soul and wasted heart? What about I've been lost in the desert and someone led me to the well? No, thank you, I'm supposed to say primly. I'd rather die.

Yes. Tonight I will have to do that: close the magic back up in the box. Tonight at nine. And we both knew where. The summer house. Very clever of Tom to assume I'd figure it out. Made me wonder about . . . but never mind. There would be no autopsy results at nine, only our date. Our last.

Sam, Deidre, and Bernadette had strung themselves and their belongings all over the living room: jackets, gloves, books, soda cans, notebook pages covered with pen drawings of grisly headless and limbless ghouls (probably Deidre's artistic output). Bernadette, who had adopted our living space as her bedroom, had piled several changes of clothing on a chair. She had converted the coffee table into a dressing table, arranging hairbrush, comb, and toothbrush in my precious Art Deco glass vase, and scattering a few ponytail scrunchees here and there. Snacks were out—Wheat Thins and a plate of fruit that Bernadette was passing around. The TV blared one of Sam's usual shows, featuring characters with skin as lumpy and cratered as the surface of the moon, one man with a fan-shaped hairdo, another with the ubiquitous Mandarin collar favored by people in spaceships. Just once I would like to see a normal human being on my television screen.

In between jabbing slices of apple, Bernadette poked Sam with her fork. "Say hi to your mom."

"Hi."

The doorbell rang.

The fork clanked onto the plate as Bernadette dropped it and leapt up. "Suppose that's Dunkie?"

Sam hastened to the window for a peek outside. He actually moved fast.

"Is it him?" demanded Bernadette.

"Does he know Dunkie?" I asked.

"No," said Deidre.

"The guy's old," said Sam. "And fat."

"Not Dunkie," said Bernadette. "Thank God." She fell back on the couch and hooked a leg over the armrest.

"I assume Dunkie's your boyfriend."

The bell rang again.

"Yes. Short for 'Duncan.'"

"I'll get it," I said. "But keep the TV down, it's too loud."

Deidre plucked the remote from between two pillows and re-duced the volume a notch. The sound wasn't really too loud, but I was feeling so beaten down that I needed to issue a request for the satis-faction of having it obeyed.

By the time I answered the door, he was edging backward down the front path. "Billy, oh my gosh, I forgot."

"I guess she's here like you said," he called to Mr. Woffert, hard at work covering his Tyvek with clapboards.

"You getting a security system?" Mr. Woffert asked.

"Who's that talking?" His wife called from a second-story win-dow. "Tom McKee's brother," said Mr. Woffert, as if she couldn't see for herself.

"I'm not getting a security system," I announced loud enough for everyone on the block to hear. "Billy, I am so sorry, my head's a fog, I forgot our interview. I feel terrible. Come on in."

He wiped his feet on the mat many more times than was neces-sary, and snatched his baseball cap off his head as if he were enter-ing church. "I waited around," he said hesitantly, "and when you didn't show, I thought I'd troll on by."

"How'd you find out where I live?"

He pulled a short strand of his curly hair.

"How'd you find out where I live?" I asked again.

"Is this your boyfriend?" Bernadette called from the living room.

"No. Would you stop with that?" I turned a friendly smile on Bill. "She's always kidding me."

He chuckled.

"She's got a secret life," said Bernadette.

"That's enough, it's not funny."

He laughed boisterously. I thought this reaction was a comment on my relationship with his brother. The heat rose up my neck, my face was about to be bathed in red, when he said, *"Babylon 5,"* and I realized that he was amused by something on TV, who knew what?

One of the most infuriating things about these science fiction shows is that the humor is incomprehensible to all but the faithful.

I introduced Billy to everyone. He had an affable conversation with Bernadette and Deidre about a character named, I believe, Vir, and then I butted in and hustled Billy into the kitchen. It was time to put my gumshoes to work. I would interview him here. It would remind me that I had a profession and a brain—always a therapeutic thing to recall.

Keeping up a steady stream of charm and chatter, I got him to shed his jacket. He was sporting a silky horizontally striped shirt, the worst thing a chubby could wear. It rippled over settling and resettling flesh. When he sat at the breakfast table, as invited, his wide bottom lapped over the seat, and he kept himself anchored with his two thick-soled, high-topped black leather shoes planted as far apart as chair legs. His eyes would light on mine, then dance off. He couldn't stay focused on any one thing.

I confided, or appeared to. "What in the world should I do about mice? I'm divorced," I added, as if the mouse problem and my marital state were connected. "Are you married?"

"Tom's married," he replied.

"I know," I said airily, bustling about, putting up water for tea, hunting for something to snack on. "I haven't met his wife yet. But are you married?"

"Kinda. I'm separated. Tom runs the business."

"I see." Possibly the only person who thought more about Tom than I did was Billy, the younger brother, the tag-along kid.

"Mice go for peanut butter," he said. "You've got to buy traps and lay on a spoonful. That's some snap when you catch them." He paused, enjoying the thought. "If you like, I could set the traps for you."

"Thank you. That's really nice." I was pouring corn chips into a bowl as Bernadette took a giant step into the room.

"I just realized who you are," she declared.

"Who am I?" asked Billy with genuine curiosity.

"Lily, could I speak to you privately?"

"Can't it wait until later?"

"No."

"Excuse me," I said to Billy, and followed Bernadette into the hall. "What's this about?"

Bernadette sulked. Her lower lip curled out, her eyebrows crunched into a wavy scowl.

"What is it?" I asked.

"He's my story, not yours."

"What story?"

"I called him today. It was the first article ever that was my idea, and you completely put it down at the meeting."

"What?" I was dimly aware of Deidre in the living room, twisting around on the couch, and even more faintly conscious of the significance: Deidre had antennae for drama.

"You said that there was no murder, so that meant that my story all about locks was really stupid."

"I'm not tracking what you're talking about, Bernadette." Sam was now riveted, too.

"Art liked it."

"Is something wrong?" Billy lumbered out of the kitchen. "I could come back another time."

"Nothing's wrong."

"I phoned you today," said Bernadette.

"Huh?" Billy slowly wiped the back of his hand across his mouth, sprinkling off corn chip crumbs.

"*I'm* supposed to interview you. Me, not Lily. Art said I should call Sakonnet Bay Security. Why didn't you return my call?"

"Tom usually—didn't he—?"

She cut him off. "I hate to make calls, so that is really mean. Did Lily ask whether you have more business?"

"No, I didn't ask him."

"Why is he here?"

Billy looked over, obviously wondering himself.

"I was going to ask about that," I acknowledged, "but I arranged the interview last Saturday night, before Art assigned you that story."

"Last Saturday, well, that doesn't make any sense. You're kind of a fake, Lily, no offense." Bernadette even had the nerve not to lose her temper, behaving as if she were the more mature being. "Imagine, coming in this afternoon all weepy and moping like someone broke up with you, when I'm the one in the breakup and you're the one about to do something underhanded. Come on." She grasped some of Billy's voluminous sleeve and yanked.

He cast a last, helpless gape in my direction while Bernadette threw his jacket at him and dragged him out the front door.

I grabbed my coat and chased after them. "Bernadette, please, we can talk about this." Honestly, she was such a child, this was such nonsense. "You're overreacting, this is no big deal." As she was about to climb into his four-by-four, I placed a hand on her shoulder. "Take it easy, sweetie, slow down."

She whirled around. "You are sick and lonely."

I slapped her across the face.

It was Deidre who suggested that I go back inside, after Bernadette had begun crying hysterically and she and Billy had taken off. "Do you want to come indoors, Mrs. Davis?" I heard her whisper. Instead, I swerved away down the block, avoiding the Wofferts who, among others, must have been thinking of selling tickets to "The Lily Show."

I had slapped Bernadette across the face. Me. I had never before hit anyone.

"Mom, wait up."

I traveled faster, past three deer nuzzling through bushes. Autumn leaves crackled under my shoes. Tom had a leaf of his daughter's resting on his dashboard. Alicia collected leaves.

Sam scooted up behind me, and soon I was flanked on my mad

walk by two quiet creatures. Deidre's legs, so much longer than mine, took enormous strides, one for my two.

"Where are you going?" Sam asked.

I shook my head.

"This way." Deidre led us into a vacant lot overgrown with dry brush, which reminded me of brittle hair and Deborah's Hair and Nails, and how happy I'd been right near this corner holding hands under a kind moon not two days earlier. Real life had been mercifully suspended.

In the back corner of this untended acre there was a hideaway. Large branches had cracked off a tree during a storm. They had fallen in an arc, creating a shady natural cave. Sam and I bent to follow Deidre and then sat on the damp ground. Secluded and still. Nearly dark now, too, and I was so close to these two oddball kids that I could feel their body heat. And I needed it. I yearned to be warmed by their breath and their affection. Sam and I sat identically, compressed like accordions, arms wrapping legs. So we *were* related.

I started to cry.

"Mom, don't"

"I slapped her."

"Big deal."

Deidre, who betrayed no emotion, kept a careful eye on me.

"I can't get a grip, I don't know why. I want a grip."

A woeful plea that no one answered, and the piteousness of it made me want to wail. Sam's thick arm landed on my back. It lay there like a log, then slowly his hand tightened on my shoulder.

"Stop, Mom, okay?" He was begging.

I raised my head to smile so he wouldn't worry. His eyes, inches from mine, blinked rapidly. I saw kindness there, but also fear.

"Bernadette's kind of crazy, Mom." His grin came out crooked.

"I guess."

I rested my head on my legs and wished for oblivion. After a while, Sam removed his arm. Deidre began amusing herself by putting leaves on her thigh and flicking them off. I knew because I peeked to see what the clicking noise was, in case it was the behavior of a large predator bug.

My nose was dripping, and no amount of sniffling could stop it. I had cried more in this safe village in two months than I had in Manhattan during the last ten years. Enough. I pelted myself with insults like ridiculous and ludicrous. The tears ran right through them. I sat up and banged my head against a branch. This brought another enraging onslaught of self-pity. "Come on, kids"—it seemed important to identify the adult—"we should go home and have dinner."

I began to plan my recovery, the knockdown doll bouncing back, this boomerang tendency of mine an uncontrollable tic. After dinner, I'd take a hot bath. I'd lace the water with salts and oils, and luxuriate. Then I'd snuggle into bed. There might be a good movie on Bravo. I didn't need to go anywhere tonight at nine. It wasn't necessary to meet to break up. Meeting to break up could make life only sadder and worse.

Big City Eyes

BY LILY DAVIS

I WAS RETURNING from the movies last Saturday, when police cars
wailed by. I was alone and, being a newcomer to Sakonnet Bay, feeling adrift, a state that can make a person lose sight of good common
sense. My dashboard clock read 10:15, still prime time but approaching the heart of night. The moon was full, a phase thought to
stimulate passion and wildness, and the sky was lit so brightly that
misty clouds·could be seen to pass across it. I followed the cars,
which was how I happened to get into trouble. Mine or hers, I wasn't
sure. As I said, the moon was full.

Her bare feet protruded from under an inkberry thicket at the edge of a bird sanctuary on Neetles Lane. Each toenail was painted a different antisocial shade of polish. Neither black nor dark green, to name two of the colors, is sold locally, at either Bright's or Deborah's Hair and Nails.

One officer, taping the crime scene with yellow to secure it, suggested that the victim had a niece or little sister who liked to play at giving manicures. But he should not draw conclusions until the evidence is in. A policeman should not do that. I don't know this cop— not really. I can only hope he's as sensitive as he seemed. He should pay close attention, read not only the words but between the lines.

I think she was from Manhattan. Like me. City women are more shocking in their choice of nail polish and more reckless in their choice of men.

I had been certain that the cause of death was rowdiness. Out-of-control partying, perhaps at one of the few summer houses visited in the off-season. Recreational drugs, overdose, subsequent panic, the half-clothed body hastily buried. She was not, as one rumor has it, decapitated, but some of her face, shoulder, and left breast had been gnawed by animals, possibly raccoons that dug up the body. I was wrong in imagining that party/drug scenario. I was wrong that evening, and impetuous. I got carried away.

The autopsy revealed a puncture wound in the lower back of this 105-pound, blond-haired, blue-eyed female. Estimated age, 20 to 24 years. Suspected weapon: a deer dart shot from a blowgun. She died of asphyxiation brought on by a lethal combination of ketamine (an animal tranquilizer) and Valium.

Police Chief Ben Blocker refused to speculate on who might have had access to deer darts. It cannot have escaped his notice that at the recent town meeting, Coral Williams rushed the stage and knocked over a display of immunization and tranquilizer darts. Every person present, or any friend of someone who attended, had access to the darts. Furthermore, according to the autopsy results, the blond woman had been dead four to six days. The town meeting took place five days before the body was discovered, a bull's-eye in the estimated time of death.

What brought the young woman to this peaceful cove that turned out to be her undoing? Did she think it was safer here, but away from familiar things, did she find herself more vulnerable? Maybe she had a crazy boyfriend or fell for a married man. Maybe she was killed by a distraught wife, unhinged by the loss of her husband. Maybe she realized she had to end a relationship and was foolish enough to meet her lover to break up. A mistake.

Meeting to break up is either an invitation to continue or an opportunity for more sorrow and pain. What are telephones for? Once I even avoided ending a relationship by phone. I stood the man up and never called to tell him why, never spoke to him again, because the sound of his voice would have been enough to wither my resolve and send me tumbling back into the briers. Did he understand that my ruthlessness was only self-protection? I don't know. I hope he forgave me.

LePater's has sold twice as many doughnuts this week. A dead body is good for business, the gossip mill churns. I would like to quash two egregious rumors. First, my son was not questioned by the police for this crime, and he is not a member of Aryan Nation. Second, when I screamed before entering my house late last Saturday night, I was not escaping from a kidnapper, a person in a black SUV, who sped away from my corner. The police are not hunting for this person. They do not believe I was the intended second victim of a serial murderer. If I were not such a patsy, emotionally speaking . . . if I had not let an overwrought hysteric move into my house, neither of these rumors would have started.

There is an illness known as moon blindness, an eye ailment affecting horses. It results in loss of sight. While it has nothing to do with lunar effects, as far as I know—I came across the term in a dictionary only by accident—I like to think that it does. I like to believe that there is such a thing as an inability to see caused by the delirium of romance: an incapacity to perceive danger and, most especially, the consequences of one's own acts. Perhaps that young woman had moon blindness. Oh, how I sympathize.

THE FRIDAY morning that my column on the dead woman landed on Sakonnet Bay doorsteps, I arrived at the office early. All the paper's employees had keys in case they wanted to write at odd hours. I struggled with the rusty lock, jiggling and twisting the key, hoping that my difficulty in accomplishing something this simple would not be emblematic of the day. When I pulled the doorknob toward me, the key turned easily and I entered. I dropped my purse inside so I could use both hands to haul in a stack of papers, tied in twine. They had been left by the printer around dawn. My column was on the front page, boxed in by a double black rule.

With a quick glance around the reception area and the advertising department to the left, I could see that the shabby offices were strewn with the hysteria of Thursday's closing—the weekly late-night process of putting the paper to bed. There were sheaves of edited copy, marked-up proofs of ad pages, and sitting open on Peg's desk, a pizza box with one slice left. Cold pizza is so depressing—the sight of melted mozzarella now the consistency of hardened glue. I carried the box to the kitchen and dumped it, washed the coffeepot and a few dirty mugs. I started the electric coffeemaker brewing again and went upstairs to my office with a copy of the paper.

I swept the old proofs off my desk, crushing the pages together and stuffing them and some of my own rage and frustration into my wastebasket. My desk was empty now, except for my computer. Rob had two framed pictures—one of a small sailboat, the other of his fiancée in a bikini on the boat's deck—to keep him company while he worked. Bernadette collected pigs: a tiny ceramic pig angel, a dancing pig wind-up toy, pig salt and pepper shakers. These knickknacks behind her computer were all knocked over, as if they were the casualties of a pig war. Bracelets of tightly woven string hung like ornaments off the arm of her Luxo lamp. I had yet to stake a personal claim to my space.

Out the window I had a view of the parking lot and the back of several stores on Barton Road. I could see the very location where Tom and I had last hooked up. "Meet me in the parking lot behind Bright's." I could recite all our casual yet charged exchanges. They were stuck in memory the way childhood poems and nursery rhymes got stuck: useless but nevertheless there for life. A busy spot in plain sight is the least suspicious. Was I the inspiration for this cleverness, or was I the beneficiary of expertise from previous infidelities?

Ever since Jane had shamed me back to reality four days ago, and I had not kept my evening date with Tom, details of our flirtation had begun to nag at me. He had arranged our rendezvous so shrewdly, sneaking a coded message into our conversation about the autopsy. Nine o'clock. Oh, sure, of course, I get it. And then he was even more brash to assume that if he gave me the time, I'd deduce the place.

At least we had not made love on a pallet where a dead body had lain. "Deceased four to six days," the autopsy had stated. We'd spied that woman in the summer house almost a month before. She'd been either sleeping or passed out, as Tom had suspected; and this news, while a relief, was disconcerting. I had been so sure. Her arm had dangled so peculiarly. I hated to be wrong.

Three SUVs pulled into the lot. Most villagers could glance out a window, as I was doing now, and figure out who the drivers were, because of a bumper sticker or a dent in the door. Jane could reel off the assets and personal history of all potential home buyers and sellers. Everyone here kept tabs on everyone else. Maybe that's why Tom hadn't worried about what Billy knew—because it was inevitable he'd find out . . . or because Tom would tell him. Perhaps the brothers exchanged tales of sexual conquest.

In retrospect, my conversation with Tom on the bleachers especially bugged me. I was in danger from him? Danger? How self-important was that? Tom was bold, flirting even when calling off a flirtation, so confident of his own seductive gifts. "We're not even going to be friends." What an adorably tragic line. Tom was sly enough to live in the city. I hadn't been sophisticated enough to detect country wiles. Not really country, though. That's what Mrs. Woffert had pointed out. I had mistaken a place with a farmstand and a doughnut machine for country. This was just countrified suburbia. Shallow. Not innocent at all.

Had I surrendered a lifetime of cynicism and reserve to an insincere man? That notion was almost unbearable.

I opened the metal cabinet to replenish my desk supplies. Some new black pens. New pens with fine points were always refreshing. "I am fine," I reminded myself, sitting down in my chair and opening the paper to enjoy my column in print. "I am fine." Wouldn't it amuse Tom to know that "fine" had become my mantra.

I heard Rob taking the stairs two at a time. "Hi," he said, strolling in. His handsome preppy face was annoyingly unlined. Not a visible worry. He lay a small paper bag on my desk.

"What's this?"

"A doughnut."

"How sweet, thank you." I looked inside. "Cinnamon, my favorite."

"I liked your column," he said.

Peg pretended to knock at the open door. She carried potted yellow mums. "Cheer-you-up flowers, honey."

"My goodness, those are beautiful." How did she know I needed cheering?

Peg fussed at my desk, turning the crock this way and that to give me the best view of the flowers. "You've hardly been here long enough for love trouble."

"I'll say," said Rob.

"What are you talking about?"

"We read between the lines. There, that's perfect." Peg stood back to appreciate her gift.

"Not to get too personal." Rob sat on my desk and ate a doughnut of his own. "But were you dumped?"

"No, I wasn't. How could I have been dumped if I wrote that I had stood someone up?"

"I thought you implied."

"Implied what?"

"Forget it. Don't get mad at me. You're the one who wrote, 'read between the lines.'"

"I said I was going to break up with the guy. Me. I was going to break up. And it was ages ago, anyway."

"Sure," Rob agreed much too quickly and threw Peg a look.

She leaned down and patted my cheek. "If you need a shoulder, honey, I'm available."

In that leafy den with Sam and Deidre, I had sworn not to shed another tear. I owed it to Sam. When I'm upset, he's frightened. But having made that pledge, I may have contrived circumstances that would render it nearly impossible to keep. An office of sympathizers, a cheek-patter. Peg and Rob regarded me with tenderness reserved for puppies.

Bernadette flounced in, thank God. The evil princess here to break the mood. "Bad morning," she announced. Rob hung up my coat and his on the door. "What about mine?" Bernadette asked, wriggling out of a down parka.

He held out his hands, and she tossed it over. "Bad morning," she repeated, glaring at me.

"Be kind, Bernadette," said Peg.

"I am, sort of, it's just that—" She squeezed out her bid for compassion, that helpless squeak in the voice. "If anyone cares, I'm trying hard to do a good job."

"And you are," said Art, stopping in on the way to his office.

"My article looks really nice, doesn't it?" Bernadette waved the front page in our faces.

"Yes," we all chimed, but she turned sullen anyway. "Lily didn't have to insult me in her column and reveal my whereabouts."

"I didn't identify you, so I couldn't have revealed your whereabouts. Besides, you're not there anymore." This was true. After absconding with Billy, she had not returned, and I had deposited a shopping bag of her belongings on her desk the next morning.

My phone rang, and I tensed. "Calm down, it's just the telephone," said Bernadette. I had been nervous about the phone all week, wondering if Tom would call, but he hadn't. He would never call me now, now that he had read my column. "Hello. Lily Davis here."

"Lily, it's Coral. Coral Williams."

"Hello, Coral."

"That McKee is not worth it."

"What?" I sat up so quickly that the seat slipped out from behind me. I hit the floor, still with the receiver to my ear. "What are you talking about?"

No response. "Hello? Hello?"

"You yanked the cord out," Rob said, plugging the wire back in as Peg helped me up.

"Coral?"

"I'm here," she chirped. "I don't think he's reliable. He seems sweet, and I guess that's what you fancied, but"—her voice lowered ominously—"don't repeat this, you swear?"

"Yes."

"Well, once he put his fist through a plaster wall. Besides, if you ask me, he's in love with his wife."

"He is?"

"Yes. I'm glad you stood him up."

The office crowd was riveted. No one made any pretense of doing anything other than stare at me. "I hate to think of you having a broken heart," moaned Coral.

I forced my eyes wide open to prevent my willful tear ducts from kicking in.

"That man was sulking, twisting his hulk around every three seconds to look at the clock. I finally had to boot him out. It was five o'clock and we were closing."

"You were closing?"

"'Meeting to break up.' I loved your column. I love how you expressed that."

"Oh my God."

"What's wrong?" asked Coral. I heard a whack and clinking coins. She must have been at the cash register, cracking open a roll of quarters.

"Do you think I was involved with Billy McKee?"

"It's nothing to be ashamed of," said Coral.

"So that explains it," whooped Bernadette.

"Explains what?" asked Art.

"How she happened to see him on Saturday night and horn in on my story."

"I am not involved with Billy McKee," I told Coral, while

scowling at Bernadette. "I was going to interview him at the café and forgot all about it." How could anyone think I was involved with that inarticulate baby? "I hope you haven't told people that he was my boyfriend."

"Not a soul."

That was a lie. "I have never been involved with anyone from Sakonnet Bay. I hope you'll convey that to everybody who comes into the Comfort Café."

As I disconnected, Bernadette was complaining about my devious behavior. Art shooed her toward her desk. "Come into my office, Lily."

In the hall, he stopped for water, offering me a cup first. I declined. He straightened the thin cushion on the chair near his desk before inviting me to sit.

"Good grief, I hope you don't pity me, too. All I did was write one pathetic line, really, how I sympathized with the dead girl's plight. Her imagined plight," I amended.

"The whole column is sad," said Art. "It reeks. Alone, adrift, however you put it. And that stuff about your son will probably make folks feel terrible for gossiping about him. Besides, you are a bit of a match girl."

"A match girl?"

"You seem like somebody who needs a winter coat."

"I don't. I have two, and one is filled with down."

"That doesn't help, either. Comments like that are so"—he fell silent as he reviewed a calendar of upcoming events, and made puffing sounds with his cheeks. "Yeah, you're plucky. Have you been to the dispatch office?"

"Yesterday afternoon."

It had been a stressful experience.

The dispatch office was outfitted with a closed-circuit TV, its screen divided into four equal parts so that Sally could view simultaneously the entrance to the building, the two jail cells, the central hallway, and the small interrogation room. This television was a fancy piece of equipment. Blocker had shown it off proudly at our first meeting. I had avoided looking at the screen as well as the wall chart that indicated who was on duty. Tom's presence on either might freak me out. I raced through the log, alert to the tread of any approaching footsteps—they could be his—while Sally chatted on the phone with her mother about plans for Timmy's third birthday, and whether he was too young for a baseball mitt.

"A handicapped plate was stolen," I told Art. "I was thinking of writing about how hard it is to find parking in the business district. While I sat in my car last Monday, eating potato chips, I had to get rid of ten drivers who were after my space."

"Parking?" He pressed the tips of his fingers into his forehead as if to ward off a headache.

I pushed harder. "With a handicapped plate you can plant your car anywhere. You won't even get ticketed in a red zone or in front of a hydrant. That's probably why one was stolen. It's a new crime, the first new crime of the twenty-first century." It was always exciting to give a story millennial significance. "In the twenty-first century, people will spend more time trying to park than they will having sex."

He looked startled, and I was, too. How did sex sneak its way into parking?

"Good idea," he conceded.

Safe idea was more accurate. "I'll do it for next Friday."

"Can you cover the school board meeting tonight?"

Tom was on the school board. "No. Maybe Rob can." I needed air. "Do you mind?" I tugged at the window, banged the frame, and tugged again before it abruptly flew upward. A wind swished several papers off Art's desk before I could pull the glass down to a reasonable level. "Sorry."

I collected the papers for him, sat, and noticed my hands. How chafed they looked—ugly beet-colored paws. When I was anxious, my skin could go from milky to red in seconds, especially my hands.

"Do an article on ketamine, a short analysis of the difference between its effect on animals and humans. It's the drug of choice for club kids."

I'd been busy hiding my hands under crossed arms. "Excuse me?"

"Ketamine. The animal tranquilizer," said Art. "It's big. In the rave scene. You're from Manhattan, you should know all about it."

"No."

"Kids call it Special K. I've got some information here somewhere." He started mussing papers around on his desk.

"Ketamine, that substance in the dead woman, is a recreational club drug?"

"A hallucinogen, as I recall."

I was cold now, bumps popping up along my arms. I closed the window. "Maybe I'm getting sick, my temperature keeps jumping."

Rob put his head in the door. "Lily, the phone."

"Take a message for her," Art instructed, still flipping through pages.

"I think I'm thirsty, after all."

I went into the hall and took my time at the water dispenser. Did Sam know about ketamine?

"Hey, I've got it, come back here, Lily."

I took a few reluctant steps into his office. He waved a Xeroxed sheet. "Here you go. Hey, why don't you come to dinner sometime? Bring your son."

"Thank you." I read the headline: Hip, Cheap, and Potentially Lethal. "I wonder if the dead woman hung out in clubs."

"Could be," said Art.

"Lily, the phone again," Rob yelled.

"I think I'll get that, if it's okay."

"Sure."

Sam couldn't be into ketamine. It wasn't possible. I picked up the receiver. "Lily Davis here."

"Mrs. Davis?" A man's voice. Familiar.

"Yes."

"Chief Blocker."

I scouted the room for a private spot. There was no such thing. Rob, busy loading the office camera, was listening to my conversation. I knew because I listened to all his conversations when I had nothing better to do. Bernadette, her back to me, stiffened, her whole body on alert to eavesdrop.

"What's up?" I said. They would get no clue from me about who was calling.

"Would you come down to the station, Mrs. Davis?" Before today, he had always addressed me as Lily.

"What for?" I inquired neutrally.

"We need some information. We need to talk to you about something important."

"And may I ask what?" I might have been talking to Jane, well, not Jane, someone more in the acquaintance category.

"Is there some problem? Is your son sick today?"

"My son?"

"Yes."

"No, of course not. He's in school."

"We'll discuss it when you get here."

"Wait."

"Yes, Mrs. Davis?"

"Suppose I get there in a half-hour, forty minutes at the latest. Would that be cool?" I went overboard selecting a relaxed adjective.

"As soon as you can would be the best."

"Bye," I bleated, sometime after he'd already hung up.

I crammed the ketamine article in my purse, grabbed my coat, and started down the stairs. I tried to move quickly, but my legs felt as heavy as sandbags. Peg seemed to glide in slow motion from her desk to the supply cabinet. I seized the front door and noticed my inflamed hands. Deidre had poison ivy. How had she gotten it?

I ran across the parking lot, hurrying to a place that I wished I would never reach. My vision blurred. The air rippled, buildings undulated, cars acquired strange shapes. No sounds penetrated, but echoes ricocheted from one side of my brain to the other. Deidre's machine-gun laughter. Sam's giggles after Bernadette had announced the discovery of the body.

The slam of the car door shocked me into normal time. I rammed the key into the ignition and fired the car with ten times more gas than it needed. I backed out of the space and heard someone swear. I hit the brakes. Slow down. Proceed with caution. I conjured up an imaginary friend to talk me home. She warned me against driving too fast, ordered me to take a right, to change lanes, to check rearview and side mirrors. I let her guide me down the block and into my driveway, even kept her along so I could amble up the walk and wave carelessly to Woffert.

"Mary, she's home," he called. His wife threw open their door.

"How are you, Lily, dear?" she asked.

"Fine." I practiced the word some more.

"Would you like to come in for a cup of tea?"

Had they read my column? Did they feel sorry for me, too? Was the whole town reading between the lines? "No thank you, that's very kind, but I'm in a bit of a hurry. Work and all."

As soon as I was inside, I tore up to Sam's bedroom. It was hard to know where to begin. With clothes strewn from one end to the other, the place already appeared ransacked. I pulled out the ketamine article and set a record for speed-reading. The liquid is usually stolen. From veterinarians. Often mixed with vanilla for flavor. Baked until solid. Any fool can do it in a home oven. Three hundred fifty degrees on a glass plate. I owned one Pyrex baking dish, that would do. After the substance cools, crush into powder, then sniff. Sam could know all about ketamine. He could be a pro.

Did Deidre steal ketamine at the town meeting? Did they plan to use it for recreation, then decide to get some Klingon kicks? *Klingons like to kill people.* The woman was shot with a dart. They could have hidden anywhere and plugged her. Where *did* Deidre get that poison ivy?

How stupid of me to assume all the clues were linked to the same person. The house, the assignation, the tire marks. Who the young lady hung out with or made love to might not have had anything to do with her death. Of course, it was possible Sam knew her. He could have known her from the clubs.

I scoured the boxes, clothes, drawers, his bed. Under his pillow, I found the condoms I'd given him, the package opened. What a pleasing discovery. I searched his medicine cabinet, the laundry basket. I wasn't sure what I was looking for, but expected that it would declare itself, possibly a cache of tranquilizer darts or a vial of unidentified liquid. I opened the extra-strength Tylenol and the boxes of toothpaste and soap, and examined the toilet paper tube. I reminded myself how methodically Tom had dissected the Nicholas house and started over, working the room section by section.

Nothing.

I sat on Sam's bed, trying to figure out what I had missed, then gave up and collapsed backward. Thank God, I hadn't found anything—although that might only mean he'd covered his tracks. I flung my arm to the side and let it dangle off the mattress. I drifted back to that unearthly day when we had first entered the Nicholas bedroom. The erotic shock, Tom's grip on my shoulders. Our fateful return weeks later. *I haven't known you long enough for "never."* Tom and I had almost rolled right off the bed while making love. Stop this madness, get up, I scolded myself, and as I swung my legs down, my shoe crunched something in the thick shag carpet. I felt around and from between the scruffy yarns extracted a vial not taller than a thumbnail. Amber glass. Too unusual and too remarkably bitsy not to contain bad news. I unscrewed the tiny black top. Brownish-white powder inside. I shook some onto my palm, and the smell wafted upward. Delicious. I might have thought there were vanilla-flavored cookies baking in the oven. No parental guide for this moment. Not in the normal range.

This was evidence. Except it wasn't. All this proved was that Sam had ketamine. Anyone present at the deer meeting might have it, too. Should I call Allan?

I pinched the powder back inside. No, I did not want to talk to Allan. How disheartening. The only person as invested in Sam as I am is someone I can't stand, someone with whom I never agree, someone determined to blame me for everything wretched about my son. Not necessary, since I already blame myself.

The phone rang. I didn't answer, wanting to keep any hellish tidings at bay as long as possible. But this might be Sam's one permitted phone call from the Police Department after his arrest. "Hello."

"Mrs. Davis?"

A woman. And the second person today to address me as Mrs. Davis. "Yes."

"This is Glenn Hall, Deidre's mom."

"Oh, hello."

"I've been meaning to call. Sam and Deidre are spending so much time together."

My lord, you'd think they been hanging out in the sandbox. "Oh yes, I've been wanting to meet you, too."

"I felt awful when I read your column this morning. I realized that you hardly know a soul here. Can you come to dinner next Friday and meet our family? You and Sam both. Sam's such a funny kid. We really like him."

"I think— Can I call you back? You caught me in the middle of . . . my hair's wet. I'm late."

"Of course."

"What's your phone number?"

I wrote it down along with the rest of the information. Deidre's, dinner, seven p.m., Friday.

Sam couldn't kill anyone. He couldn't be a murderer. Murderers don't get dinner invitations. Murderers aren't funny kids who have meat loaf with their mothers at their girlfriends' houses. Murderers hide evidence; they don't drop it on the carpet. I'm fabricating this whole thing. Out the window are trees I can't identify, animals that aren't on leashes, fresh air. The only air I breathe easily is the air that alters from moment to moment with the aroma of bagels, burgers, stinky garbage, hot sugared peanuts cooked on a skillet on an outdoor cart. I miss busy stores. I miss that bestial urge on a crowded street to bean an old person so he'll move faster. The sky here shelters a strange world. And it is so vast. It is not my sky.

How can I know what I think?

I hid the vial in the back of a kitchen cabinet, inside a mug shaped like Santa Claus. I phoned the police before leaving, and left a message with Sally to tell Chief Blocker I'd be right there. Again supervising myself as though I were driving with only a learner's permit, I got myself to the station.

THE POLICE station was located just outside the village proper, up a winding hill. Here its modern utilitarian concrete-block architecture could offend no one's aesthetic sensibilities.

I expected to be squired to Chief Blocker's office, but Sally escorted me down the hallway to a cubicle not larger than six by eight. The interrogation room. I recognized it from the video screen in the dispatch office. A disconnect set in, my ironic double marveling that I should ever in my middle-class life be led to the hot seat in a police interrogation chamber. My son seemed a distant appendage, something that might or might not come up, and I might or might not acknowledge our acquaintance.

Footsteps—a deliberate, even pace down the stairs—and I turned to see Maureen Mooney, the only detective on the force. She was big-boned and self-possessed, and had probably ordered her conservative brown suit from a catalogue. She held her head haughtily, cranked at an upward angle, her eyelids raised only a lazy halfway, the minimum necessary for her to look down her freckled nose at me. When Mooney was a patrol officer, according to Art, she had been known to issue tickets to drivers speeding one mile over the limit.

"Mrs. Davis?"

"Yes."

"Come on in."

She waited for me to precede her and then indicated one of the four gray metal folding chairs at the rectangular Formica table. I sat, wondering whether I was an accessory simply from hiding that tiny amber bottle in a Santa Claus mug. She took the chair opposite.

I placed my purse on the floor next to my feet and clasped my hands in my lap. We exchanged polite smiles while we waited, although I didn't know for what. I was not about to be tricked into filling her silence. That was my technique for getting information, too.

"Thanks for coming over." Chief Blocker burst in and commenced a nervous hopping gait from one side of the room to the other. Following him, more cautious and circumspect, was Tom.

"Hello, Lily," he said. He didn't sit, either.

Blocker brushed his hand through his fuzzy hair. "You okay?" he asked.

"Excuse me?"

"You're squinting."

I was, I realized. I had been trying to reduce Tom to a blob, the way I had with that mouse.

"I'm a little tired. What's going on?"

"Sergeant McKee mentioned that you were in the Nicholas house together."

"What?" My foot involuntarily kicked up and toppled my purse. I bent over to shove the contents back in.

"Over a month ago—the day we saw the dead woman," I heard Tom say smoothly as I set the purse upright and resumed my composure. Oh, that day. "Only, of course, then, she was alive." He spun a chair, lopped a leg over the seat, and sat. This guy had moves even when it came to chairs.

"We were wondering," said Blocker, "if you could cast your mind back to that day. We're trying to identify the body. Perhaps if you'd describe what you remember, the woman, the room, anything."

This isn't about Sam. This has nothing to do with my son. Not yet, at least not yet.

Detective Mooney slipped a small notepad out of her pocket. She selected a sharpened pencil from the paper cup in the middle of the table and tapped the eraser impatiently.

I pretended to think. I made some clicking sounds with my tongue and scratched between my eyebrows.

"Lily?" said Blocker.

"I don't remember anything."

"That's impossible. You must. Think back. You and Sergeant McKee entered the driveway—"

"I told them that you came in," said Tom.

My God, did he imagine I was keeping silent now because on that day I'd promised him off-the-record confidentiality? He'd obviously fessed up to Blocker. "I'd injured my ankle. I'd been bitten by a dog and was pretty flipped. Otherwise, I would never have gone into that house, and really, I don't remember a thing, except those painted toenails. I was not myself. No, I wasn't. In fact, it's as if I was never in that overdesigned mansion, ever—that's how much I've blanked it out."

I rested my eyes on Tom to make my point: We never happened. He stared impassively back. Then I smiled broadly at Chief Blocker and Detective Mooney, who was looking peeved.

"A locket around the woman's neck, perhaps. She was undressed, I understand."

"Yes, naked. I don't remember her face, I think that's why, because I was so startled and then I tried not to look."

"How about a purse? Did you see any clothes?" Blocker leaned toward me, pressing his palms into the tabletop.

I shrugged helplessly.

A weary calm settled over him. While I was certain that his big toe was wiggling in his shoe, functioning as an exhaust valve, the rest of him wilted. Poor Blocker. He could have been a farmer in a drought: it hadn't rained for weeks, and now the one possibility—the only cloud on the horizon—had evaporated. I didn't feel guilty. I had nothing to contribute. Tom was what I remembered and intended to forget.

I was about to stand, to let them know that the meeting was over, when it crossed my mind that I was not allowed to excuse them. They were the dismissers; I was the dismissee. I waited.

"Are you absolutely certain?" Blocker said, with a sigh he couldn't suppress.

"I couldn't tell you the color of the bedspread." A limpid inviting peach. "Or the pillows." Crisp organdy that wrinkled as easily as linen. Her bare skin and ours. "Not even the length of her hair." That was true. "Everything I did in that house feels like an accident."

"Huh?" said Detective Mooney. "I'm not following."

"It's clear to me," said Tom.

"Traumatic but fortunately, mercifully erased."

Detective Mooney closed her notepad and deposited the pencil in the cup. Tom got up, whipped his chair around, and slotted it back in. "Thanks for coming over," said Chief Blocker. He gestured toward the door.

As they filed out after me, I inquired about whether I could report the fact that the victim had been seen three weeks before she died.

"Nothing's on the record for now," said Blocker.

"Is George Nicholas a suspect? Has he been interviewed, has anyone else?"

"No comment."

"Nice to see you, Lily," said Detective Mooney. With the interrogation over, I was Lily again. She punched Tom not too gently on the arm. "I heard your brother, the stud muffin, has been giving Lily a hard time."

"My brother?" That mini-grenade shook some suave out of him.

"Coral Williams started a rumor about your brother and me, that we were involved," I explained.

"I read your column," said Mooney, with an astonishingly girlish giggle. "You're having some sort of man trouble, or I'm not a detective."

Heat of tropical proportions rushed from my head to my toes. I must have turned shocking pink.

"Leave her alone," said Blocker. "Stop giving her a rough time."

"I'm not having a rough time. I'm fine."

"You heard the woman," Tom said. He clapped Blocker on the back and thanked him for ruining his afternoon off. "Take it easy, Lily." Very curt. He could not have been more curt, before he strode away down the hall.

DRIVING DOWN the hill, along a residential street, I passed a woman carrying out garbage and a man covering a motorboat with a tarp. At the sight of these everyday tasks, I suffered acute envy of the ordinary. I was living with the kind of anxiety that a person must get when she receives a dire medical diagnosis. I have crossed a line and entered the other side. I inhabit some science fiction world where the species to which I belong carries an overwhelming burden of dread. That's what distinguishes us from others who have only workaday worries. This envy of strangers might have been misguided—who knew what grim prospects the man with the motorboat might be facing—but under the circumstances, it seemed forgivable.

My deep funk was not from my interchange with Chief Blocker or Detective Mooney, or from the coolness of relations with Tom. I had handled all that with aplomb. I had to confront Sam.

After swinging right, off the road to the police department, I traveled Main to the big intersection, took a left on Barton, and followed it past the better shops. Out here the picturesque looks of Sakonnet Bay took a dive, with a jumble of dilapidated structures: an abandoned one-pump gas station; an auto-body shop; a junk store, its perimeter strewn with stacks of wooden doors and windows, bathroom sinks. Things perked up half a mile later, thanks to the presence of the old-fashioned three-story all-American brick high school.

After parking on the opposite side of the street, I cut across the broad, well-kept lawn, and hurried into the building, and down the hall to the main office. I needed my son, Sam Davis. I showed the woman my driver's license, establishing my identity. Would she please get him out of class, so I could take him home, it was very important.

As I waited in the corridor, watching a supposedly normal-range boy—at least he had normal-range hair (NRH)—open his locker and try to stop everything inside from falling out, I considered the best way to confront Sam, the way that might produce the truth, much as I might not want to hear it.

Sam gave the impression that he had awakened from a deep sleep. As he slouched toward me, his face knotted with confusion, his eyes blinking, he appeared to be adjusting to daylight. Only the spout on his bald head was jaunty, a small, hardy plant on the surface of the moon.

"What?" he greeted me.

"I need to talk to you."

"Is Dad okay?"

"Yes, he's fine. I have to talk to you, that's all."

"You got me out of class to talk?"

"It's important."

He groaned—I was obviously exhausting his boundless goodwill and patience—and left the building ahead of me.

"Sam, wait up." I chased after him, hearing him mumble. "I can't understand what you're saying."

He repeated his words, "You're getting really nuts, Mom," then dodged several vehicles to cross in traffic. When I got into the car, he was already ensconced, biting a nail. His army surplus jacket had bunched up around him, the collar jabbing into his chin. He dropped his grimy backpack to the floor between his legs.

"Why is your backpack caked with dirt?"

"Chuydah."

"Sam, if you speak Klingon, I swear, I'm going to throw you out the window."

That was not how I intended to begin. Truly not. "Look, I'm sorry." That wasn't how I intended to begin, either. With an apology. We started down the street into the center of town.

"What was in your column today?" he asked.

"It was about the woman who died. Why?"

"Some kids were talking about it."

"What were they saying?"

"Nothing."

"Nothing?"

"Shit, Mom, what do you want?"

"Don't talk to me that way. It's rude. Don't." I pulled over in a red zone to try to collect myself. Somebody banged on the windshield and held out a white paper bag. I think we were being offered doughnuts. I shook my head.

"Who is that?" asked Sam.

"I have no idea. Someone friendly. Look, I found a small bottle, yellowish, on the floor of your room. What's in it?"

"I don't know."

"Sam, please, don't lie to me. Is it ketamine? Is it Special K?"

He slammed against the door as he yanked the handle, and almost fell out. In an instant he was down the block, weaving through shoppers. I got out to bolt after him but realized there was no way I could chase my son down Barton Road. Why is that kid tearing through town when he should be in school? Already someone was speculating, mentioning the curious fact to a shopkeeper, who would relay it a few minutes later to his mother-in-law. I walked briskly in the same direction Sam had gone, straining to spy his lumbering form, peeking down alleys between stores; I had to set a pace closer to hurry than panic. Four or five folks said hello as they strolled by. I didn't see him anywhere. I doubled back, now peering into shop windows, feigning an intense search for exactly the right gift. Another hello. A bright, cheerful greeting, that I felt forced to simulate in return. It was that damn column. I should never have said I was alone. Worse, adrift. Now people were going out of their way to be friendlier than ever. They'll feel bad for gossiping about your kid, Art had warned. A memory of blissful anonymity overtook me, a recollection of being on a Manhattan street—hordes of people, and not a single one making eye contact. Privacy in a public place. What an undervalued asset. Then the big, beautiful soap bubble popped as a mittened hand wagged amiably in my face.

I wound through LePater's, in case Sam was cowering behind the paper towels, then the Variety Shop, where Tom's wife had bought him grease-flavored jeans. Out again and into the parking lot. I investigated, row by row.

When I returned to my car, Officer Scott was writing a ticket. "Sorry, Lily," he said. Twenty dollars for parking in a red zone.

Now I tracked Sam in the car, hunting up and down the streets in our neighborhood. I searched the hideaway in the vacant lot, tooled down Linden Lane past Deidre's inviting shingled house, where bikes of various sizes were propped against the porch and Indian corn decorated the door. I worked up a lather of apprehension, charged blindly through stop signs, then halted in the middle of an intersection, jolted to attention by a red-and-white flash in my peripheral vision.

Finally I went home and sat in the living room, flipping channels, awaiting Sam's return. I settled on the cooking network, narcotized by directions for making sweet potato tamales, chicken mole, and Mexican corn soup. I brewed tea and forgot to drink it. The phone rang, and racing to answer, I cracked my knee on a kitchen cabinet—was even my spatial judgment skewed? It was Jane, only Jane, lamenting that she'd had no idea until she'd read my column that I was coming down off something big. "Are you all right?"

"It's long over. A New York thing. And it wasn't big."

"I mean, are you all right this second? Your hello was weird."

"I was napping."

"Lily—"

"What?"

"That was strange, your putting in all that speculation about why the woman died. A jealous wife . . . as if I could do that."

"Of course you couldn't do anything like that, Jane. I'm really tired, could I please get off?"

"But—"

"It wasn't about you."

"I didn't think it was."

"Jane, I'll call you tomorrow. I promise."

"All right."

Was she angry? I was too worried to care.

At three-thirty, I phoned Deidre's. Her mother answered, and I accepted her dinner invitation. "Is my son there by any chance?"

"No."

"He has a dentist appointment. He must have forgotten."

"Just a second."

I heard her shout for Deidre, as well as referee some small children, before returning to the phone. "She hasn't seen him today. She thought he was home sick."

"Oh, no. He was home for a while but . . ." Now I was really in over my head. I forced a laugh. "It's too complicated to explain. Tell Deidre that even though it's Friday, he might not be able to see her this evening. If they had plans or something—"

"Don't worry. We'll enjoy having her to ourselves."

I realized I couldn't ask her to tell Sam to call if he showed up there. I had implied he would be otherwise occupied. This was such a muddle. "Sorry to bother you."

"You're no bother," she said, and I hung up.

I wasn't going to notify the police that he was missing. Not yet, anyway. There was nothing to do. Nothing to do but wait. My most hated scenario.

Aside from informing the paper that I was working at home, I stayed off the telephone.

I paced to the window again and again. The flagstone path to the front door faded in a gray twilight. I flicked on the porch light, a beacon for Sam. Except for that glowing yellow orb with a few moths flitting about, the world outside was now black. Black and very still, devoid even of the wind's rustle. Occasionally a car whooshed down the block and away.

At about seven-thirty the telephone rang. A hang-up click. I hit *69, but didn't recognize the local number. When I dialed it, no one answered. At eight-ten the phone rang again. "Sam," I shouted into the receiver, "don't hang up." But the phone clicked, and *69 got me to another unfamiliar, unanswered local phone.

Now I was furious with Sam—for torturing me, for being so reckless. If only I knew he was all right. If only he would come home so I could kill him. At nine, the telephone rang again.

"Hello."

"Lily, it's Allan."

The last person I wanted to hear from.

"You can relax. Sam is here with me."

"With you?"

"He took the train."

"You're kidding." From here to New York City, then up to Boston? "I didn't realize he had that much money. Or energy."

"He won't tell me what this is about. Did you two have a fight?"

"Not exactly." Oh God, how should I handle this? "It's between Sam and me."

In the background I heard a woman's voice. Allan's wife, Joanne, was always coaching him when he talked to me, suggesting things he might not have thought of.

"Allan, would you please send him back? Don't let him spend the weekend. Put him on a plane tomorrow."

"Hold it." More back-and-forth with Joanne, until he announced in his reedy, nasal voice that he would do as I asked.

"Thank you. Thanks a lot, Allan, I really appreciate it. Put Sam on, please."

"He doesn't want to talk."

"So what? Put him on."

"Hi, Mom."

"Sam, you're flying home tomorrow and we're going to talk. When you get here, we're going to talk about everything."

"Yeah."

"Is that a yes?"

"Yes."

"Okay, sweetie, I'll see you tomorrow."

So he was fine, at least physically. And I was not—couldn't keep my head up from the events of today and the prospect of tomorrow. I turned off the lights and lay on the couch under a quilt. On the TV, a chef flipped pizza dough into the air, then smoothed it on a wooden board. The chatty show and the cook's lively confidence as he sprinkled on a confetti of green and yellow peppers, mushrooms, and baby tomatoes lulled my eyes closed. I zapped the television and was soon asleep.

The sound that awoke me was skittering. Squirrels perhaps, outside the window. Then a firm crunch of ground. Not squirrels now, not deer, not animals at all. Too precise and cautious. The clock on the VCR read eleven twenty-three. A branch fluttered against the window, and I discerned two more quick but heavy treads. I pushed the patchwork cover onto the floor. The feet padded outside. I could hear them circling from the living room window around to the enclosed porch, my office. Had I locked the porch door? I slithered down off the couch so whoever it was couldn't see me through the window. I didn't want to turn on a lamp. A flash of light might trigger rashness. The maniac might burst in. I crawled across the living room, feeling the way with my hands to avoid collisions, trying to recall precisely the landscape of the room. The nearest phone was in the kitchen.

I scuttled more quickly on all fours across the hall. The rustling had now reached the kitchen door. I heard someone try the knob. I pulled the phone from the counter and dialed 911. "This is Lily Davis," I whispered hoarsely. I didn't know the night dispatch officer. "Three-twenty-five Windham Street. Someone's trying to break in."

The officer told me to hold on and I could hear my SOS relayed over the wires. I felt for the cupboard under the sink. Let there be no mouse, I prayed as I opened it, pushed back the bug spray, sponges, and dishwasher detergent, and squeezed inside. The plumbing pipes butted my shoulder. The cordless receiver was jammed under my chin. I couldn't speak—it was too cramped for my jaw to open—but I wouldn't have dared anyway. The dispatch officer repeated that I should keep calm, help was on the way. I managed to shut the double doors—the first easily by gripping the edge, the second by hooking my fingernail under the bolt that secured the outside handle and teasing the door toward me. I was now stuffed inside an airless, pitch-black box.

Contorting even further, I contrived to press my fingers into my ears. If the intruder entered, I'd rather not know. He could blast the cupboard open. Suppose I ended up a pulpy mush of bullet holes? Suppose I was nailed by a deer dart?

"Lily, Lily." Loud kicking rattled the back door.

"Tom?" I rolled sideways and fell out of the cabinet. "Tom." I sprang up and was about to turn on the light, when I stopped myself: Was he safety? I hadn't heard a cop car, or the blare of an approaching siren. He had called my name, but he hadn't announced himself officially as the police.

The door shook, even the hinges strained as Tom pummeled. Why was he kicking? "Lily," he shouted.

I approached as to my death. I turned the light on. I rotated the security bolt. The door flew open.

Tom had a young man snared. With one hand on the collar of the kid's mangy sheepskin jacket and the other clenching his wrists behind his back, he shoved his prisoner inside. A beanpole of a boy I'd never before seen, his face spatter-painted with freckles, and his watery blue eyes rimmed with a stubby fuzz of eyelashes slightly more orange than his strawberry-blond hair. He smelled of fish.

"Do you know Duncan Cates?" said Tom.

It took me a minute to find my voice. "Duncan? Is this Dunkie?"

The boy was crying now, his nose a leaky faucet of snot. Tom pushed him down into one of my breakfast chairs, then took off his own jacket and wrapped it around me. "You're shaking, take some deep breaths."

I did as I was told.

He opened a few cabinets, found a glass, and filled it with water. "Drink slowly." He watched me before turning to the boy. "Are you out of your mind, Duncan? What the hell is this about?"

Duncan wiped his nose with the hem of his T-shirt. "I was looking for Bernie."

"Bernie?" I was so frazzled, so disoriented. "Do you mean Bernadette?"

"Bernadette Lester?" asked Tom.

He sniffled an acknowledgment.

"What makes you think she's here?"

"In the paper. What she wrote?"

"My column?" I lowered myself carefully into the chair next to him. "Did you read my column?"

"My mom did. You had something in it about Bernie."

"The overwrought hysteric?" Tom suggested. "How she let an overwrought hysteric move in?"

"Yeah, that's it. My mom said that sounded like Bernie."

"Your mom's right, but Bernadette moved out."

"I just wanted to talk to her."

"That's probably all he did want," I told Tom. "You need a bath, Duncan."

"I know. I didn't shower since the boat."

Tom checked with Dispatch, letting them know that everything was under control—a true statement in only the most immediate sense. He peppered his call with lingo and numbers, ending with "Ten-four." I would be in the log. I was now a log item.

Mr. Woffert, rifle in hand, knocked on the back door. Tom sent him away. I relaxed enough to offer Duncan a Coke and a hero sandwich. While devouring the sandwich in huge chomps, he fretted about Bernadette, and how they'd had a big fight because he sprayed her with the hose when he was washing his car.

"There's got to be a better way to express affection," said Tom.

"I really respect her," said Dunkie.

"That's what Bernadette said," I confirmed, handing him a second paper napkin, which he used to wipe his mouth and then to collect the crumbs on the table.

I observed him the way one might a stray cat invited in for milk, finding myself reluctantly won over, resenting that he was more adorable than I'd originally thought. Tom seemed similarly affected; at least I fancied that I detected amusement mixed with his exasperation.

"I don't want to press charges," I told Tom. "Can we let him go?"

"Where's your truck, Duncan?"

"Around the corner."

Tom jerked his head in the direction of the door—the boy could skedaddle. Duncan put his plate in the sink and his napkins in the garbage, and thanked me over and over.

"Did you phone here a couple times and hang up, Duncan?"

"That was me," he said, turning pink. "Can I still leave?"

"Yes."

He hustled out the door.

"He's well brought up," I observed.

"Yeah." Tom was hot-wired with energy, pacing across the kitchen and into the hall. He raked his hair. Finally, he stopped, his brain having apparently arrived at some destination.

"What is it?"

"I'm trying to think what I want to say. Although I understand that you want nothing to do with—" He caught a look on my face. "I'm sorry. I'm out of line. This was a tough night. You had an awful scare. Are you all right?"

"I have a lot on my mind."

"Do you want me to leave?"

"Yes. I really do." I held out his jacket.

He took it as he came past me through the kitchen, collected his cap from the table, and whacked it against his leg a few times. Then he opened the back door.

"This is not about you," I said by way of good-bye. "This is not about what happened or didn't happen between us."

The door closed, the screen banged, and I was left with my gnawing terror about Sam. I sat back down at the table and buried my head in my hands.

"Lily?"

I screamed.

"I'm sorry, I didn't mean—I don't know what I was thinking, I thought you heard me come in again. Jesus, I'm screwing up all over the place."

"Sam has ketamine."

He flinched.

"I found some in his room."

"Are you sure?"

"Yes. I found the powder form, which means he probably had the liquid."

Tom pulled a chair very close and sat down. "Your son couldn't do that terrible thing."

Then it all poured out—the nasty Klingon stuff, and Sam and Deidre's inappropriate remarks and giggles, and every loner-gone-berserk story I could remember from the nightly news. I found knowledge at my fingertips that I didn't know was in the vault, for instance, that Timothy McVeigh, the Oklahoma City bomber, had parents who were divorced, and that his father had insisted that Timothy's antisocial strangeness dated from their separation. "Parents never know what their kids are up to. I've noticed that again and again. They never know." I was babbling, mixing up my fears with my facts. I told Tom about the steak knife, the reason we'd moved here. I even revealed the most damaging bit, that Sam had split when confronted.

Tom picked up my hand and opened my tight fist. He smoothed his fingers across my palm and rubbed it hard with his thumb. Then he curled my hand up and returned it to me. "Lily, look, I have to patrol. Come for a ride with me."

"No."

"You're going to go crazy in this house."

"I'm not going with you."

"You'll feel safer."

"I don't know anything about you, Tom. Do you realize that? I don't know a thing."

"What do you want to know?"

"Nothing."

"Lily . . ."

"How old are you?"

"Thirty-five," said Tom.

"That's what I thought."

"What else?"

"Nothing."

"Come with me."

"Was I the first—?"

"The first what?"

"Woman?"

"That I was unfaithful with?"

"Yes."

"No."

I got up and stumbled backward, turned and headed into the living room. I heard Tom's voice behind me. "When I saw you that first day—"

I began rearranging things on the mantel, moving around the photo of Sam, when he had normal-range hair, holding the hammock that we'd hardly ever swung in.

"You were taking everything so seriously, that idiotic woman, that loon of a dog." He took the frame from my hands. "Where do you want this?"

"I don't know."

He placed it in the center. "The whole thing was so stupid, freaky. I had to pop a pitcher off a dog's head, and all I'm thinking is, That scribbling pixie is going to steal my soul."

"Tom, please. Let's be honest with each other."

"You don't believe me?"

I said nothing. He grabbed my arm. "Okay, you tell me what you felt."

"When?"

"On the beach, whenever we talked, when we made love."

I tried to assemble something conclusive, something decisive, something sarcastic. "I thought—"

"Not what you thought, what you felt."

Staring into his expressively sincere eyes, I had to admit to a serious limitation: Opinions came easily to me, knowledge was more elusive. "I felt—" I said weakly.

"The truth."

"Completely fulfilled."

"Me, too." He put up his hands, indicating he would back off. I sat down abruptly.

"My brain's been fried since I met you, trying to figure how this happened and what I was going to do about it. At the station . . ."

"What?"

"When you said we meant nothing—"

"You were so slick, Tom."

"Yeah, sure."

I couldn't tell if he knew it. The fact might have depressed him.

"Come on, Lily, let's get out of here. We'll circle the town five hundred times before dawn."

Tom bundled me into my coat, taking special care, as if I needed help even locating the sleeves. He buttoned me up, fastened the collar under my chin, and undertook other necessary tasks that I might be too upset to execute properly, like turning out the lights and locking the door.

We drove around, confiding secrets.

It turns out that the most private place in Sakonnet Bay is a police car at two in the morning. Rolling down tree-lined streets, past blurs of happy homes, we would have talked our throats raw, except for Tom's near-lifetime supply of Myntens. A cop car is not as cozy as a regular automobile, I was relieved about that. Too much technology—radar box, jabbering walkie-talkie. No, not cozy, but secure. A veritable safe on wheels. For as long as the night and our ride lasted, nothing bad could happen.

We toured Tom's past—his childhood haunts and teenage hang-outs, including a favorite fishing pond and necking spot. With his powerful red-and-white official police light rotating on the car roof, he lit the place like a Manhattan theater on opening night; only in this case the stars were in the sky and the crowd was a spidery thatch of towering trees. We sat on the front bumper, drinking sodas and ad-miring the view.

Among other tales, he told of trains, which reminded me of Sam's getaway. My son was hovering always, a worry barely held at bay. Tom used to ride from town to town, anything to escape his enveloping family. "No privacy," he said. "None." A brother, two sisters, parents, and a parade of aunts, uncles, and cousins stopping by unannounced. "Fun, noisy, endless," he said. And all the men were cops, his dad and three uncles.

"So there was no question about your future?"

"None."

"But you're not quite suited."

"No," he said bluntly. "The uniform isn't a perfect fit."

I confessed why I got divorced, that I sold out Sam's innocence because I was bored, numbingly bored by Allan's awesome gift for tedious conversation. This fact revealed me as a spoiled brat of a woman, something about which I was both embarrassed and ashamed, particularly now in this chaos of trouble. I tried to explain how the divorce had altered me as a parent. It seemed significant, even though I didn't know why I needed to tell Tom or how, exactly, I was differ-ent. Less natural, and something else—my relationship with Sam was out of whack: we mattered too much to each other. Yet how could that be possible? How could a mother be too important to her child, or vice versa?

The car's interior, with its faint dashboard light, was so protec-tive. All the things we said or felt could be present but not proclaim themselves. I could marvel at Tom and not be found out. He loved to talk, and from one sentence to the next, his mood could be as variable as weather. And he listened . . . listened as keenly as if we were in the wilderness and my voice were the only human sound. I had never known a man as open or accepting.

"You didn't know who you were," he said.

"When?"

"When you got married."

"That's a very kind way to put it."

"How would you put it?"

"I was immature. Careless."

"Good God, Lily, cut yourself some slack." I was thrown by his vehemence.

"All right. All right, I will. I was a kid. A baby." It felt nice to kiss the guilt good-bye. *Adiós,* at least for tonight. "Did you know who you were?" I asked him.

"When?"

"When you got married."

"I guess. I always knew who I would marry."

We were pulling into the Town Beach parking lot, one of the few places where we had history. He shut off the engine and we rested awhile. The waves were thunderous, providing pounding drama an invisible distance away. "Do you know why guys become cops out here?" he asked.

"Why?"

"Because of retirement. Out at forty-five. Great pension."

"How strange. It's a dangerous profession, but a safe choice."

"Yes," said Tom. "All safe choices until you."

We were both absolutely still. Outside was the noisy surf, inside the gargle of the walkie-talkie, but between us lay a quiet too precious to break.

Tom lay the back of his hand against my ear and neck. "Are you okay, are you warm enough?"

"I like the cold. Tonight, anyway."

"Would you do it again, Lily?"

"Do what again?"

"Get divorced."

"Oh, Tom."

"Tell me."

"You mean, if I had a child? If I had children, like you?"

"Yes."

"My son has a broken heart."

Until then, until I had the pressing need for Tom to understand the havoc we could wreak, I never understood myself what had happened. "Sam's dad and I broke his heart." I could see my son's heart right now—a valentine with a zigzag line across it. To Mom, it was addressed, in Sam's slanting, almost indecipherable scrawl. "One day it will heal," I told Tom, although tonight it wasn't easy to project Sam's future. "The surface will be smooth, the pain paved over with good feelings, but underneath there will still be a telltale hairline crack."

"Children are resilient," he said.

I didn't want to argue, but there could be no self-deception, not for Tom or me. "They adjust. That's different."

In a pale blue dawn, we pulled up to my house. "I suppose you have to interview Sam." I was looking at the army of squirrels hunting for breakfast on the lawn.

"Maybe. I hope not. I think the murderer was someone who had keys to the house."

We were back to the case, a more neutral subject for conversation; and I was thinking about how I dreaded going inside. Discussing the crime would delay our separation, even if it increased my anxiety.

"We're working our way through Mr. Nicholas's family and friends," said Tom in his sergeant's voice.

I wished I had paper so I could take notes.

"What about the contractor and the housekeeper?" I inquired.

"They have alibis."

"The pool man? Oh, no, I forgot, he doesn't have a key."

"How do you know that?" asked Tom.

"Jane. Jane Atkins. She knows everything."

"How does she know?"

"She's a realtor. This is a small town."

"The town's not that small."

"Come on, everyone knows everything about everybody."

"Not about the summer residents. Did she broker his house?"

I faced him without thinking and was struck anew by his good looks. "Maybe—I don't know." I tried to recall my first conversation with Jane on the subject. I tried to slow my brain down to think clearly. If she had brokered the house, she might have a key, too.

"I pumped her for information one night. She was a wreck about her husband, imagining that he was cheating, which he wasn't, but I was obsessed with us. I wanted to talk about that summer house because it had to do with us. I wasn't really even paying attention to Jane. How ruthless. Passion can make you reckless with your friends, your family. It's like you could step on dead bodies."

I didn't know if I was talking about Jane or me. I looked at the squirrels. One carried a nut as large as an egg. Tom drummed his fingers on the steering wheel.

"When is your son coming back?" he asked.

"Tomorrow. I'll have to check, but probably early afternoon."

I suddenly thought I must look terrible. I must look as though I'd been up all night. I ran my hands through my hair, slicking it behind my ears, arranging my bangs.

"Leave quickly," said Tom.

I was almost out of the car when he caught my hand. "I'm in love with you, Lily."

"Let go, please." I ran for the door.

AS MY SON slunk off the plane, he found excuses not to look my way. With apparent fascination, he watched the greetings of others: air kisses between two well-dressed women; a toddler hurtling himself at his dad; and trooping out with a flight attendant, one little boy with a backpack, a version of Sam flying solo years before. Even the floor was a thrilling diversion. I inferred nothing from his refusal to connect with me, except that he might be ashamed of something, and then I decided not to infer even that.

Declining to settle for his skimpy hug, I gripped him tightly. "You scared me to death, Sam."

"Sorry, Mom," he muttered.

I let that worthless apology go by for now, and didn't attempt conversation on the way home. My only kindness was the drive-through window at Burger King. We snacked on fries and Sam wolfed down a

Whopper. I hoped that the silent ride, with his mom making no attempt at small talk, would unnerve him.

When we entered the house, I announced that we would convene right away in the living room. He would have no time to collect himself or phone Deidre. One other thing that I had planned ahead: I told him to sit on the couch and lodged myself by his side. Seated as we were, inches apart, it would be hard for either of us to shout or insult. If Sam was going to try to pull the wool over my eyes, he would have to do it at close range.

"You tell me," I began.

"Sex," Sam blurted.

"What?"

"The K. It was for sex."

"You mean, the ketamine? That's what you used it for?"

A smile turned up the corners of his mouth. He clapped both hands over it. His eyes grew large and buggy. I recognized the reaction—he was trying to counter an overwhelming compulsion to grin.

"It's not funny."

He removed his hands and appeared contrite.

"Did Deidre get it from the deer meeting?" He nodded almost imperceptibly. "Did you bake it into powder?" No answer. "Sam?"

"She brought home darts," he whispered. "She didn't know."

"What?"

"That it wasn't just for deer."

"So you told her?"

He took a deep breath. "We baked it. You're weren't here, after school. I knew how. We mixed it with vanilla, because it's easier to sniff." He was finding his voice now, and a long-repressed ability to converse. He twirled his spout around his finger. "Woffert was on the ladder, banging away, and I was scared he could see inside, or he was going to come over, he's so nosy, but Deidre stuck her head out the window and yelled at him."

"She yelled? What did she yell?"

"Just hi." He started to grin again, but stopped himself.

"She's got nerve."

"Yeah." Now he was sober.

"When we talked that night after the deer meeting, why did she describe what the dart looked like, if you'd already seen it?"

Sam shrugged.

"Sam, come on."

"We were kidding around."

"You mean misleading me?"

"Yes."

A teenager's gift for lying is awesome. She'd sipped my cocoa and lied a little. Cocoa obviously has some power, but I'd overrated it. This was only one of my many errors in judgment: Cocoa is no truth serum. "So go on."

"That's all. We made it and took it."

"Did Deidre have extra darts?"

"Maybe."

"Sam."

"She got rid of them when that dead woman was found. She didn't want to have them anymore, she told me, so she rode her bike somewhere and buried them."

"Where?"

"I don't know, Mom, why?"

"Is that how she got poison ivy?"

"I guess."

If there was a culprit here, I'd bet my money on Deidre. Sam had been chattering—my God, full sentences, with modulation and spirit. While he sometimes had trouble making eye contact, he still leaned toward me, all earnestness. But now that we were discussing Deidre and her disposal of the darts, he fidgeted. She was such an odd, unflappable girl. She had tempted a nosy neighbor to catch them with drugs, brazenly refused to speak to me in English for weeks. How far would she go? Had she hidden in the bushes with a blowgun and a dart? Sam tapped his foot, and his tongue twitched around and slid under his lower lip.

"Why did you run away? It was so frightening. You must have been very upset about something."

"I don't know."

"Yes you do." I wanted to envelop him. Why wasn't I a bear of a person, instead of this runt whose arm couldn't reach across her own son's shoulder?

I tucked my arm under his and snuggled closer.

"I don't want to hurt your feelings," said Sam.

I couldn't think of how to respond. By treating me like an invisible housemate, he'd been hurting my feelings for years.

"You've been so weird, Mom."

"Me? I've been weird? Don't put this off on me, please. I haven't been speaking the language of an intergalactic race."

"Mom, I'm serious, okay? You're . . ." His body lolled sideways, and surprisingly, his head ended up in my lap. And then he got comfy, stretching out on the couch.

I smoothed the prickly growth on his bald head. "Have I been scaring you?"

"We should go home, Mom."

"Home?"

"You know."

We should go to New York? He should leave Deidre? I was confused. I didn't doubt his sincerity. At that instant, I knew Sam's single motive was concern for me and an instinctual grasp of his own needs. But I had this niggling worry. Why would a madly-in-love teenage boy want to leave his girlfriend? I was about to ask this when the telephone rang.

Sam sat up. "It's probably Deidre."

I couldn't tell whether he was pleased or not. I decided to answer. Sam and I should visit Deidre's anyway. Sam, Deidre, Glenn, and I should have a talk.

I was about to pick up the phone when Sam waved to catch my attention from the couch. "Do you love me, Mom?" he asked.

"More than anything."

He sighed.

"Hello," I said into the receiver.

"Lily, it's Sally."

"Who?"

"The Police Department dispatch officer. Hold on." I heard her exchange her official voice for something more chummy. "Get red crepe paper. Timmy loves red. One second, Mom." She returned to me. "Sergeant McKee requests that you come down to the station. Oh my Lord."

"Sally?"

No response.

"Sally, are you there?"

"Come down here right now, please," she ordered. "Sergeant McKee thinks it would be helpful. I've got to go."

"Wait." Too late—she'd disconnected. I slammed the phone down. "She's got to go? She's 911. How can she have to go?"

"What happened, Mom?" Sam had wandered in and was removing an old slice of pizza from his backpack.

"I don't know, honey, I really don't know. I have to go down to the police station."

"How come?"

"I don't know."

He gathered his backpack in his arms and started up the stairs. "I'll be in my room."

I would like to claim that I inferred nothing from his hasty retreat and that all the way to the station I was as calm as a yogi. In fact, I was wondering whether I should call a lawyer. Mentally, I thumbed through a list of connections—a classmate who had gone into criminal law, a guy I'd dated a few times whose father was a judge. At worst, if Deidre was involved, Sam could be accused of being an accessory, although clearly he was not. He might know something, a little, that's all.

Even before parking, I could see the department was abuzz: many more cars in the lot, extra vehicles from Suffolk County, mobile units from two local radio stations. I pulled my notepad and pen from my purse. If other press was there, I should act like them. No one would think that my son was a suspect or that I was about to be questioned. There it was, the ultimate foolishness—I still imagined that there could be such a thing as a secret in Sakonnet Bay.

I squeezed my way through many insistent reporters demanding the scoop. At the open door, Sally held them back with outstretched arms. "Chief Blocker will give a press conference in two hours," she repeated as I ducked under her fence. "Lily Davis is here," she shouted.

I climbed the stairs past the dispatch office, where three officers were coping with the continuous ringing of telephones. "Did they identify the body?" I inquired, but an officer shooed me into a hushed hallway, where, clustered at the far end, I saw Tom, Chief Blocker, Detective Mooney, and Jane. Why is Jane's hair pinned up as if she just got out of the shower, I was thinking, when she fainted.

Big City Eyes

BY LILY DAVIS

JANE ATKINS and I met on the day that I decided to move to Sakonnet Bay. She found a house for me and my son, and was with us on the lawn to cheer as the moving van rumbled in six hours late. When the lights blew during a recent nor'easter, I lit candles that she had given me. A transistor radio, her other housewarming gift, kept me sane during bursts of wind and hail. When I wanted to gab, when I wanted to have fun, when I found life to be more than I could handle, I phoned Jane. Of course she could have tea, lunch, dinner, go to the movies. Did I want to trundle off with her to open houses?

With Jane, I could talk until the sun set in Sakonnet Bay, get tipsy over margaritas, wipe my tears with tissues from the packet that she kept in her monster of a purse. From the first day, as Jane whirled me from one end of town to the other, I knew I would grow old with her.

Now life is a lot more than Jane can handle, with the arrest last Saturday of her husband, Jonathan Atkins, for the alleged murder of a young New York City woman named Tracey Kenniston.

According to police sources, Atkins met the young woman by chance. When one of his Internet stock transactions did not go through, Ms. Kenniston called from the brokerage company to inform him that the computers were down. A phone flirtation ensued, then clandestine dates.

Jane kept a key to each house she brokered. Over the years, she'd accumulated enough to fill two desk drawers. Each key was wrapped in white bond paper and secured with a double-twisted rubber band. On each piece of paper she had printed the address and any necessary instructions. This was how Jonathan Atkins was reportedly able to enter vacant summer mansions, following his wife's written directions for disarming the security systems. The Nicholas house on Ocean Drive, along with other real estate she sold, was a trysting spot for her husband and his lover. They had planned to run off, but according to Ms. Kenniston's friends, she changed her mind.

Perhaps the suspect meant only to detain Ms. Kenniston by such crude means, the tranquilizer dart. Perhaps he was trying to deter her from leaving him. He might not have known that ketamine, a drug that can sedate a deer, can kill a woman . . . especially if it is shot into her . . . especially if she has already ingested Valium.

Chief Ben Blocker praised the brilliantly intuitive detecting of Sergeant Tom McKee, who picked up Jonathan Atkins on a hunch.

As people have gathered in every conceivable location to hash and rehash WHAT WE KNOW ABOUT THE CASE, I have been thinking and rethinking gossip. I have come to believe that gossip contains an element of malicious glee, whereas this other activity that bears a strong resemblance to gossip is just people trying to make sense of life. Folks munching on facts as well as doughnuts are trying to understand how this terrible hurt could have come to pass, to deplore it and construct some version of the facts that protects them from believing that such madness could happen to them.

At one time I would have seen these events through the eyes of Tracey Kenniston. I would have tried to figure out what needs this older man satisfied in her. She fell in love, tried to escape from it, and as a result, she is dead at the absurdly young age of twenty-three. At one time, not only would I have sympathized with Tracey, I would have been willing to do what she did: blindly follow her heart. Giddy and extraordinary passion is compelling, and a life lived without that paradise painfully incomplete. It is self-delusion to imagine otherwise. But at my own stage of life and in my own circumstances, I suffer from myopia and see this tragedy only through the eyes of my friend. If the accounts are true, I wonder, how could her husband betray her so brutally? How will she ever survive?

Jane Atkins is a realtor, but her job was simply a concrete, money-earning outlet for her need to mother. She found us homes and made sure our families were safely stowed. Now her own house is coming down around her . . . except that no one in town will let it.

Each day when I visit, attempting my own hapless version of good cheer, there are at least twenty other Sakonnet Bay residents doing likewise. Meals are cooked, clothes and dishes are washed. Hearts and heads advise and console. Jane bucked us up, and now we are all trying to give something back. Last night even a deer appeared to pay special heed, and passed up her leafy hedge for one next door.

JANE AND I were lying side by side on lounge chairs in her backyard, both bundled in wool blankets. The stubby grass had a film of frost and the bare trees provided no shelter. Through the back windows, we could see Coral moving from kitchen to dining room, laying out the never-ending buffet of snacks. Jane's daughter, Carrie, helping Coral, paused every so often at the window and sent her mother an encouraging smile. She and her brother Simon had come home from college.

In the almost three weeks since Jonathan's arrest, Jane had dropped pounds. Her full cheeks had hollowed out. With haunted eyes looking larger, taking up a disproportionate amount of her face, she had a romantic look: the heroine of a nineteenth-century novel, wasting away with something tragic like consumption.

"I gave them evidence, you know."

"What do you mean, Jane?"

"He said he'd never met her, but I was sure he'd taken the key. I told them. They found his fingerprints there."

She couldn't stay off the subject for very long, and that was part of Jonathan's curse. His crime possessed her.

"Phone bills, too, with his calls to her. I gave them everything. I won't talk to him."

"Of course. Is he going to plead guilty?"

"Simon says he claims he shot her with that blowgun by accident. There are no witnesses." She barked a brief laugh. "Maybe he'll get off."

"Bye Jane, bye Lily." Coral called from the back door.

"Bye. And thank you. Thank you, thank you, thank you." Jane livened up, summoning years of practice as a happy, outgoing person. "Are you cold?" she asked me. "We can go in."

"Not unless you want to."

"No. I like it outside." She slumped back and pulled the cover up higher, around her chin. We rested awhile, listening to animal sounds, a few hoots and coos that I didn't recognize.

"I went into the village yesterday. Carrie took me to buy groceries. She thought it might help me to do a chore."

"Did it?"

"Well, I bumped into my old life."

I sat up. "It's inescapable. In this town, I know I'll turn a corner and there will be what I'm avoiding on the day that I'm missing what I'm avoiding so much that my head hurts, so then what's going to happen?" I stopped as I realized that I had managed to get Jane's attention off herself.

"My God, you were involved with someone."

I took a tissue from the large box I carried around Jane's house and planted on the ground or floor near wherever she landed. Very handy it was. I blew my nose.

"Did you fall in love?"

I couldn't see my friend right now through the watery blur, so I just waved my hand—she should forget it.

"If you miss him, Lily, call him."

He had phoned me. Many times. I had a stack of pink re-minder slips at the office, all with the same message. "Tom McKee. Call me at the station." Peg had probably thought they were related to the Atkins case. Yes, every day after Jonathan's arrest, I received calls that I hadn't returned, until my column appeared. The one on Jane. "It's over. He knows it's over. He read it in the paper."

"Huh?"

"I'm joking."

"Oh."

We fell silent again, Jane's mind drifting off, probably to some endless replay of Jonathan's madness.

From somewhere down the block, a leaf blower roared into action. "I hate that sound. Hate it."

"You're leaving," said Jane.

"I don't know. I'm thinking about it."

"Billy McKee hasn't driven you out, I hope," she teased.

"Did Coral tell you? She can't get off him. She assured me that he's better now, in case I care. He's joined AA and goes to meetings in Patchogue."

The clues weren't all linked to the same person. I'd been right to conclude that, but wrong about which ones did link. Another mis-guided intuitive leap. The tire tracks weren't Jonathan's. They could have been left by Billy, amusing himself on security patrol after knocking back a few.

"Why don't you come to Manhattan and live with us? You could sell real estate in the city."

"I could, couldn't I?" A glimmer of possibility. Jane reached out.

Her cold, thin hand tightened on mine. "I'm not going to be all right for a while."

"No."

On the way home, I stopped at LePater's to buy fried chicken for dinner. "Daddy." I heard a chirpy voice. I was certain it was Alicia's. I turned and saw a curly-haired tot in a stroller, pointing to a stuffed bunny she had dropped on the floor. Her father was in uniform—the matching green shirt and slacks of a local gas station mechanic. He picked up her toy, and also opened a box of animal crackers for her. Behind them, out the window, a police car passed by. I paid for my chicken and left the store.

I cut down the pedestrian alley, the same one I had limped through after Baby chewed my ankle. I was starving, and as I dug into the takeout container for a drumstick, Tom walked into the alley at the other end.

I bolted back out of the alley, and into traffic, pressing the tub of chicken to my chest while attempting to keep a grip on the cardboard top and drumstick. "Wait up," I called my alibi to no one, scrambled around cars, and ignored the honking. I hurried down the sidewalk on the opposite side of the street and into a cleaner's where I knew there was a back exit. "Your clothes aren't ready yet," the woman told me as I rushed past the conveyor belt of dry cleaning and out the rear. I came to my senses only after several minutes of meandering among garbage cans behind shops.

"Hi," said a woman. "Oh, it's you."

"Me? I guess it is."

Becky Ray, stylist at Deborah's Hair and Nails, was locking the shop. She held the key gingerly between thumb and forefinger. After dropping it into her quilted tote, she blew on her nails.

She walked directly toward me. Her lips tightened prunishly as she drew close.

"Deer only know flight," I said.

"What?"

"Nothing." I stepped aside, realizing I was blocking the way to her car.

"Did you change your hair?" she asked.

"No. It's just windblown."

"It looks good."

"Really?" I took a bite of my drumstick.

I waited until she drove off, then ambled by a circuitous route to where I was parked—all the way down Barton so I could enter the lot at the far end. The cautious stroll gave me time to assess my panic. Running away wasn't a sign of weak character, I decided, when the only other choice was giving in.

IN THE half-hour since the moving van left, Sam and Deidre formed a mournful tableau, clinging together, lovers in sacrificial heroism just before the *Titanic* sank. Every so often Deidre wearily raised her head to gaze with red-rimmed eyes at Sam, recharging them both to hug ever more desperately.

As soon as Sam had suggested that we return to Manhattan, and vented his fears about having such a crazy mom, he'd reversed himself. He didn't want to leave, he moaned, this was the first place he'd ever been happy, we'd just arrived. A total flipflop—mercifully normal range. When he wasn't complaining, he forgot to be miserable (also NR). There were small but telling indicators. While I read at night, he sometimes came into my room, collapsed on my bed, and kept me company. He laughed more often, and when he did, he sounded happy. His bedroom door was occasionally left open, and the giant-killer thump of his tread moving about the house was definitely lighter.

Yes, someone actually was fine—how amazing that it was my son. Because I was going back to the city, as far as I could ensure it, another woman's children would be fine as well.

I left Sam and Deidre on the doorstep and took one last wander through the empty house, trailed by Bernadette reading aloud from her latest piece of reportage.

I hadn't had the stomach to cover the Atkins case as a dispassionate observer, and Rob, the logical second, had been away on the weekend when Jonathan was arrested. With coaching from Art and me, Bernadette had dived in. She researched diligently and wrote with a driven intensity. She sat inches from the computer keyboard, her eyes boring into the screen. She disdained the more efficient route to finding synonyms—the thesaurus built into her word-processing program—and preferred instead to involve us all in her drama. "What's another word for 'fast'?" she cried, snapping upright. "Swift," she proudly answered her own question. "'The case came to a swift conclusion.'"

Sam had celebrated Thanksgiving with his father. I had spent mine with Jane, as I had every other spare moment.

Jane's real estate office kindly arranged for us to break the lease on our house with only the security deposit forfeited. After considerable begging on my part, our New York City tenant agreed to relocate. "It's your office, not your home," I nagged him. For three weeks after Thanksgiving, I wrapped up our Sakonnet life, quit the paper, hired movers, packed our worldly goods.

I had arranged with Deidre's parents for Sam to return to Sakonnet Bay after the Christmas holidays. He would finish the last few weeks of the semester with them, ordered to share a room with one of Deidre's younger brothers, sleeping on an upper bunk. Deidre, who was rarely allowed out on school nights, had a remarkably high grade-point average. As I had suspected, it was not possible to have a low IQ and master the entire Klingon vocabulary. Sam's grades were improving. He would flourish in the Halls' stricter family life.

And then, because Deidre's parents were so fond of my nutty son, they would be happy to have him visit on weekends during the spring term. Deidre would visit us.

"'Having struck a bargain with the Suffolk County district attorney, Jonathan Atkins pleaded guilty to second-degree murder,'" Bernadette continued to read her article as I noticed, in the living room, a plaster crack making a crooked path across the wall. The ceilings were low, the windows looked puny. Dust particles swirled in the mellow afternoon sunlight.

I hadn't properly appreciated the bright welcoming light in this house, but it didn't matter now. The same sun enlivened our apartment in Manhattan. I couldn't wait to sit there and be warm while I read the morning paper. No, I wasn't about to discover charm in Sakonnet Bay on the day I was leaving.

Bernadette rolled up her *Sakonnet Times* and whacked Sam on the butt as we passed the distraught teenagers on our way out of the house. "God, you're practically coming right back," said Bernadette. "Get in the car already."

Mr. and Mrs. Woffert came out to bid us good-bye, and we swore never to lose touch. Deidre kissed me shyly and Bernadette threw her arms around me and squeezed. "You're becoming a wonderful reporter," I told her.

They all lined up at the curb to see us off. As Sam and I pulled out, Deidre sniffled and waved broadly, a wiper on slow speed.

We left Windham Street, its porches and windows strung with Christmas lights. At Main, instead of turning left into town, we drove the other way. Sam opened Deidre's farewell gift—a black scarf in which she'd wrapped some beach glass, a lock of her pasty blond hair, and a silver ring with the grim face of a skeleton engraved on it. He tried to jam the ring onto his pinkie, with no success.

"We can have it enlarged in the city. You can get anything done in the city," I reminded him.

"Deidre's going to love the subway."

"She will?"

"Franco's, too."

"What's Franco's?"

"Old CDs, tapes. Second Avenue and Seventh. Wait until she sees Sal."

"Who's Sal?"

"The cook at Nick's Pizzeria. He's got a tattoo on his forehead."

"I hope you never do that, Sam."

"I'm not nuts, Mom. Deidre says sometimes you have to go someplace to find out who you are."

"Deidre's very smart."

"She says that's why she has to come to the city. She's meant for it. Do you want to stop for hot dogs?"

"What a great idea." We were talking with the easy intimacy I'd always wished for. "Let's hit that stand on Route 23." I checked the rearview mirror and saw, directly behind us, a swirling red light. "Oh, dear."

"What?" said Sam.

"The police."

I moved onto the shoulder of the road and stopped. In the side mirror, I observed the approach of Sergeant Tom McKee.

"Mom, tell him that you worked for the paper. Tell him who you are."

"He knows who I am."

"Maybe he won't—"

"Won't what?" asked Tom.

"Give us a ticket. What did I do, Officer?"

"You forgot to say good-bye."

"It wasn't possible."

Tom looked around, as if on this raggedy stretch of road outside town there might be something to see. "Nice sunset," he said.

And so it was, pink and purple fireworks streaking through the evening sky.

Sam scooted low in his seat to get a better view. His ring rolled onto the floor.

"This is my son, Sam," I said, while he dug around under his seat. "Sam, this is Sergeant McKee."

"It's nice to meet you," said Tom. He took off his cap and rubbed his arm across his forehead.

"Jane may come to live with us."

"I heard."

"After the new year."

"I'll be back all the time," said Sam, popping up after retrieving his ring.

"Not you, though, huh?"

I shook my head.

Tom's eyes searched mine, looking for the answer to another question.

"I hope we don't hit traffic. The trip will be so difficult. Unbearable."

"Forever," he said.

I moved my hand from the steering wheel to the window ledge and his closed over it.

"Good-bye, Tom."

"Good-bye, Lily, take care." He leaned in and kissed my cheek.

I watched his retreat in the rearview mirror. He looked back once, and then again.

I will jump out and chase him. I will leave my son and his skeleton ring sitting on the side of the road. I will have the chance to forget who I am and who Tom is, and find out more about him and me than I ever dreamed.

Sam jabbed me. "Let's go."

Tom's patrol car swung a wide U and headed toward town.

"Absolutely, let's go. What shall we listen to?"

Sam fiddled with the radio till he found a noisy, battering beat. I was going to have sauerkraut on my frankfurter. Yes, the works—

sauerkraut, relish, and mustard. I would make a deal with Sam—his station until we eat, then I would get to choose. I resisted the desire to touch my cheek on the sacred spot where Tom had placed his lips. Maybe *Car Talk* would be on the radio. I love that show.

By the time *Car Talk* is over, we'll be winging our way through the suburbs. We'll salute familiar landmarks, like the sign to Francis Lewis Boulevard. I'll switch to 1010 WINS for the latest news and traffic.

When I hit the rise to the Triboro Bridge, I know my heart will skip and flutter at the parade of skyscrapers, that dazzle of stone and steel and glass. The music of Manhattan will grow louder and louder until I shudder from the bang and clatter of cars and people, jackhammers, buses, and talk, talk, talk. The whir of city life will welcome me back—the distraction of endless choice, the promise of things familiar. I will get over him there. Won't I?

ACKNOWLEDGMENTS

I am grateful to many, many people who shared their knowledge and their world with me. I would like to thank the East Hampton Village Police—all the members of the force who took the time to talk with me. Police Chief Glen Stonemetz and Sergeant Mike Tracey were especially generous, kind, and patient. I could not have written this book without them. My thanks also to Donna Prisendorf of the *Berkshire Record* and to Bridgett Leroy of the East Hampton *Independent*. All references to Klingon in this book are taken from the *The Klingon Dictionary*, an amazing volume, by Marc Okrand. My apologies to Mr. Okrand for a few liberties taken with spelling to aid in pronunciation. To Faith Sale, my deep gratitude, and also to Lorraine Bodger, my thanks and love.

Big City Eyes

DELIA EPHRON

A Reader's Guide

A Conversation with Delia Ephron

Q: What inspired you to write this novel?

DE: The Log column in the local East Hampton newspaper. I visited friends in the Hamptons and got hooked on it. This column lists incidents that have been reported to the police—things like "three geraniums disappeared off my porch." I loved the innocence of the crimes, and the idea that crimes could be innocent. I began to think: suppose a woman is a crime reporter in a place where there are no serious crimes. Then something big happens. Would people believe it? This was the germ of the idea for this book. I also began to think of all of the things that I'm interested in. Divorce and its effect on children is one of them. I like to write about things that people find terribly sad, find the humor in it, and make people laugh and cry.

Q: Lily argues, "Divorce is the destruction of childhood." Is she speaking in your voice?

DE: Well, I am not Lily, but she has concerns and interests that I share. I am a stepmother, not a single mother. However, I have seen how my stepchildren have been affected by divorce. I have written nonfiction about divorced kids and have interviewed a lot of these kids. I have seen the anger and hurt. Parents have to get divorced with blinders on to some extent; they don't always want to acknowledge what their decision means for their children. It can lead to years of grief. This is what happened to Lily's son. For Sam, divorce was the end of his innocence—the first time he realized the world was not a safe place. It is a dramatic moment, a terribly big moment. I wanted to write about the long-term effect of this on Lily and Sam's life.

Lily faces a huge moral dilemma in this novel. Suppose the man you fall in love with is married with children? Do you want him to leave his family knowing what it will do to them? Lily knows first-hand what it will do to his children.

Q: What kind of research did you do?

DE: I went to the Hamptons alone in the winter. I hung out with the cops, who were unbelievably generous, especially Sergeant Mike Tracey. They let me ride around with them. We once rescued a man who had had too many martinis. This was the first time I had lived in a place where the animals weren't on leashes. I grew up in Los Angeles where there is no natural vegetation, so I was terrified. I didn't recognize the sounds at night, and had never lived in a place that got truly dark. I became so anxious that I had a car accident in the police department parking lot and ended up in the police log myself.

Originally I had thought my main character would be a Sakonnet Bay native. Then I began to think, maybe she would move there from the city. It helped me as a writer because I don't know the names of plants and animals—writing vegetation is not my favorite thing. It enriched the story to have Lily discover in the course of the novel how a small, rural town worked. I also spent time in Great Barrington, Massachusetts, and visited all my friends in Maine who live in small towns. I always do a lot of research for my writing.

Q: **Lily's terror of the great outdoors provides some of the funniest moments in this novel. Would you agree that this novel is, among other things, a celebration of urban life?**

DE: Absolutely. Lily is confused and trying to cope with life in the country, but she cannot forget about life in the city—the pleasure of walking the streets of Manhattan and having nobody recognize you. She misses anonymity. And the smells of pizza and garbage—and everything else—that come at you. In her loneliness and alienation, she romanticizes city life, fondly remembering Sixth Avenue being shut down because Yassir Arafat was in town. It is interesting what people think is lonely. For Lily, living in an apartment building stacked and sandwiched with other people is not lonely at all.

Q: This novel includes so many elements—comedy, mystery, coming-of-age, family drama—that it defies easy pigeon-holing. How would you describe it to your readers?

DE: This is a story about different kinds of love and the sacrifices we make—Lily's love for her son, her passion for Tom McKee, her loyalty to her best friend Jane. I threw a murder into the mix, and that is also about love. And let us not forget Sam's romance with Deidre, the Klingon. There is such a focus on genre in publishing nowadays, but I find it more fulfilling and fun to mix things up. Lily writes the column for the weekly newspaper and this column appears periodically throughout the novel. She uses the column to communicate secretly, and accidentally, she reveals secrets about herself. The whole town begins speculating about her. Lily is a writer. Writers have experiences and they make them into essays or stories. Lily writes about the murder, but she also writes about getting a bad haircut, losing her mind at a roadside stand, and being the subject of gossip.

Q: Lily declares, "I was doomed to spend my life out-of-step and over my head." Does this apply to any of the other characters in this novel?

DE: Not really. Tom McKee has the opposite problem. He did exactly what was expected of him. He married his high school sweetheart and became a cop like his other relatives. Lily brings out his passionate, adventurous side. She represents the path not taken.

Q: Was Sam, who is so nonverbal, a difficult character to write?

DE: No, I love writing kids of all ages. Writers have things they are comfortable with and, for me, that's kids.

Q: Where did the character of Deidre, Sam's Klingon-speaking girlfriend, come from?

DE: I was browsing in a bookstore one day and came across the *The Complete Klingon Dictionary*. That someone had taken and translated this language struck me as divine and insane. All I could think of was "his poor mother." Obviously the author is a complete Trekkie who grew up and decided to write this book. I had heard that there were such things as Trekkie camps where kids go and learn to speak Klingon. I thought it would be great to create a teenager that spoke this language. How frustrating would that be for a parent?

Lily thought she would take Sam out of the city and save him, but what does he do? He meets the only person in town who is as odd as he is. In the end, I think Sam saves Deidre. She is meant for the city. When Sam arrives, he really opens the world up for her.

Q: **Lily's internal dialogue about Sam's increasingly disturbing behavior is hilarious, especially the not in the normal range scale (NNR). How would Sam rate his mother's behavior?**

DE: He would rate it DMC—driving me crazy.

Mothers have told me again and again that they really identify with this normal range business. It's confusing to raise a teenager. We are constantly reading about teenagers that go off the track. So at some time or another we find ourselves wondering: Have I got one of those kids? And lying is what teenagers do best. We all lied when we were teenagers, yet still it's shocking to think that your child is lying to you. Sam and Lily have to learn to trust each other again.

Q: **What are readers to make of Tom McKee? Is he ultimately trustworthy?**

DE: First of all, he is a cop and a complicated guy. He is genuinely mad about Lily, but he is not a simple man. If you think a good guy is a guy who is faithful and a bad guy is a guy who is not, then you would judge him harshly. But I would not.

Q: This novel is populated with an appealing supporting cast of characters. Do you have a favorite among them?

DE: No, I don't. I love them all, but I did especially enjoy writing Deidre and Bernadette. Lily has a powerful effect upon Bernadette, who is a cub reporter. Bernadette is a person who notices everything and never understands the significance of anything.

Q: What came first to your mind—the murder mystery or the emotional relationships—in terms of structuring this novel? Was it difficult to set up the murder mystery?

DE: I knew the murder mystery would be secondary to the love stories, but it would be the motor that drove the book. I am a fan of murder mysteries and was looking forward to writing one, but I am interested in emotional relationships, not autopsies. I needed to keep focused on my characters' emotional lives.

Q: Did you always know how this novel would end? Did you ever consider a different ending?

DE: I knew that Lily would make a sacrifice. She was willing to sacrifice two years of her life to get Sam through high school. But she ends up making another, much bigger sacrifice that she did not anticipate. I didn't know about this sacrifice at first. This novel is about the sacrifices we can and cannot make.

Q: What writers have influenced you?

DE: I love to read—and write—a good story, which is why I so admire many English writers—George Eliot, Graham Greene, Jane Austen, John LeCarre. I also love Anne Tyler's stories. I just love great storytellers. When I was a child I remember sitting in a chair with a plate of chocolate-chip cookies and reading *Anne of Green Gables* by L.M. Montgomery. I was swept away. As an adult, I want to pass on that feeling—of spending an afternoon someplace else. I want to keep you in the chair eating chocolate-chip cookies.

Q: **How do you structure a day of writing?**

DE: I sit down after breakfast, work until lunch, and begin again after lunch. I write a lot, but don't have a really rigid schedule. I just don't have a problem with writing. I used to get up and move around more during the day, but now the computer is so much fun. I spend a lot more time at my desk going online and writing e-mails.

Q: **Your body of work is wide-ranging, from nonfiction to humor to novels to screenplays to children's books. Do you have a favorite genre?**

DE: No. Each offers something different. With scripts, a certain number of them don't get made, and some of the ones that do may not resemble what you actually wrote. Writing a book is pure because it is just me.

Q: **You have also produced several movies. Has this work affected your writing in any way?**

DE: No, producing is completely different. I love the isolation of writing—of being alone in a room each day. But once a movie is being made and you are producing it, you are running around to meetings and doing all kinds of things. It is a very different experience from writing.

Q: **What is up next for you?**

DE: I am working on a new novel, which is very different from anything I've written before. I am also working on some screenplays, but I am not sure which is going to be up next.

Reading Group Questions and Topics for Discussion

1. How do Lily's "big city eyes" deceive her when she first arrives in Sakonnet Bay? How does her opinion of this sleepy village change over the course of the novel?

2. What do you think Lily's life was like in Manhattan? Do you think Sam is the only one who needs saving?

3. Lily finds the natural world around her threatening. Can you relate with her concerns and anxieties? What is your opinion of the vast night sky?

4. Lily is tortured by the fear that her son is a freak and she is to blame. How much responsibility do parents bear for their children's behavior? Where and how do you draw the line?

5. Lily tells Tom that she and Sam matter too much to each other. Do you think this is an accurate assessment?

6. Throughout the novel, Lily struggles over how to protect her son while still giving him space to grow. Do you think she manages to find some balance? For parents, when is it time to intervene?

7. Lily's life illustrates how difficult it can be to juggle single parenthood and romance. How does a woman (or man) balance the responsibilities of parenthood with her (or his) own emotional and sexual needs?

8. What is your opinion of how Lily handles the issue of Sam's sex life? What would your approach be?

9. Lily suffers from great guilt over the effect of her divorce on her son. Do you agree with her opinions regarding the impact of divorce on children?

10. How do you think Sam would respond to his mother's opinion that his parents' divorce broke his heart?

11. Do you think Lily gives us an accurate portrait of her ex-husband Allan? How do you think he would describe her?

12. Discuss the importance of an intact family versus the needs of individual members. How do you keep these in balance?

13. What effect does falling in love with others have on Lily and Sam's relationship?

14. What do you think of the character of Tom McKee? What do you think motivates him?

15. Discuss the motives behind the infidelity in this novel.

16. Did your opinion of Sam, trapped in the throes of teenage angst, change over the course of the novel?

17. Did you enjoy Lily's columns? Did you have a favorite among them?

18. Were you surprised by the identity of the murderer?

19. Besides Lily, which characters were your favorites and why?

20. One reviewer has remarked, "By presenting a wider set of obstacles and a detective who needs to find out more than just 'who done it,' Ephron's *Big City Eyes* lets the reader share a triumph wider than simply catching a killer." Do you agree? Do you find the mix of genres satisfying?

21. Do you think Lily made the right decision in the end? What would you do in her shoes?

22. How does your group decide what to read? Why did the group choose this book?

23. How does this novel compare with other works the group has read?

24. What is the group reading next?

Excerpts from reviews of Delia Ephron's *Hanging Up*

"Compassionate, funny, and tremendously satisfying. Among the many pleasures of *Hanging Up* is the way grave and ludicrous events ricochet off one another, scattering sentiment and anger and hilarity in all directions. . . . *Hanging Up* is honest and deeply felt, and Ephron's comic timing is flawless. *Hanging Up* is full of life and ultimately . . . love."

— The New York Times Book Review

"Ephron's gift for particulars and nuances of dialogue and her smartness keep *Hanging Up* near its goal as weighty work with a quirky sense of humor."

— Chicago Tribune

"Quietly comic . . . with gentle humor and deadpan observation . . . Ephron handles it with a deft, delicate touch, never allowing her characters to descend into caricatures."

— The Boston Globe

"Hilarious . . . A charming, entertaining read. Ephron offers perhaps the most realistic depiction of the complex interplay between sisters since *Little Women*."

— Los Angeles Times

"Ephron's comedic talents serve her particularly well with her cast of characters, who are specific enough to feel like real people but broad enough to prompt sardonic laughter. True to her strong comedic instincts, Ephron can't help leaving us with a laugh when *Hanging Up* finally rings off."

— The Philadelphia Inquirer